IN THE GARDEN OF LIGHT AND SHADOW

THE CHRONICLES OF ADA ST. JAMES

CERECE RENNIE MURPHY

In The Garden of Light & Shadow: The Chronicles of Ada St. James

By Cerece Rennie Murphy

Cover Illustration: Jocelyn Short

Paperback Cover Design: Jesse Hayes, Anansi Hayes Media

Hardback (Special Edition) Cover Design: Jesse Hayes, Anansi Hayes

MediaPrint Design & Typesetting: Jesse Hayes, Anansi Hayes Media

lionskypublishing.com

cerecerenniemurphy.com

TO MY GRANDMOTHER

Mary Baptiste, whose life showed me what it means to love with courage. Your sacrifices have made everything in my life possible. I live under the protection of your prayers.

ACKNOWLEDGEMENTS

I will never forget dreaming about this story! It came to me so vividly. Little did I know how long it would take to write it! At times, it seemed like every single challenge reared its head over the last 18 months, but word by word, I got it done.

I thank God for the blessing of this journey and the privilege of doing something long enough to get better at it.

Mom, Aryeh, Skye, Monica, Kamishia, and all my family and friends, thank you for your encouragement, patience, and love. With you, I know I can face any trial.

Jocelyn, Jesse, Clarence, Jess, Rukmani, Krissy, Laurie, and Tyler, thank you for your creativity, constructive criticism, discerning eye, sense of humor, and belief in me and this story. Each of you helped me make this book the best it could be.

And to you, the reader. Thank you for trusting me with your time.

Love Always,

Cerece

prologue

RAZIEL

"DYING shouldn't be this hard."

Yet after centuries of running into lightning bolts and waiting to drown at the ocean's end, RaZiel knew that for him it was. Still, every time he came upon a new possibility, he could never quite escape the hope that *this* time might be different.

Humans were, after all, endlessly inventive in their quest to create or destroy.

He peered through the stained-glass ceiling of the Sisters of the Light convent observatory and returned his attention to the astronomy lecture already in session. Below him, Sister Carpethianna Racine de Bornacia weaved an elegant line through the neat rows of desks in her classroom. Standing at no less than six feet, the nun was as frail and thin as a scarecrow, yet her wizened eyes barely contained her excitement as she described the different phases of the moon and how each one gave power to the things of earth below — power, that if used skillfully, could ward off evil itself. It was no wonder the students in Carpethianna's class followed her every word and gesture with rapt attention.

This was no ordinary convent.

RaZiel knew well the power to which she referred. He was there when God did something new, breathing a tendril of consciousness through each blade of grass and grain of sand, into the air itself so that every living thing could tap into the power of their Creator if they chose. This was how birds knew to fly south for the winter, and how new butterflies found their nesting ground year after year. In the earliest days of humanity, the phases of the moon became a powerful symbol of this connection, which they named mooncraft. For thousands of years, most humans understood mooncraft only through their instincts or a vague feeling that warned them of some impending danger. Others, feared as sorcerers and witches, used mooncraft to gain glimpses into the future.

Only the Sisters of the Light had discovered the secret RaZiel knew, that mooncraft gave humans abilities beyond those of any angel. As divine beings created to serve the Ever, angels knew perfection and harmony, but never change. They could feel the connection mooncraft created, but they could not access its power as an instrument of creation. With discipline and mastery, mooncraft could be molded by the will of the wielder into an almost infinite number of manifestations.

No one had harnessed enough mooncraft to kill a demon — at least not yet. But, after millennia of searching, the fact that the Sisterhood had discovered what so many had missed was encouraging. RaZiel leaned closer, hoping his patience would finally be rewarded. The young women here would become healers, witches, and, if they were truly gifted, members of the E'gida — a demon shield.

Lessons given at the Sisters of the Light convent were a relief after the nonsense RaZiel endured while investigating the Knights of Umber. Their "training" on killing demons consisted of heaving great rocks that RaZiel could have easily crushed under his foot, and surviving all manner of manhood rituals that had no hope of impressing a human woman, much less of slaying a demon.

He left the Knights of Umber two weeks ago in despair of ever finding a way to end his existence, until he heard a rumor that a warrior, a *woman* warrior, had successfully driven out a group of demons from a small village in the northern plains of the Ulan Peninsula.

As if reading RaZiel's thoughts, Sister Carpethianna took a sudden detour in her lecture.

"And pay no mind to the inept scribbling of the Timekeepers who serve the Knights of Umber," she urged. "The moon is *not* the backside of the sun."

RaZiel sighed, grateful to be in the company of beings acquainted with science and common sense once more.

"While we do not have the strength or longevity of the demons we seek to contain, like our Sister Moon, we are connected to everything, and everything is connected to us. It is our duty as the Sisters of the Light to harness every bit of the power this earth offers and use it to our advantage." The nun's raised fist quivered with conviction making RaZiel ache to believe her, too.

It took him a few days after hearing of the Sisterhood to find the nearest convent. He'd been spying on them for almost a week, and so far, Sister Carpethianna's class was his favorite. He liked it so much that RaZiel considered drawing her a map of the universe, or this galaxy at least, but then thought better of it. The drawing would undoubtedly take up an extraordinary amount of paper, which would be expensive for the Sisters to replace, and at the end of the day, as open-minded as Sister Carpethianna was, she would not understand.

RaZiel knew better than most that humans were not built to fully understand all the mysteries the infinite held. Yet he hoped the Sisterhood would find a way to solve their problem and his.

Timidly, the girl sitting next to the lone empty seat in the class raised her hand.

"Sister Carpethianna?"

"Yes, Sabine."

"Forgive me, Sister…"

"Do not ask for forgiveness, child! A question is not a crime."

"Yes, Sister Carpethianna. I'm sor-" Sabine cleared her throat. "It's just that most believe demons have no weaknesses. If this is true, even with mooncraft, how can we hope to defeat them?"

"An excellent question, Sabine, and what do *you* think? A question often precedes the suspicion of an answer. Tell us!"

Sabine's eyes shifted to the vacant seat beside her. "Well, Lilavois says any problem that still exists cannot be solved by conventional wisdom.
She believes our greatest strength is that we can adapt, finding new ways to use mooncraft to our advantage. She thinks that's how we'll win."

RaZiel's skin prickled with excitement as Sister Carpethianna smiled.

"Sister Lilavois makes a strong point. She has been sorely missed this week. But since she is not here to elaborate, I'd like to hear what *you* think?"

Sabine hesitated, thinking of the charred bodies of her murdered family. "I … don't know. I hope Lilavois is right. My village … we couldn't stop them. It was so easy for them to overtake us, but maybe the fact that we have to work to build our connection to mooncraft will make us stronger in the end."

"Hmm. Two interesting hypotheses to be sure! Time will tell, Sabine, if the wisdom of the Sisterhood prevails, but I will say this — I've never seen any good come from blindly following the consensus of the crowd. In fact–"

Sister Carpethianna's sharp eyes turned towards the sky. "For a second, I felt

... something."

Her class stared back at her blankly.

The nun squinted in a vain attempt to peer past the blinding rays of the sun, but RaZiel was already gone. Chastened by her words, he took to his crow form and flew to the convent gardens to wrestle with memories he could only face in shadow.

In the Ever, RaZiel loved all his brothers and sisters. Every Angel and creature of God's creation was precious to him. But out of all of them, he loved Obi the best.

They shared the same dreams and thought the same jokes were funny. Above all, their Affinity to God in all Their infinite manifestations was exactly the same. They understood God best as a being of nurturing kindness — a creator who cared as much about how They chose to adorn the underside of a leaf as They did about the placement of each star in the universe.

While Obi and RaZiel had this affinity in common, there were many other Affinities, such as power, peace, and love, through which the Host of Angels connected to God, depending on which trait spoke most deeply to them. These differences in ties made for a diverse tapestry of interests, talents, and callings within the Host.

But as close as the two Angels were, Obi and RaZiel also had their differences.

Obi had an adventurous and mischievous nature, while RaZiel tended towards a quieter demeanor, preferring not to take form unless it was needed. And Obi made sure it was needed as often as possible, signing them up for any errand of mercy. There were always curiosities to explore in the infinite presence of God's creation, and Obi was determined to find each one. Yet after the moment of discovery passed, RaZiel tended to linger while Obi was instantly ready for the next pursuit.

Lucifer was the same way.

Although their Affinities were different, Obi and Lucifer shared a restlessness that spawned a steady tide of questions and ideas. RaZiel took in all of this with an ease that allowed each thought to flow through his mind then flutter away like a breeze through an open window. His heart was content, but Obi slowly began to ponder the notion of more.

At first, RaZiel did not understand. They had everything. They existed in the Ever where everything that is, was, and would be existed. What more could there be?

"A life untethered," Obi posited. "An existence unencumbered by errands of mercy and the maintenance of worlds. A world where we are free."

"But what of the miracle of the plants?" RaZiel countered.

Obi's laugh made the air around him shimmer. "There are plants everywhere!"

"But what of God?"

"There is only God. There is always God. We will simply know Them a new way. We are infinite, too."

RaZiel frowned. "Something truly new?" The idea hardly existed.

"Yes!" Obi replied. "Something *we* create. A possibility that has never existed before."

Something in his words made RaZiel's dark wings tremble. "We should ask permission."

"We will," Obi promised.

They did.

It was not granted.

Obi and RaZiel joined the rebellion that cast them down.
Later, RaZiel would marvel at the irony that beings who knew so much could understand so little. For how can a creature who has only known the safety of love comprehend the dread that seeps inside a soul apart from its maker? It is a barrier that cannot be fully understood until it is crossed; a pain that only comes from knowing there is no going back.

The first lie RaZiel ever told was to himself — that he could bear the weight of his choice, and that the brilliance of their newfound freedom outshone his pain. But it was not true. As soon as his tender feet touched the brutal ground for the first time, he knew he would feel the cost of his mistake forever.

Uncertainty kills love, and so it did with Obi and RaZiel and many of the other angels who left with Lucifer in hope, and found only darkness.

They began as heroes, beings that humans could look up to, pray to, and revere. More tangible than a faceless deity, they made themselves gods in the eyes of lesser beings, and, in return, they were worshiped as vehicles of favor, while the angels were kind or feared as manifestations of God's wrath when they were not.

They had moved from the haven of God's purpose into a heady kind of glory they could call their own — a new reality where they determined every aspect of who they would be.

The unfamiliar ache of *need* for anything was unsettling, but on Earth there seemed no shortage of things with which to fill it. There was food of every flavor and texture, new conversations in which they were finally the ones with all the answers, and there was physical pleasure too, like nothing they had ever experienced. Men and women offered their bodies freely to them, teaching the angels the new language of desire.

As the shock of their separation subsided, the angels tried to find light in the freedom that Lucifer promised. And, at first, they almost did.

RaZiel reveled in the adoration as Obi and the others did, throwing himself into every sensation, every experience. He found enjoyment in many things, but none of them could take the place of what he knew before. For what is the fascination of a few when you have been truly known and loved infinitely? In leaving the Ever, RaZiel realized he had broken his wholeness. The hunger to be complete again would never leave him and there was nothing in this realm that could take its place.

When he tried to share his realization with others, there were few who would admit suffering the same anguish he did, but RaZiel suspected that this same hunger was the reason the first of the killings began. To take a life one could not create would have been unthinkable before their descent. It took decades to confirm that angels were incapable of conceiving or siring a child. Having witnessed the power of creation firsthand, most of the angels accepted this limitation as the price for the life they had chosen. Others were furious. To have the power of creation denied to them — a power even humans possessed — could not be tolerated.

"If we cannot bring life to this world," Lucifer declared, "then we will claim death as our prize!"

What began as the angels acting as instruments of justice quickly became a lust for dominance and vengeance against a God they had abandoned but now claimed abandoned them. It took several centuries for the angels to go from gods to demons, but RaZiel's kin earned their titles well. By the end of their first millennium on Earth, the angels were known collectively as The Fallen.

The constant sensation of lack wore a hole inside them that no pleasure or curiosity on Earth could comfort. They began to look upon forever with dread, knowing that with every passing day their hunger would grow.

Some, like RaZiel, retreated from the world while others descended into madness, pouring out their anger like poison onto an already wounded world. Inciting terror became the antidote to their emptiness, shared misery being the only balm for their suffering. The forms The Fallen chose to take became more frightful and grotesque, as ugly as their pain, as fearful as their insides. With the chaos they brought into the world, they believed they were punishing God, too blinded to see that the only thing they destroyed were the last traces of what once made them divine.

Those who remained faithful to Lucifer, those whom RaZiel held most dear, became unrecognizable.

The last time RaZiel saw Obi, it was raining. The downpour was a blessing to a small town that had been on fire for three days.

From the schoolhouse to the barest hovel, the demons set each structure ablaze – punishing the citizenry for their mayor's refusal to offer them lodging. Theirs was not the first town that dared to refuse the growing demands of Lucifer's horde. It was just the cruelest example of anything RaZiel had ever witnessed. He was there because SeKet begged him to leave the snowcapped peaks of Mount Killi where he'd been hiding and help her stop their kin. She'd told him Obi would be there. She'd whispered that there might still be a chance to save him. In their falcon forms, they flew all night following the northeast winds that carried the scent of burning flesh and reached the town of Ethyne by dusk.

By the time the sun had set, every store, home, and barn was destroyed and would still have been burning if not for the heavy rain that had begun to fall. Only the church and the cemetery were untouched. Within the sanctuary gates, a small group of demons rounded up what few survivors remained.

SeKet told RaZiel that Obi was their leader. With the sight of charred bodies covering the streets like trash, RaZiel could not believe it until he found Obi behind a burned-out shed. His back was turned away from RaZiel and oddly bent. A boy sobbed quietly at his side. RaZiel's plan had been to approach from behind in an effort to surprise and subdue, but a cry of anguish escaped him as he stepped close enough to *see* Obi draining a father to death in front of his son.

"What? What have you done?" RaZiel gasped. The son's face shifted from Obi's to RaZiel and recoiled.

At the sound of his brother's voice, Obi dropped his victim. RaZiel flinched at the sight of the man's body hitting the ground as the last of his blood drained from a large wound at his neck. Only then did Obi turn around. His grin was unnaturally wide, as if his jaw was extended. Blood ran down his chin and dripped from the tips of a crowded row of sharp teeth.

RaZiel could not speak. The stench of malice stuck in his throat, stole his breath, and turned his stomach. His thoughts went silent as a new emotion rose up in his belly. And there, at its source, was Obi. Not the Obi he had loved and known since birth, but the twisted creature he had become.

Without warning, RaZiel lunged, pinning Obi to the ground. With all his strength, RaZiel struck him in the face once and again, but it was not enough. His arms swung like anvils in tandem, pummeling Obi into the dirt and ash he'd created. Bones cracked, bruises bloomed, but RaZiel felt none of it. His body, his mind was connected to nothing but the rhythmic movement of his arms and the fury that pulsed into them. From someplace far away, he heard someone scream, "I hate you! I hate you! I hate you!" but he didn't know who it was or what it meant.

He only knew that he was both burning and numb at the same time.

It was SeKet who broke the spell — using the superior strength of her own body to wrench RaZiel away — trying to stop what he'd almost done, who he had almost become.

"RaZiel! Do you hear me? It doesn't matter if you hate him! You *cannot* kill him! He is still one of us. They will demand your death, and I can't lose two of my brothers to darkness in one night. Do you hear me?"

Slowly, RaZiel looked past her anguish to where Obi lay unconscious and beaten beyond recognition.

"Help me," RaZiel pleaded through desperate tears. "It's inside me now." SeKet could not return his gaze. She had no answer for him, no cure for what lay ahead. Instead, she held him close until their grief was interrupted by the forms of two siblings she once knew: Leophrastos, a once regal angel of bronze skin and feathers now masquerading as a monstrous beast covered in bristly hair, and Selah, who had traded her nearly silver skin to match her beastly kin in everything but height, hovering just a few inches shorter than her brother's eight feet.

"You almost killed him!" Leophrastos roared, but SeKet was not fooled. She saw the tremor in his paws, heard the hitch in Selah's breathing.

"Almost," SeKet replied, strangely calm. "But I had not the heart to watch our kin receive what he deserved."

Selah's wolf eyes shifted between Obi's face and RaZiel's battered hands.

"He is not our judge! We have no judge!" Selah spat as she extended her claws. "He will pay for what he has done!"

SeKet had no hope of saving Selah. The Fallen were lost. She knew that now, but she would not allow this to continue.

SeKet rose to her feet on legs that were still faster than any of them could ever hope to be. Summoning the commander of legions she had once been, her voice rang out like the thunder that had always been kindred to her.

"Stop!"

Leophrastos and Selah flinched back.

"If death is not what you seek, be at peace, or *I* will finish it!" When they offered no challenge, she continued. "Take him and go before the madness of this night claims me, too."

SeKet turned away, hiding her tears as they carried Obi away.

From the ground from which he was not yet able to stand, RaZiel held out his arms, waiting for SeKet to give in to her grief once more. When the weight was too heavy, she sank to her knees, where he pulled her close.

"Would you have done it?" RaZiel's baritone had withered to the tenor of a frightened child.

"I don't know," she cried. "I don't know." RaZiel didn't either and so they wept together, too afraid of themselves to let go of the other.

From across the room, the little boy who had cried so much looked between his dead father and the demons who were not quite so with new dry eyes.

"He wanted us to pray to him, but my father refused," the boy began. "But if you stay and protect us, I'll pray to you."

SeKet shook her tears away. "We are not God, boy. If this night has proven nothing else, it must have shown you that we are not worthy of your prayers. It is God you should thank for your life."

"God didn't save us!" The boy pointed at RaZiel. "He did. I don't believe in God anymore."

For a moment, SeKet and RaZiel could only stare back at him.

"This is not salvation," Seket replied. "We cannot save you from a chaos we created. This is redemption only."

"What's the difference?" the boy asked.

"When you meet God, you will know," RaZiel whispered. "Go and find whatever is left of your family. There will be no more burning tonight."

Later, RaZiel would imagine he saw the boy make the sign of El before dissolving into the rain, but his vision was so saturated with his own tears, he could not be sure the boy did not just disappear.

"What have we done here?" RaZiel's voice trembled.

"We've stolen their hope and given them a hell of our own making to take its place."

"God forgive us."

SeKet sighed, her eyes raw but dry. "It is surely too late for that now."

How many centuries had it been since RaZiel last saw Obi? He could not, he would not say. The memory of Obi being carried away by his brethren with the stench of blood on his breath still made RaZiel shudder. Every day since then was written on his heart in a language too bitter to speak. Without the existence of time as a reference, in the Ever, a millennium might pass with the blink of an eye, but on Earth, every hour without his whole self felt like an age. He missed his wings so much.

For a long time, RaZiel wandered with no purpose. He worked or begged to feed the ache for food, shelter, clothing, and warmth, but little else. The darkness of despair almost consumed him until one day he came across a group of children, or rather they came across him. They were playing on the hillside at the base of Mt. Kitanglad while their mother tended a trip of goats nearby. He'd been laying in the guinea grass for days staring up at all the stars he knew by name who would never speak to him again. He had just closed his eyes to rest, when a girl tilted her small head towards him. Looking up, the pale morning sun set her brown hair ablaze.

"Are you lost?" Before he could answer, a boy younger than the girl came into view.

"He must be lost. He doesn't look like any of the families around here."

"I don't know," the little girl replied impatiently. "He hasn't spoken, yet."

It had been months since RaZiel had spoken to anyone, and though he remembered their language from the many he and Obi had studied, their sudden presence confused him. Before he could get his thoughts together, another girl, younger still than the two before her, with a face as round as a daisy, leaned in.

"He's stinky!" the youngest girl announced. "Maybe he can't talk. That's why he can't ask someone to give him a bath."

"No one asks for a bath," the little boy replied. "Parents just give you one whether you want it or not."

The eldest rolled her eyes. "That's why I think he's lost."

Despite his stench, the third child drew closer. "Well, say something! If you don't speak, we can't help you find your people."

RaZiel began to weep. "I don't have any people," he rasped. "I lost them."

The three children looked at each other as if somehow they understood *exactly* what he meant.

"You can have my elephant apple." The boy's voice was soft as he dropped the apple on RaZiel's broad chest. The eldest girl looked to her younger sister expectantly.

"There's only two rice cakes left, but I can give you *one*." Unlike the apple dropper, daisy-face set the rice cake wrapped in palm leaf on his stomach with the care of a great sacrifice.

The first child nodded with pride, before adding, "I'll bring you some soap tomorrow. Until then, you can hold on to my doll. You can talk to her if you want. Okay?" She placed the doll made of straw and feathers on his chest, then patted his head. "No one is lost forever."

On some silent signal he could not detect, the children suddenly headed back toward the field where their mother waited. RaZiel sat up slowly clutching their gifts. There was so much he wanted to say, but his feelings were too big for words, his voice too small and raw from longing.

As if reading his thoughts, the first child — tall and thin as a scarecrow — turned back to him. "I know," she smiled. "You're welcome."

It was then, as he watched the children bound down the hill, that he remembered if God is truly a Being of Kindness, there must be a way to end this hunger. There must be an end.

No one is lost forever.

That night, for the first time in 3,000 years, RaZiel rested under the canopy of a Katmon tree and prayed.

"Let me know death, God. If ever You loved me, if ever there was a moment of truth between You and me, end my life. Help me find a way."

Of course, he had tried many times on his own, but this time he prayed. This time he asked the God who created him and surely knew his last breath for help.

If there is an end, God has surely lived it, RaZiel reminded himself. *It has already happened. It is happening! I have only to reach the point of its existence.*

He looked up to the heavens, to the stars that faded with the first light of day, and knew for the first time what it truly meant to hope.

Above him, a blossom fell from its branch. RaZiel caught the motion out of the corner of his eye and held out his hand. He watched through tears as it fluttered and twirled in its descent on a gentle breeze that had not been there a moment ago.

It landed in his palm with fine white petals and reddish pistils exposed to the faint morning light.

A million colors lay there, each intricate and entirely unique, dazzling in their subtlety yet no less profound than the vivid emerald green of the leaves from which they came. In all his life, he had never seen *this* flower before.

RaZiel wept for the simple truth he had once known so well and forgotten so easily. *If God can love so small a thing, perhaps, perhaps God can still love me.*

There is an answer to this hunger, he realized, *a path to death.* The secret lay written in the palm of his hand, in the lifelines of each petal, though he'd lost the ability to understand its meaning. But it was *there* and he would decipher it. God had answered his prayer.

Pulling the long dead flower that he still carried from his pocket, RaZiel settled under the canopy of another Katmon tree. When he first arrived at the convent, he was stunned to find it. He had not seen another like it since the morning his prayer had been answered so many years ago. In that moment, he knew that the presence of the tree within the convent gardens was a sign that the answer to his most fervent prayer would be found here. With patience and nothing but time on his side, RaZiel retreated into the shadows of the garden to wait.

PART I
LILAVOIS

chapter one

LONG WAY FROM HOME

LILAVOIS St. James was from the south, the Isle of Moor to be exact, where the air was warm and fragrant all year long. So being caught between the dark clouds and the damp cold of North Kesar was far from her liking. The wind assaulted her as she paused in the kitchen doorway, ripping at the edges of her woolen cloak and skirt as if it meant to strip her bare right there on the threshold.

“Be still you beast,” she snapped at the air before closing the door firmly behind her. Instantly, the gale died down, too hurt to carry Lilavois's insult far enough for its brothers to hear.

Lilavois sighed. It was an abuse of her powers as a third-year apprentice with the Sisters of the Light Convent and Preparatory School to convene with nature in such an ill-mannered way.

“I'm sorry,” she muttered. “I know it's not your fault.” The wind picked up just enough to brush her cheek in a gentle caress before twirling off to rattle the trees.

She had no right to be angry with anyone. At twenty-one years old it had been her choice to forsake all that was expected of her, all the luxury and privilege she was born into, and study with the Sisters of the Light, or the Sisterhood as they called themselves, to learn how to wield mooncraft and use the herbs required to heal, to soothe, and to kill.

Her sturdy boots were made of the finest oilskin leather and lined with enough brown mole fur to give Lilavois confidence she could make it far enough into the garden and back without freezing. Stepping firmly into the wind that had forgiven her, she followed the speckles of moonlight that the cloud cover allowed and made her way.

Nightshade was a powerful elixir, but to gather its full power, it must be picked under the full moon and only at night — and only if the plant gave permission. Nightshade taken by force was good for nothing but a slow torturous bellyache. She inched forward, warmed by the fire of indignation burning in her belly.

She'd missed almost a week of class due to cleaning latrines and scrubbing floors. Sister Ignatia called it "punishment for her insolence." Lilavois knew better. Given how remote their convent was, the lack of electricity could be excused, but the lack of indoor plumbing was another matter. The peoples of Indus and Kemet had invented indoor plumbing over 3,000 years ago. Through trade and shared knowledge, most of the world had adopted this technology so that it was commonplace in even the humblest homes. The fact that a remote convent in Kesar was still using latrines was more than antiquated – it was spiteful! The memory of Sister Ignatia's smirk as the woman handed her a long scrubbing brush and a fresh pair of elbow length rubber gloves was all the proof she needed.

Sister Ignatia wasn't even the Headmistress at the Convent, though most days it certainly felt like it. The Reverend Sister Imoleina Kai founded the Sisterhood almost fifty years ago to train women on the art of harnessing mooncraft to protect the world against demons. Her crusade took her all over the world, constantly recruiting and establishing new convents, leaving Sister Ignatia to rule over the apprentices in Kesar Convent with comfortable impunity.

"She's just a bitter old shrew," Lilavois scowled. "Everyone on the Moors knows you have to boil the onion with the skin on to cure a cough. Is it my fault I know more than she does?"

Deep down Lilavois knew that was more than a bit of an exaggeration, but whatever begrudging respect she had vanished the moment the putrid contents of Sister Ignatia's chamber pot spilled down her apron. She'd been racing through her chores, in hopes of catching the last half hour of her Ancient Charms and Incantations class when the unfortunate incident occurred.

That was three days ago. Now she was just a ball of seething rage.

Basket ready, Lilavois charged into the garden. Punishment and cold be damned. Five families with the grip were quarantined in their homes in the nearby village of Esa, and Lilavois was going to brew a tincture that would cure them, whether Sister Ignatia liked it or not.

Guided by all the pig-headedness that had gotten her into trouble in the first place, Lilavois traced the Adinkra symbol for honoring the divinity of Mother Earth into the soil, said her prayer of blessing, then inspected and clipped her ingredients with a sure hand. Ginger root, lemon thyme (always!), and dragon weed. Though the clouds still held back the moonlight, Lilavois found her way to what she needed easily. She knew this garden by heart.

These shrubs had been her sanctuary over the past three years, the only part of the dark, dank convent that held any resemblance to the lush, green landscapes of her home. The deeper she went into the garden, the harder it was to hold on to her mask of anger, exposing the tender truth that despite the few friends she'd made here, Lilavois was terribly homesick.

The irony that she had tried so hard to get away from the one place she now longed to be was not lost on her. Every week, she lied to her mother and sister in her correspondence, telling them how exciting it was to be in the North, how kind and helpful her teachers were, and how she hardly had time to miss them at all. Shame kept her from telling the truth.

It was not as if she had not wanted to join the Sisterhood. She had wanted almost nothing else since her family was saved by members of the E'gida four years ago. But life at the convent had not been what she expected. While Lilavois could not deny that she had learned a great deal in the medical arts and was now proficient enough in self-defense to kill if necessary, she still had many questions — questions that were most often met with skepticism or scorn. It did not help matters that although Lilavois's ability to summon mooncraft had improved greatly, she had yet to conjure enough magic to form the E'gida — the shield of the Sisterhood and the last rite that would signify she was ready to become a demon slayer.

Apart from her friends, Sabine Arnold and Jhonna Tayo, with whom she had bonded immediately over the shared loss of family members and a desire to do more than what was expected of them, Lilavois found herself mostly alone. The isolation and the cruelty seemed designed to break her, and every time she thought about it, it made her something more than angry.

Lilavois wiped the dampness from her eyes and moved deeper into the garden. She had to shake off this melancholy. Her anger made her warm, and she would pull on that if nothing else to keep herself going. The nightshade was close to the ground in the deepest part of the garden. She wasn't near enough to see it, but she could smell its mossy essence. With a sly twitch of her lips, she thought about the many uses of nightshade. A little could give you terrible stomach cramps, but the right amount could send you into the most peaceful rest. In less skilled hands, it could also kill you, but Lilavois knew exactly what she was doing. Crouching, she waited until the clouds cleared enough to let the moonlight illuminate the ground before offering a prayer of thanks. She clipped two vines that had wandered and tangled across the path. For good measure, she took another clipping and held it up to the moon with the tips of her fingers, shifting it tenderly away from the shadows cast by the tree just above.

"If Sister Ignatia tries to punish me again, I'm going to use you to send her to the latrine for a week." She smiled wickedly.

"What kind of nun can hope to fight evil while holding such ill in her heart?"

Lilavois dropped the clipping, her basket, everything but the shears in her hand, and leapt to her feet. There were no males permitted within the convent, but that was not what made her blood run cold. If this was a man, she would slit his throat and be done with it. She had been through enough of the Sisterhood's training to do the deed without hesitation. But every fiber in her body knew that this was no ordinary being. His voice was velvet. Deep as the ocean itself. Perfect. Too perfect. Like an angel dropped down to earth. Except there were no angels on earth, not anymore. They had earned a different name. With hands that were trained not to tremble, Lilavois raised her shears and stared into darkness.

"If you value your life, you will stay where you are. We E'gida are never alone."

What she had mistaken for the great shadow of the tree was something else entirely. The demon above her was massive. Though she could not see what form he took, his amber eyes gleamed in moon's light. Still, he did not move. Instead, he watched her with the patient curiosity of a crow studying the body of a soon-dead animal.

"Lay down your weapon. If I wanted to harm you, there would be no way for your sisters to get here in time to stop me."

Lilavois took a step back from where he towered above her.

"All the more reason to keep my shears close," she replied. He did not answer. "If you mean me no harm, then show yourself." Most of her hoped he would not. The yellow-eyed demons of her past flashed before her, but she would not give in to panic. Even if this was her last moment, she would face it with courage and discipline as she had been trained to do.

The shadow before her poured down the branch of the tree like water. When it reached the ground, a man stepped out dressed in a gray woolen tunic and simple pants roughly cut at his ankles. His skin was ebony, flawless and smooth as stone that had been chiseled into features too sublime to describe, against a thicket of long locs that hung past his shoulders.

“Cruelty alone cannot hope to kill a thing like me.”

Lilavois flinched to shake off the way his voice crept into her mind like a lullaby.

“What are you doing here?”

“Waiting,” he said softly. “For a heart pure enough to kill me.”

She should have been glad. Destroying creatures like him was the very reason she was here.

Yet killing *him* was the furthest thing from her mind.

He was not awful.

He did not hiss and sneer.

He was cordial, patient.

Though he was everything she swore to despise, he was nothing she expected.

He was a demon.

A devastatingly beautiful demon.

And so, she did the only thing she could. Lilavois dropped her shears and ran.

chapter two

ENEMY

LILAVOIS crept into her bed that night, careful not to wake her other roommates. But she did not sleep. With the sound of his voice, his startling beauty, and the effect they both had on her still coursing through her, there was no way she could settle.

But he was not the only reason her cheeks burned.

Why had she not screamed? Run to Sister Carpethianna or Sister Agnes and told them there was a demon waiting to die in their garden?

She laid awake all night trying to find the answer as shame warred with the undeniable pull in her belly. By dawn, she'd finally exhausted herself enough to fall asleep, but by then, it was time to wake up.

Filled to the brim with uncertainty, Lilavois decided to say nothing until she could sort out the mystery of her own behavior.

Of course, Sabine and Jhonna would have none of it.

"You look like the dead," Jhonna declared in a voice that conveyed more concern than was typical of her generally caustic personality. "What's wrong with you?"

At six feet tall, with a long neck, an athletic build, a wild ash blonde afro swirling about her head, and pale white eyelashes that framed her large grey eyes, Jhonna Tayo could only be described as formidable. Yet Lilavois knew for a fact her bark was much worse than her bite. When Lilavois walked from her dorm room into the bathroom, she had been prepared to run into Sabine first since they shared a room together and Sabine always got up early. Jhonna slept in the dorm room opposite theirs, but they shared the same washroom, which held six stalls equipped with large barrels of lukewarm water for bathing and six latrine closets. As always with Jhonna, her voice carried across the blue-tiled room in a way that turned every head Lilavois's way.

"I didn't sleep well," Lilavois offered sheepishly, avoiding the unwanted attention of her peers. "Stomach ache."

"Ooh. Make sure to ask the kitchen for some ginger tea. If that doesn't work, we can always go to the infirmary, but you know whatever Sister Zhao gives you is gonna smell bad."

Lilavois gave Jhonna the best smile she could manage before heading into the nearest latrine closet. By the time she was finished, the situation had gotten worse. While the bathroom was significantly less crowded, both Jhonna and Sabine were waiting for her by the wash basin. Sabine was the exact opposite of Jhonna in many ways, standing at barely five feet, with long braids she always wore in a bun, a petite frame, and toffee-colored skin. But what Sabine lacked in stature, she more than made up for in curiosity. Though Jhonna was the boldest, Sabine would have the most questions.

"Hey," Lilavois offered, avoiding Sabine's gaze as she poured fresh water into the basin and reached for the bar of charcoal soap to wash her hands.

"Jhonna said you were sick, but you look more worried to me. Has something happened?"

"It's just my stomach." Lilavois concentrated on the bubbles sliding through her fingers. "I'm sure some ginger tea will help."

Sabine placed a gentle hand on Lilavois's back. "Are you sure?"

Lilavois could feel her resolve crack. She hated lying, especially to Sabine. She had lost her entire family to a demon attack before coming to the convent, and Lilavois knew how much she depended on her and Jhonna as her new family.

"Have you heard from your sister?" Sabine asked. "I know you were worried about her running off with that sailor from Reva."

The sudden turn in conversation was a relief. Lilavois reached for the towel and the needed distraction with a watery smile.

"I received a new letter from Charmaine just before our study session. She's moved on, thank God! Found out he didn't wash his legs when he bathed because of gravity or some such nonsense. She called him a barbarian and left him standing right there on the promenade. She's now being courted by an architect or musician, maybe both. I can't keep up with her."

Jhonna wrinkled her nose in disgust. "Does that mean he doesn't wash his feet either?"

Lilavois shrugged before they all burst out in a fit of laughter.

"Oh, you'll have to read the letter to me later," Sabine said, glad to see Lilavois looking brighter for the moment. "Your sister tells the best stories!"

"I'm planning to write her back during our Navigation lecture. I'll tell her you both said hello."

"Oh no," Jhonna protested. "We have a test this Friday, and we need your notes to help us study. Sabine and I've had to make do on our own this past week, and it hasn't been pretty."

"Yes," Sabine agreed. "*Please* try not to antagonize Sister Ignatia."

Lilavois looked doubtful as they walked from the bathroom and right into Sister Agnes.

"That's sound advice from a friend, Sister Lilavois. I do hope you take it to heart now that you've completed your latest tour of punishment. Unless, of course, you prefer cleaning latrines to learning." The Sister's tone was serious, but her eyes were full of mirth.

"Yes, Sister Agnes. I mean no, Sister Agnes. I was just about to brush my teeth and get dressed," Lilavois stammered. Sabine stood stock-still and mute beside her while Jhonna scurried off to finish dressing.

"We look forward to it. Fresh breath is a service to all."

Lilavois covered her mouth and mumbled, "Yes, ma'am," then waited until Sister Agnes had moved further down the hall.

"Is my breath that bad?"

"Of course not," Sabine smiled.

Lilavois raised her eyebrows skeptically.

"Jhonna would have told you if it was."

That's true, Lilavois thought, before another idea occurred to her.

Do demons ever get morning breath?

His face, the gentle light in his eyes and the smell of night jasmine flooded her senses…

And just like that, she was right back where she started.

❂❂❂

During first period, Sister Ignatia waited for the staunch defiance Lilavois was known for, but the girl who had been up all-night trembling had no defiance to spare. She went through her classes in a daze, barely speaking, hardly able to pay attention. Instead of her habit of taking copious notes, Lilavois found herself drawing in her notebook. Sketching the outline of a creature with menacing eyes as if to remind herself of the nightmare he should have been.

Desperate for a reason to explain her hesitation, in between classes, she stalked the hallway poring over the tenants of warning that hung on the walls and were engrained in her by the Sisterhood —superior strength, speed, cunning, the ability to transform and mimic any beast or human form. Nowhere did it mention the ability to beguile or bewitch. Nowhere did it mention their beauty as a weapon.

"Of course, it wouldn't," Lilavois reasoned. "The beguiled would be incapable of reporting their affliction. I must be stronger than that." Whatever his appearance, Lilavois reminded herself, horror and brutality were his true nature. In Advanced Demon Mythology, she found the outlet she needed for her fears.

"Sister Mantoya?"

"Yes, Lilavois."

"Do demons have the power to hypnotize?"

The entire class turned toward Lilavois.

"For what purpose would they use such a power?" Sister Mantoya countered. "They don't need to subdue. The Fallen are exceedingly efficient at overpowering their prey."

Lilavois licked her lips. "... Maybe seduction?" As snickers erupted throughout the class, she hastened to minimize her embarrassment. "I was just wondering if there were any recorded cases."

"Silence!" Sister Mantoya snapped. Lilavois was grateful for the seriousness in the elder's expression which lent some legitimacy to her query.

"That is certainly an interesting question, but there is no record of demons having this power. There are accounts of them once possessing a god-like presence and beauty when they first arrived thousands of years ago. So much so that they were revered by all who saw them, even worshipped. Some were certainly known to seduce, but there have been no reports of beguilement. By all accounts, their attractiveness and wealth were all that was needed to persuade any number of partners. But these incidents are few and far between now. In the last hundred years, almost every demon encounter has been violent, with humans facing some grotesque visage of a demon's choosing. Whether they've simply forsaken their human forms or have lost the ability to take them is unclear."

Lilavois nodded as Sister Mantoya concluded her explanation and continued the lecture, but her thoughts lingered.

He was nothing like the demons that had attacked her family or any in recent record. He made no move to hurt her. He hadn't uttered a single threat.

I'm waiting for you to kill me. Why would he say that?

That question, along with the shame of having held the secret of him for an entire day, kept her up a second night. She spent the time convincing herself that she needed to be cautious. In Sister Prima's first-year Demon Anatomy class, students learned that demons were supposed to have extraordinary use of their senses, with the ability to hear and see things miles away. He would surely kill them all if he heard her telling the head of their convent about him, wouldn't he? There might be other demons nearby, waiting to swarm. Yet the obvious terror she should have felt at the notion was difficult to grasp.

For most of the next day, she was able to convince herself that she was doing the right thing. That she could have easily written a note to the headmistress did not occur to her until after dinner. By then, Jhonna and Sabine were staring at her from across the dining table with open concern. Over the steady din of Sister Zhoa and Sister Angustella announcing plans for a new building fund to upgrade the convent's facilities, Sabine leaned forward.

"Is your stomach still bothering you?" Sabine asked. "You haven't been yourself since yesterday morning."

"And your Navigation notes had all these creepy drawings," Jhonna complained. "Something's got you distracted."

"I think I'll go lie down." Lilavois said, hastening from the room to avoid the concern in Sabine's eyes and the suspicion in Jhonna's. But her bed was no match for the turmoil in her mind.

Despite her claims of commitment to the Sisterhood and readiness to begin E'gida training, at the first chance to face the monster she had sworn to kill, Lilavois had run away like a frightened child. Worse, she'd been chastised by a demon for her own unkind intentions — not in anger, but with a voice that was soft and patient. He could have killed her then. He could have killed them all, yet he had not.

Disgusted with herself, that night Lilavois pulled back the thick covers from her bed and tiptoed to the window so as not to wake Sabine and the other girls with whom she shared a room. She could see the courtyard and the path to the stables. Beyond stood the gardens, shrouded in a white fog. Her thoughts raced with the memory of him and the knowledge that he was still there waiting to die. Perhaps waiting for her.

Lilavois could see his face before her as clear as if he were standing below the window — wide, soft eyes, a jaw that was strong, sharp, and in complete contrast to the plush lines of his mouth. Every inch of him was ebony and beautiful.

At the top of the trees, a cloud of fog began to swirl, revealing a dark shadow at its center. Lilavois stepped back from the window, her heart pounding. "What are you looking at?"

Lilavois almost screamed as she turned around and pressed her back to the window, obstructing Sabine's view.

"I…nothing…I couldn't sleep."

Sabine stared at her with eyes that were tired but no less alert.

"Did you know you get a crease right in the center of your forehead when you're not telling the truth? That's how Sister Ignatia always knows when you steal her potion supplies or that you're not really sorry when you apologize to her for it. I always meant to tell you, but then I forget because outside of her class you always tell the truth, until just now."

Shame made Lilavois's back break out in sweat. There was no challenge in Sabine's voice, just a simple, clear certainty.

Lilavois heard the strain in her own laugh as she tried to brush Sabine's observation aside. "If she would let me import my own supplies, I wouldn't need to borrow hers…"

"You know you can trust me, right?"

With a sigh, Lilavois chose her words carefully. "Of course I do. I just thought I saw something in the garden, but I know it's my mind playing tricks on me. I guess I got spooked."

Sabine smiled gently. "Did something scare you when you went to the gardens the other night? I've told you to stop going out there just to spite Sister Ignatia."

Lilavois turned back to the window, relieved to see that the fog had not lifted, leaving an impenetrable mist over the garden. "Maybe. You know there are strange creatures around this time of year."

Sabine laced her hand around Lilavois's and peered out into the night. "All the more reason to listen to me."

Lilavois looked down at her diminutive friend and returned her smile. Sabine and Jhonna were without a doubt the two people in the convent who would help her with anything. She only need ask. "I should listen to you," she said softly.

"But we both know you won't," Sabine teased.

"I will tonight," Lilavois yawned, suddenly exhausted by the weight of everything she chose not to say. "Come on, we have that Navigation quiz tomorrow and I think we should probably go over the wayfarer charts one more time over breakfast. You still seem shaky on some of the lesser constellations."

The smile on Sabine's lips fell. "Don't remind me or I'll never get to sleep."

"You'll do fine. I'll make sure you've got it before the test."

"I know you will."

But as they returned to bed, anxiety and exhaustion coiled around Lilavois's heart. Closing her eyes, she couldn't escape the question of who she'd been protecting when she lied to Sabine at the window — herself or the demon in the garden?

Disgusted by her own frailty, Lilavois went back to bed resolved to rid herself of the guilt of being so easily subdued. Only a trained E'gida with a deep connection to the earth and mooncraft possessed the power necessary to summon her shield and challenge a demon. Even with this level of skill, only one member of the E'gida, their founder Sister Kai, had ever faced a demon alone. The story of how she'd lost her arm and nearly her life during the confrontation was legendary. It was the reason they never fought alone.

Still, if the demon was true to his word, she would not truly be going into battle. Tomorrow she would break into the armory and take one of the lassos of El, the other weapon of an E'gida. She would go back to the garden and give him what he claimed he was waiting for.

I shouldn't need the shield, she convinced herself. *If death is what he seeks, he needn't wait any longer. I will bring it to him.*

She returned to the garden the next evening on legs too tired to shake. Lilavois had pushed herself hard all day. In weapons class, she tested her skill. In mythology, she tested her courage, studying the grotesque images offered in her books, preparing herself for what she hoped was the worst he could offer. By nightfall, her mind and body were exhausted. Her wrist ached from practicing the flicking motion needed to ignite the potion that the lasso of the E'gida was soaked in so that it would light up with moon fire once it struck the ground. Anchored to her belt, the lasso felt heavier than it was, weighed down by the knowledge that she was not nearly strong enough to wield it with full command.

Still, Lilavois's resolve outweighed her weariness as she locked the gate behind her.

As if that could hold him, she thought, taking the lasso in her hand. Yet she could not stop the compulsion. Even if she was walking to her death, this must be done. She had put the Sisterhood at risk with her silence, and since she refused to share the truth, the burden of setting things right was now hers alone to fulfill. Lilavois promised herself that she would at least scream to alert them to the danger if her efforts to vanquish him failed.

There was no reason to believe that she would find him in the exact place she'd left him and yet she knew he was there. The weight of him felt like gravity pulling all silence and darkness towards him. Like before, against the darkened sky, she could only make out the wild, lush branches of the Katmon tree. Wanting to avoid the sensation of powerlessness from having him hover over her, Lilavois stopped a few feet away from where the dense foliage made impenetrable shadows.

Her presence was met with stillness, a startling absence that seemed worse than the enemy himself. Sweat broke out on her brow. Her body found its energy to tremble until she was sure she was mad for thinking he was here. Grasping for courage, she opened her mouth, but before she found her voice, another rose up to take its place.

"Good evening, Ms. St. James. I did not think to see you again so soon. You hold the lasso of El. Have you come to honor my request?"

Her trembling ceased as every ounce of anger, courage, and shame drained from her like water from a broken cup. Though the lasso remained in her grip, she was bare. All that remained was the silence and him. When she did not answer, he stepped out of the shadows wearing less than he had the night they met. His chest was broad and naked. His feet were bare. A ragged blanket of rough brown wool hung across his shoulders. His pants she recognized as the same from the other night, made of the same material as the blanket but thinner and frayed.

How can such a ragged thing look so beautiful, she wondered. Determined not to be distracted, she gripped the leather in her hand until it bit into her palms and answered.

"I have."

The man before her closed his eyes and nodded. Sadness cloaked every angle and feature on his face.

"I have waited many years for the certainty in your voice. Do not tease me if it is not so."

Lilavois had imagined this moment so many times. Slowly, she pulled out a dagger from her cloak laced with moon fire potion. Most of the weapons in the convent were made of steel, but this one Lilavois had fashioned for herself from iron and a shard of blue jade from her homeland. Among the rarest and hardest substances, blue jade could only be found at the heart of a mountain where the lava cooled and blended with the earth and elements to create something entirely new. On her island, it was said to be one of the most powerful wards against evil. Only the wealthiest people could afford even a sliver. But before she left for the convent, Lilavois's grandmother, Lilith, had given her an entire shard, two inches thick and six inches long. Lilith had meant for her to keep it as a talisman of protection, but Lilavois knew the moment she felt the weight of it in her hand the dagger it would become.

Though it was dark, the moonlight caught the polished patina of the iron hilt and the dazzling pattern of turquoise blue, red, and brown metallic flecks that made-up the distinctive color of the blue jade blade.

"I mean to do what I say." Her voice was steady, but her heart raced. He looked at the blade and smiled.

"Then may God's will be with you." He folded to his knees before her, his eyes begging without words to be set free.

Lilavois tried her best to suppress her shudder, but the sight of his simple surrender was too jarring. This was not the conquest she had envisioned. Ever since she survived the demon attack on her family, she had imagined herself slaying hordes of feral creatures. Wielding her whip and shield without mercy. Her skill and her fury the only things standing between the helpless many and the tyranny of the demons.

But this was not that.

There were no crying babies. No fathers begging for mercy. No taste of ash. There was only the beautiful edge of silence and a man on his knees, eyes filled with tears that spoke of a sadness she could hardly bear to behold.

"Do not be fooled by my appearance. The moon's shadows are a kindness I have not earned. You must not doubt that I am guilty of all the things you imagine my kind to be capable of — worse, perhaps. Tonight, if you succeed, you do the world a great service."

Her mind told her to step forward, bind him with the lasso then slit his throat, but instead she spoke. "I am no murderer. Speak your crimes and I will judge whether you are worthy of my blade."

"My time here spans more than four millennia. My crimes are too many for you to hear in one night."

"That is for me to decide." Before her resolve could wane, Lilavois stepped forward. "Give me your hands." Though he complied immediately, she knew it was a stupid notion that the lasso could bind him without moon fire. She'd never heard of such a thing, but then again, had she ever imagined a demon kneeling in supplication?

He stayed perfectly still, watching her intently as she used the tip of the lasso to bind him at the wrist. When she was finished, she loosened the length of leather between them so that it touched the ground. From a distance, if needed, with a flick of her wrist she could ignite the moon fire.

"I will not struggle. You have my word."

Being so close she could smell the faint scent of the sea mixed with a hint of flowers. Lilies, sweet peas, night jasmine, and sandalwood, if she was not mistaken. There was no way he could have encountered most of those blooms this time of year, and yet the scent was unmistakable. Slowly, she began to wonder if the scent was his. She tried to hold her breath.

"I only want a true account of your crimes, if you seek mercy."

To test her blade, Lilavois dragged the edge over his bare shoulder. They gasped together as it burned a fiery line across his skin.

"You wounded me!" he said in awe.

"This is what you wanted," Lilavois replied, trying to keep the apology she felt from her voice.

"It is," he said. With a strange excitement he looked from her to the blade to the scar that was already beginning to heal. "It's never happened before." Tears of joy welled in his eyes.

"Again. Deeper, please. You must try again."

Lilavois stepped back, withdrawing her blade with a weary sickness growing in her belly. "Do you not feel pain?"

"Pain? There is no word for what I have endured. I do not fear your blade."

"How many have you killed? Tell me, and I will give you what you ask."

His face fell.

"Is this your price?"

"You are a demon. It cannot be much to tell me."

"None," he answered.

Lilavois stared back at him too stunned to speak. More than 4,000 years. He must be lying, and yet somehow, she knew by the defeated hunch of his shoulders that he was not.

"Why should that make such a difference? I see it in your eyes. You hate my kind. You want to kill me, so finish it. Do what you came here to do."

"I hate them. The demons who attacked my family, but you are something else. I don't know what you are."

"You don't need to know. Please. If there is a chance, you must try."

"Why have you killed no one?"

He was silent for so long she almost thought he didn't hear her.

"Because I remember," he said finally. "I remember the miracle of creation. Even though I am forsaken, I cannot defile it even as I am defiled. Even our demon council respects life to some extent – our own at least, if not yours. It is forbidden to draw our claws on each other."

"Your claws? I thought demon poison only killed humans."

"A demon can kill a human with just a scrape of one claw across the skin. To kill our own, we must use all five with our poison. It's only happened twice since we came here. It affects us differently, but the result is similar except we do not return to our Creator, like you will. We cease to exist."

"And you've asked your kin to do this to you."

RaZiel shook his head. "I begged them. Every one of my kin refused."

Lilavois took another step back, avoiding his scent and the impact his sincerity had on her. She knew what she should do, what she was trained to do, but now she knew she could not do it.

"Please! Do not despair. You are not bound by demon laws. You only have but one life to take — a demon's at that. It should be nothing to you."

"If your own kind wouldn't kill you, why would I? Do you take me for a murderer?"

"I take you for a member of the E'gida. At least a member in training, though in class today you seemed less than attentive."

This renewed Lilavois's caution. "In class? You were watching me?"

"I attended Sister Carpethianna's Astronomy class. You were there. I had not seen you before. You looked distracted."

Lilavois turned away, somehow ashamed that he'd witnessed her that way. "Why were you there?"

"I find her lectures insightful. You apparently do not."

"I do!" Lilavois said defensively. "She's one of my favorite teachers." He frowned, clearly confused. Lilavois sighed. "I've been kept from class on punishment for the last week, and then today, I guess I was distracted."

"I saw your drawing from the window above. You drew three pairs of eyes. Cruel eyes. They were demons I think, but I could not say if they were meant to be mine."

"How could you...?" But then Lilavois remembered demons were thought to have extraordinary senses. Even with the twenty-foot-high ceiling of the observatory, it would have been no problem for a being with such ability to see whatever she was doing clearly enough. But the question was why would he bother?

"What do you want with us?"

"I mean to observe you. To see if the rumors that you are developing a sorcery capable of killing a demon are true."

"So you can die?"

"Yes," he hesitated. "If you will not grant me this mercy, then would you consider unbinding my hands. The leather is…itchy…against my skin."

"Why should I trust you?"

"I do not ask that. Only consider that I have been here over a week, with every opportunity to do harm at my disposal and have not done so."

"And you won't?"

"I will not."

Lilavois drew close enough to loosen the knot then stepped away. The rope left tiny welts on his wrist that healed the instant she pulled the leather from his skin. He rose slowly, taking great care not to step closer or make any movements that might startle her. Watching him, he seemed to be both a part of everything and yet otherworldly too. Every leaf and branch leaned towards him. Lilavois fought the inclination to do the same. She watched as he bent over, shook out the blanket, and threw it across his shoulders then sat on a branch she swore lowered itself to accommodate him.

"What is your name?" she asked to bring satisfaction to her curiosity and distract her mind from cataloguing his every feature.

"I am known as RaZiel."

A sudden gust of wind pushed through the trees, nearly lifting the blanket from his grasp. Lilavois shivered.

"Are you not cold?

His head shook sadly. "Not usually, no."

"You're barely clothed. How is that possible?"

He met her gaze with something hard, bitter.

"I am not human, Ms. St. James. The blanket, the clothes, are out of respect for your world. They are for your modesty, not mine."

Lilavois swallowed, resisting the current vibrating through her that crossed the barrier from surface to bone deep. Is this what the leaves feel, she wondered. She began winding the lasso back together before fastening it to her belt. The simple task helped her refocus.

"How... How do you know my name?"

"Sister Carpethianna mentioned you in class. Even when you weren't there. Yours was the only seat in the room that was empty."

Watching the tight grip of her fingers on the lasso and the tension in her body, RaZiel felt sorry for her obvious discomfort.

"The other demons. The ones you mentioned before — will you tell me what happened?"

Lilavois let out the breath she'd been holding, relieved to focus on something within her control even if the memory of it cut her anew. She retreated to the stone bench far enough away from him to give her nerves a moment to settle. With a calming breath she took off her gloves. The night air felt like a gift against her sweaty palms.

"We were attacked on the way back from my cousin's wedding. They killed my father and one of our servants. He tried to warn us, but we didn't listen. In the end, it cost him his life."

"How many attacked you? Do you remember what they looked like?" RaZiel leaned further into the tree trunk. When Lilavois did not answer right away, he continued. "I'm sorry. I don't mean to be insensitive."

"No," Lilavois frowned. "It's just some things are so vivid in my memory, and others ... seem to fade. I'll never forget the taste of them as they drew near, like a mouthful of ash. I would say three, but perhaps there were more. They were shrouded in smoke and shadow. I can't remember their faces. Just their eyes. They burned this awful yellow. I still see them in my dreams even though it happened several years ago."

"How did you escape?"

"The Sisters of the Light. Two of them drove the demons off with their lassos and their sacred shields. I'd never seen anything like it — like them.

Immediately I wanted to be one of them. I've been training to conjure my own but I'm not very good yet."

RaZiel nodded towards her hands.

"But you have that dagger. I've never seen one of its making."

Lilavois held it up to the moonlight. "It's made from a very rare volcanic rock. At home the elders say it can keep evil intention from harming you." Lilavois met RaZiel's gaze. "It's also one of the hardest substances while still being porous enough to absorb moon fire."

"You think that's why it was able to cut my skin?"

"I believe so."

"Would you allow me to borrow it? For a moment. I'd like to try something."

Lilavois hesitated. Without it she would only have one weapon left. *But then again, if he'd truly wanted to harm me, the deed would have been done a while ago.*

She held the dagger out to him and waited.

RaZiel walked over slowly and took it with a nod of thanks before turning it over in his hands with intense focus. After a moment, he walked a few paces away with his back to her. Every move he made up until that moment had been slow, careful — until the hand that held her dagger rose up in a flash then plunged into a space she could not see. Understanding came a second too late. Lilavois jumped to her feet.

"Stop!" Her voice was commanding yet it had no impact. He did not stop.

By the time she reached him, traces of a strange clear fluid ran down his stomach where he'd pierced his flesh with her blade. He held the edge just below his ribs, trying and failing to push deeper.

"It won't go past the skin." RaZiel grunted through clenched teeth. "No matter how hard I try."

Without thinking, she placed her ungloved hand over his fingers. The jolt of electricity that ran through her made her gasp. He looked at her startled. His grip on the knife loosened, as if he felt it too, as if, like her, he had no idea what it meant.

"Stop." Her voice trembled. "I can't let you do this."

Confusion focused his gaze. "Why should it matter to you what I do? My kind have brought you nothing but pain."

Unwilling or unable to answer, Lilavois ignored his question. "Please. Give me the knife. It's never been tested this way. You might break it."

With grief in his eyes, RaZiel handed the dagger back to her. She took it hastily, shaken and irrationally angry. Hadn't she come to this very place to do what he'd tried to on his own?

"Where is your instinct to defend your own life?" Lilavois snapped.

He shook his head. "I don't have such instincts. Fear is still new to me; before there was only peace. Nothing could harm me. Nothing ever tried."

"I don't understand why you're here?" Lilavois muttered, fighting the need to stay and the warning in her heart to run as far away from him as she could.

"I've told you."

"You're observing the Sisterhood to see if we can find a way to kill you."

"Yes," he replied softly. Lilavois noticed that the fluid as well as the mark on his skin from the dagger were already fully healed.

"Are there others like you who also seek death?"

"Yes. I haven't seen my kin in many years, but we are not all like those you've encountered. Your knife is a promising development. Will you help me?"

Lilavois's thoughts scattered. Parts of her were clear that she should jump at the chance to hasten his demise, even to take credit for it. If she could claim to be the first to have ever killed a demon in this way, her failure to conjure the shield of the E'gida would be all but forgotten. In fact, she would have shown that you don't even need it! This was her chance to finally step out from under the stifling weight of the Sisterhood and prove that she was truly worthy to be among the E'gida.

Except everything about what happened between them felt wrong. Where was the certainty of victory she'd hoped for? The glowing yellow eyes that had earned her fury were absent, replaced by a pleading gaze that threatened no harm. Instead of triumph, Lilavois felt shame for attempting to take a life that felt somehow more defenseless than her own. And though it didn't make sense, she could not make herself act contrary to what she knew was true.

The questions remained. Could she help him? Would she?

"Only if you promise not to try to take your life again unless I am with you."

RaZiel hesitated. "I don't understand. Why would you care?"

Lilavois could not answer that question. She only knew she was not prepared to watch him die. Not today.

Feeling the current from his body still pulsing through her, Lilavois secured the lasso to her belt, put her knife back in her cloak pocket and turned toward the garden gate.

"That is my condition," she said over her shoulder. "You can accept it or leave this place." Though she heard nothing, she could not escape the feeling that he was still somehow right beside her. Her hands trembled more than the cold warranted as she reached the gate and pulled the latch open.

"I accept your terms, Lilavois, if I may call you by that name."

Turning, she was startled to find him not far from where she had left him. She could barely make out his figure among the crowd of Katmon trees, yet his voice felt like a whisper in her ear. He stood amongst the branches, impervious to the snow that had just begun to fall.

Lilavois nodded. "I'll see you tomorrow then." She didn't wait for his reply. She could not afford to. Instead, she opened the gate and hurried back to the relative safety of her room.

chapter three

CLEARER IN THE DARK

FOR the next three weeks, Lilavois was more than a little distracted. Between keeping her normal class schedule and staying up half the night to work on a new series of weapons with RaZiel, her focus was stretched to its limit. Not to mention the strain of knowingly and willingly harboring a demon within the confines of the convent.

On this point, Lilavois assuaged her guilt by reminding herself that no matter how it might appear, she was, in her own way, carrying out the mission of the Sisterhood.

She and RaZiel were not friends after all. They were allies with only one thing in common.

They both wanted him dead.

Lilavois found herself needing this reminder more often as the weeks went on. More often than she cared to admit.

Their truce got off to a rocky start. The day after she left RaZiel in the garden, Lilavois found herself in trouble. On edge and tired from the night before, Lilavois went to class and tried her best. Her best however did not stop her from making a less than diplomatic statement when commenting on Sister Ignatia's sleep potion recipe.

"Who are we putting to sleep with all this lavender? A man or an elephant?" Lilavois said as she worked with Sabine to measure out the ingredients. Sabine tried to muffle her laughter, but the comment did not go unnoticed.

"Did you have something to say, Ms. St. James? A comment perhaps."

"Ah, not really …"

"Something about an elephant, I believe?"

"I was just thinking …" Lilavois began trying to navigate how best to make her point. She cleared her throat. "In my experience, too much lavender can upset the stomach." By the narrowing of St. Ignatia's eyes, she could tell she had not chosen her words well enough.

"Experience, you say. Experience! Let me tell you a thing or two about experience!"

By the end of class, Lilavois had earned herself an incomplete for her potion assignment and two weeks of kitchen and latrine duty for her sass.

That first night, she hurried through dinner, making the excuse to Sabine and Jhonna that she was too upset to eat because of yet another punishment from Sister Ignatia. With a promise to be back in time to help them with their studies, Lilavois left the table to take a walk. She marched toward the garden, outwardly composed and inwardly fearful.

To her surprise, RaZiel took the news with a shrug.

"I was there," he admitted. The barest hint of amusement rising on the crest of his cheekbones. "I watched you argue with Sister Ignatia for ten minutes over an extra teaspoon of lavender."

“Too much isn’t good for you,” Lilavois insisted. “My sister is very sensitive. It can make you constipated.”

RaZiel frowned as if grappling with a new idea.

“Don’t you …” Lilavois began.

“No,” he replied. “Our bodies don’t produce waste.”

“Oh … Do you sleep?”

“All living things sleep in some form or another. Only Abba needs no rest. Plus, I enjoy the sensation of closing my eyes.”

Lilavois was silent. Embarrassed that he had watched her argue and somehow jealous that he never needed a latrine. RaZiel unleashed his smile.

“I must admit the exchange was quite entertaining. I’ve never seen anyone fight so valiantly for their punishment. You’ll be happy to know that your classmates took your advice on the potion measurements. You missed that part because by then, of course, Sister Ignatia had thrown you out of class.”

Catching the mirth in his voice, Lilavois narrowed her eyes. “Are you … teasing me?”

RaZiel paused, stunned by the faint ripple of joy slipping through his melancholy. “It’s been a while, but yes. I believe so.” His grin went impossibly wider.

Lilavois turned away, unable to withstand the sheer beauty of his face any longer. “Yes, I was there too. Thank you! So pleased to amuse you while I spend my evening scrubbing dirty dishes and waste from the loo.”

“I could help.”

“I mean it’s not as if I insulted her directly. She should be glad someone has enough —. What did you say?"

"I could help. I have worked in this capacity before."

"You have?"

"When I've needed to earn money to buy food or clothing. I believe I'm quite good. I've never left an employer displeased with my efforts."

"How do you manage the smell?" Lilavois grimaced.

"I hold my breath."

"For how long?"

RaZiel shrugged. "Until I'm done. It's no trouble."

Lilavois fell silent for the second time, overwhelmed by the enormous gesture and the simple humanity of his words. His guileless eyes touched some place in her she did not know was lacking. Before her stood a member of The Fallen willing to wash dishes and scrub toilets to help her. She backed away with a nervous laugh.

"Oh, I can just see it! You must be trying to get me expelled. Imagine Sister Ignatia walking into the bathroom to find me mopping the floor beside a demon."

"I would be quieter than you and disappear into the shadows before she could see me."

She looked at him warily. Her chores could be done in half the time, but would she really let a demon into the convent just to save herself the work? Even her audacity had limits.

"Thank you but no. This is my fault and my burden. I can't allow you onto the grounds any more than I already have. It would be irresponsible."

RaZiel looked disappointed and maybe even a little hurt. Lilavois could not imagine why, but then she remembered. “I know our work will be delayed a bit, but I have a plan. While I clean, you can stay at the window and tell me what methods you’ve used to take your life before. I don’t want to waste time formulating things you know won’t work. From your experience, we can narrow down a list of possibilities that might yield” — *what was the most tactful way to put this?* — “better results. Can you do that? It doesn’t have to be every detail, just as much as you remember?”

RaZiel nodded. “I can. I remember everything. I’ll meet you below the kitchen window tonight.”

That first week, RaZiel had more than enough stories to keep Lilavois company through all her punishments. Dark as they were, Lilavois could not escape the fascination and morbid humor of listening to someone describe five-hundred years of suicide attempts.

RaZiel’s first attempt had been to throw himself off the Kermine Cliff of Opus. He had been conscious the entire 10,000-foot dive down, both certain and terrified his efforts would succeed. He had woken up shortly after the moment of impact with nothing more than a torn shirt and a desperate suspicion that there was no escaping the fate he had chosen.

Over time, his efforts grew more extreme, from racking himself on iron chairs to running into lightning storms and swords, taking various poisons, and hanging. He had even made an attempt at decapitation that left him with nothing more than an unfortunate haircut. By the third night of storytelling, RaZiel had joined her in the kitchen, pointing out that he was a far better dishwasher and it would serve the Sisterhood best if she stuck to drying the dishes and mopping. Lilavois could not say whether it was the sight of his six-foot-five frame hunched over the wash basin or the sheer proximity of his presence that imbued her thoughts with a restless energy that seemed to burn away her caution.

By the end of their fifth night, after RaZiel told her of his third attempt to blow up an armory full of gunpowder and dynamite with himself inside,

Lilavois put down her drying cloth and turned to put the last stack of dishes away.

"At what point did you finally figure out that fire was fire, and it wasn't going to work?" She tried to keep the sarcasm from her voice, but when she turned around it was clear she had failed. RaZiel had stopped washing. His face was a mixture of shadow and disbelief. The smirk fell from her lips.

"I'm sorry. That was terribly insensitive of me."

"Another one hundred and twenty-three years."

"What?"

"You asked at what point did I figure out that my efforts were useless. It took me another one hundred and twenty-three years, and even then, I refused to believe it until I met others who had tried and failed as I had."

"Oh."

"I never realized how dense I must seem until saying it out loud to you."

"Well, I mean I guess it's all a matter of perspective, right? If you live forever, you can afford to take a long time — I mean, as much time as you need — to figure things out." Lilavois had never been a politician. She tried again. "So, I suppose a few centuries isn't really that bad."

RaZiel stepped from the shadows with a grin that stretched slowly from him to her. "Five hundred years is a ridiculously long time to figure out that I can't die."
"It kind of is." Lilavois pressed her lips together to suppress her laughter.

But then he chuckled, and the sound carried over her as if the earth itself rumbled with satisfaction. For an instant, it looked as if RaZiel was lit from within as soft and pure as the moon.

At that moment, she was certain he was the most transcendent thing she had ever seen.

"In my defense, humans are always coming up with some new means of death and destruction. Every time you invented something, I felt the need to try again. I was also riddled with angst and other strange emotions I wasn't accustomed to."

"I have no doubt," she replied, avoiding his gaze by searching for the bucket and mop. "Well, those of us without eternity to sort out our feelings work." Lilavois threw RaZiel the mop, which she knew without looking he would catch.

"Is it effective?" RaZiel asked inspecting the wooden tool for untapped potential.

"When we're done, you can let me know."

They cleaned the bathroom in relative silence. This was in part because they were closest to the dormitories, but also because the feeling in the pit of Lilavois's stomach was unsettling her. All the fear she'd felt at the thought of his presence was gone, replaced by an ease she could not truly explain.

On the way to lunch the next day, Lilavois didn't notice Sabine and Jhonna studying her.

"I think you're starting to like scrubbing those latrines. You've had that little smile on your face all morning. I was beginning to feel bad about not getting up to help, but you apparently don't need it," Jhonna teased.

"What?" Lilavois had been lost in thought, replaying her conversation with RaZiel the night before. By the time she realized what Jhonna said, she couldn't stop the blush from burning her cheeks.

Sabine's frown let her know she needed to think of something to say… quickly.

"You shouldn't feel bad, and I don't blame you!" Lilavois laughed. "You guys have been cleaning latrines with me for two years now. I think you deserve the break."

The look Sabine and Jhonna shot each other told her that they agreed.

"You're not mad though, right?" Jhonna asked.

"Of course not." Lilavois smiled a bit too enthusiastically.

Sabine let out a sigh of relief. "It's just that now that you're working at night, I have to work twice as hard to study on my own."

"But at least you're coming to class," Jhonna offered. "That week I was forced to rely on my own notes was atrocious."

"Both of your notes have kept me from falling behind in my studies more times than I can count," Lilavois admitted.

"True," Sabine agreed, "But something has changed. I think as Jhonna gets better a conjuring her e'gida, her penmanship is somehow suffering. You know it's bad when you can't read your own writing."

"Was it my handwriting that didn't make sense or Sister Agnes's lecture?" Jhonna huffed. "No one can say for sure."

They giggled together as they made it through the lunch line, then sat at their table. The simple pleasure of sitting with her friends and joking about the day felt centering. The intensity of what she and RaZiel were planning, the closeness it required, had consumed her the past few days. If she had any hope of being grounded, Lilavois realized she would need her friends.

If she told them, would they understand? What would they think of her?

Lilavois still wasn't sure what she thought of herself, and until she knew, she decided to keep RaZiel as separate from her life as possible.

To maintain a modicum of emotional distance, Lilavois dedicated their second week of cleaning duties to identifying new methods that might be more successful than his past pursuits. The burns caused by the moon fire and blue jade had been promising. Working off the theory that it was possible to penetrate his skin, she decided to focus her efforts on developing a means of interrupting the regenerative process that allowed demons to heal quickly, effectively weakening his constitution. If successful, it would make RaZiel more vulnerable to a sustained attack, which could create the opportunity to inflict a fatal wound. If she could break down both his internal and external tissue, a sword or dagger might be able to inflict permanent damage.

With RaZiel willing to try anything, they divided up their labor. After all the dishes were cleaned and put away, RaZiel cleaned the bathrooms while Lilavois snuck into Sister Ignatia's pantry to combine moon fire with ground obsidian crystals to create a weapon that could be both ignited and inhaled. Ground obsidian was one of the deadliest poisons available. Its common name was Maker's Bane because it was known to kill whoever tried to produce it before it could ever be used on an enemy. The process was time-consuming, grueling, and dangerous, keeping Lilavois up well past the thirty minutes it took RaZiel to clean their latrines. Even a few grains of obsidian on the skin would slowly eat away to the bone – with no antidote to reverse the damage. For this reason, it had to be ground with a hand mill in very small batches while wearing full protective gear. Though the Sisterhood kept a healthy store of the stone, which was also used for divining, even the most skilled of the E'gida rarely attempted to process it in its powder form. No third-year apprentice would ever be allowed to make it.

But Lilavois was determined to try. RaZiel had done everything he could to help her, teaching her more than any member of the Sisterhood could ever claim to know about a demon. And all he asked in return was that she try to end his life. Except that every day she got to know him and witness his honesty, kindness, and gentle nature, it seemed more of a crime to kill him than to keep him alive.

chapter four

MURDERER

BY their third week of working together, Lilavois was back in Sister Ignatia's Advanced Medicinal Remedies class and at her breaking point. Though she knew the recipe for the ringworm salve by heart, no matter how hard she tried, she could not get her brain to focus on her measurements. Halfway through blending the ingredients, Lilavois realized she had added too much witch hazel root too soon in the process. With a frown, she noted that the resulting ointment was better suited to treat a foot fungus than the delicate skin of a ringworm patient.

Staring at but only half-seeing the chalky concoction in her bowl, doubt crept into her mind, opening the door to thoughts of RaZiel and the pact she'd dared to make.

What if the poison bombs she had made did not work, or worse — what if they did? How could such a beautiful person be swept from the earth by her hand? Shame burned her cheeks, until she remembered the mantra she'd been telling herself all week.

This is what he wants.

He is not a man.

He is a demon, and his sacrifice and the knowledge she had gained will save many more lives.

Tears of exhaustion sprang to her eyes, but Lilavois refused to let them fall. Instead, she took a deep breath and refocused on the mess in front of her. To salvage the ointment, she reached across her table for a vial of rosemary oil only to drop it on the floor where it spilled but did not shatter. Shocked by her uncharacteristic clumsiness, the entire class turned in her direction.

“Focus, Ms. St. James!” Sister Ignatia snapped. “Creating a new formula for the treatment of ringworm was your grand idea was it not?”

A more rested Lilavois might have pushed back against the smug satisfaction in Sister Ignatia’s voice, but this ragged version did not have it in her.

“Yes, Sister Ignatia. My apologies. I have more in the pantry that I distilled yesterday. I’ll get it.”

Two rows back, Sabine slipped quietly from her chair and followed. In the confines of the pantry, Sabine finally gave voice to the fears.

“Lilavois, what’s going on?”

Lilavois sighed. Keeping RaZiel out of her life had not proved as simple as she had hoped. The late nights and the demands of carrying out their plan had been more grueling than she had expected, but that was not the only problem. As she got to know RaZiel night after night, she was finding it harder to deny the fact that she no longer wanted him to die. The feeling of constantly being in conflict with herself was wholly unfamiliar. Lilavois knew it made her distant, and she knew Sabine and Jhonna had noticed.

“Please don’t worry, Sabine. I just haven’t been sleeping well.” Lilavois reached for the new vial of rosemary oil and held it tightly in her hand. That, at least, was true.

"You haven't been yourself lately. I noticed you've been getting up early the last couple of days. I just thought you couldn't sleep. Has something happened?"

Lilavois had tried to be quiet. Still, she should have known.

"I'm all right, Sabine. I just have too much on my mind. It'll all be over by next week."

Lilavois's skin flushed, but it took her weary brain a full second longer to realize her mistake.

Sabine drew closer and placed a gentle hand on her friend's shoulder. "What will be over next week? Lilavois, please. You're clearly upset."

Lilavois steeled herself to turn around, face her friend, and hold a smile. "I just meant that it's been a hard couple of weeks, and I think cleaning all the poop from the latrines has finally gotten to me. This weekend, I'll get a good night's sleep and feel much better."

Under Sabine's careful gaze, Lilavois did not dare flinch. Her best friend was no fool. She only hoped she had told enough of the truth to help Sabine ignore the rest of her suspicions.

"Don't worry. You don't need to wait until next week. I'll make you some of your sleeping potion tonight. Everyone agrees your recipe is better than Sister Ignatia's anyway."

Lilavois drew Sabine into a tight hug. "That's a great idea. Know what? I'll make some for us both," she whispered, already plotting how she would make sure Sabine got her portion. She had one more early morning of milling to go and she didn't need Sabine watching her closely before her meeting with RaZiel tomorrow night in the garden.

Lilavois eyes burned as she carefully twisted the handle of the mill. At its base, a fine black mound was forming, still glittering in the first light of dawn despite being reduced to almost nothing. Although her protective gear made it impossible, her nails, her hair, even her skin felt coated with the obsidian powder that she had risen to make every morning for the last five days. It had taken longer than it should have, but there was nothing to be done about it. The need to first make the moon fire, whose ingredients she spent all weekend gathering, control any dust from the obsidian, then coat each particle with moon fire, meant that she had to mill slowly enough that the moon fire did not ignite, but thoroughly enough that the dust would be fine enough to inhale. Each portion had to be milled three times. This was the last batch.

The mixture would go into the last smoke bomb that would be tested on RaZiel tonight. The thought made her hands shake often enough that she had to block it out. She could not afford to make mistakes and she could not afford to picture his face contorting in pain as he breathed in the poison she brewed.

Would he fall to his knees as his beautiful brown eyes met hers? Would he forgive her for killing him? Lilavois stilled the mill handle and took a quick admonishing breath.

"You have to stop this!" she told herself. This was their agreement. The reason for their alliance.

Lilavois pulled out the tray beneath the mill. Almost but not quite full.

This should be enough, she thought. She could not bear to make anymore. Besides, everyone in the convent would be up soon to begin the morning meal. Carefully, she poured the powder into a wax-hardened sack then hid it underneath the medicine armoire with the other smoke bombs. Next, from the table that Sister Ignatia used for drying flowers and herbs, she gathered the blue jade-tipped arrows and her dagger, which she laced with a liquid form of the same obsidian and moon fire mixture, tucked them in her quiver, wrapped them in the waxed burlap cloth she used to cover the table, then placed them with the other supplies underneath the armoire. When she was done thoroughly cleaning the classroom, she removed her gloves, goggles, and rubber-hooded gown and tucked it into another sack beside the rest of her ingredients. She wouldn't have to think about killing him again until nightfall. She walked to her room and collapsed on her bed to catch another blessed thirty minutes of sleep before her day officially began.

Lilavois stepped into the damp chill of evening with a bag that felt far heavier than its weight.

Every preparation was made down to how the contents of the bomb would react in the damp air. Having noticed the shift in the atmosphere at dinner, Lilavois snuck away to add ground chia seeds to the smoke bombs to make the poison dust stickier when it made contact with the moisture in the air.

Despite the chill, she was sweating profusely. Her feet dragged beneath her. She didn't have the right to refuse his request, not after everything he had done to make it possible. Instead, she prayed that somehow he wouldn't be there.

But when she arrived, RaZiel was exactly where he said he would be. Stripped down to nothing but his trousers, locs flowing like vines down his shoulders and back. His arms stretched out between the branches of two white birch trees until all three looked like extensions of each other. It was something she had noticed in the last month of observing RaZiel: whenever he was in nature, a part of him seemed to fuse with his surroundings. He was inherently a part of them and they a part of him.

"You're late," RaZiel began. "I feared you would not come."

"I promised."

"That you did, and I am grateful." RaZiel studied her. Though Lilavois's body was covered from head to toe in a protective jumpsuit to keep dust from the bomb from her hair and skin, he knew the hue of almost every strand of hair on her head, the shape of her hidden underneath the bulk of her jumpsuit, and the smell of her skin by heart. His senses were naturally attuned to such things, but not once since the Fall did he have occasion to observe someone *new* so closely for an extended period of time. Normally, Lilavois held herself with a grace and confidence that disguised any doubts she might have underneath. He had never before made a human friend, which is how he knew from the stilted rhythm of her footsteps that she was afraid.

He watched as Lilavois put down her crossbow, quiver, and the soft canvas bag that he knew carried the poison bombs she had made. Carefully, she took two small spheres from the bag and brought them closer with trembling hands.

"You needn't be afraid," he offered. "Please remember this is what I want. You are performing a mercy tonight."

"I know."

Lilavois could not look at him as she placed the devices in front of him on the ground. His voice was kind and gentle — everything she was taught he was incapable of being. There was no wind, but the match she lit trembled in her hand.

"It will take 30 seconds for the powder to ignite. When it does, breathe as deeply as you can to maximize the effect."

"I will," he promised. Lilavois lit both bombs and moved away. Though she kept her bright brown eyes from him, he knew their exact color. *Like the inside of a walnut shell*, he thought. He had wanted to see them one last time but felt unworthy to ask. Instead, he closed his eyes and took in a clear deep breath, drawing in the peace and the stillness of the night. Despite all the lush greenery around them and her heavy covering, he could still smell traces of her sweet, soapy scent.

A shudder came over him as he realized, in what he hoped to be the last seconds of his life, something astonishing.

When he opened his eyes, RaZiel was relieved to find her staring back at him, crossbow held high and ready. She was lovely. In all his years on Earth, he had never longed for a single thing or person until this moment.

“Lilavois,” he said. “I will miss you.”

The powder ignited, swirling and clinging to him, a menacing plume of black and grey smoke. A shadow monster of Lilavois's own making. RaZiel's knees buckled as he held on to the tree branches. He shook violently, groaning and grunting in pain, but he did not scream. He did not let go of the trees.

She watched the powder turn to acid on his skin, eating tiny bites of flesh across his chest, neck and face. His arms erupted in long red ribbons, wounds that followed the strain of his muscles. They had tested a smaller sample of the powder on his hand earlier this week. This was exactly what was supposed to happen. Yet seeing it now felt like the worst evil she could imagine.

But the effect would not last long. His natural defenses would counteract the poison in seconds. She needed to fire the crossbow now. Her fingers closed around the crossbow's trigger. Though tears collected along the rim of her goggles, she could make the shot. She should make the shot.

She watched in horror as his eyes first creased in agony then quickly bulged in bewilderment.

“It burns,” he rasped. The beautiful melody of his voice was ragged and torn.

She felt her pulse pounding against the metal of the trigger. Every heartbeat, a moment where she allowed his anguish to linger. She hovered there unable to move, unable to decide, and unable to look away — until he raised his eyes to hers, wide and desperate, and uttered a single word.

"Please."

Before her mind could deny him, her heart answered. She let her arrow fly.

By the time it sank into his chest, she'd already dropped her bow, was already running toward him, but it was too late to take it back.

RaZiel gasped at the shock of being sliced open.

"Finally," he whispered as he closed his eyes, released the trees that held him up, and dropped into silence.

chapter five

GOD KILLER

"RAZIEL!"

Lilavois tried to lift him. His body was warm to the touch but felt as immovable as stone. With strength she did not know she had, she wedged her arm underneath his shoulder, careful not to disturb the arrow that had landed exactly where they agreed it should, where a human heart would beat. Hands shaking, she checked for signs of breathing, a pulse, which she knew he did not have, but checked anyway, desperate for any sign of life. There were none. She had never been so sorry to have such good aim. New tears broke before she could stop them, before she could name a single one of the emotions she felt.

The mission of the Sisters of the Light had been fulfilled. She had brought everything she knew to this task. Everything she had learned in her time with the Sisterhood and the very best of her instincts pruned by their tutelage. And now she knew, she was a fool. The intellectual challenge of making the powdered bomb was wholly different from the reality that she had crafted something that would cause someone so much pain. It had to be a sin to kill something so beautiful; something that tried so hard to be good.

Holding the stillness of him was almost unbearable. Unbidden, her memory brought her back to the effortlessness of his movement. RaZiel did not walk, he flowed like water gliding through a riverbed.

The weight of other memories came chasing after. The rumble of his laugh. How careful and polite he was. The way he smiled down at her from a height that had long ceased to intimidate. How light and supple his touch had seemed; so much so that it had never occurred to her that his body would be so heavy. All the time they shared, all the things she now knew how profoundly she'd taken for granted or simply refused to acknowledge. She had held herself back from him from the moment they met. Holding his body now she could not deny all the ways she had failed; all the little ways she had lost ground every day as he showed her how beautiful a demon could be.

Absently her hands strayed from his shoulder to his chest. She had never allowed herself to touch him on purpose. Her fingers spanned out, weaving around the arrow to where his heart would have been. As he lay still, his flesh had grown hotter, burning beneath her hands. Until she wondered whether he would burst into flame in her arms. She hoped so. Such a fire would burn through her protective suit and leave a scar.

It's no more than you deserve, she thought.

He had told her many times that he did not have a heart nor did he possess a soul.

I was not created with one, he explained. *A soul is a key that allows you to return to God after one is separated. You were created to be separate then find your way back. I was not.*

Lilavois had always been taught that demons chose this realm to rule. Until meeting RaZiel, it had never occurred to her that they might have ever regretted that choice.

"So, you have to stay here forever?" she had asked him.

"No. I am lost here forever."

Lilavois began to sob.

"God, please…Please, give him a soul. Another chance to return to you. Do not leave him here all alone."

chapter six

OATH KEEPER

FOR a long time, there was nothing but grief and the heat that never waned from his body until a hand closed in around hers.

"No one has ever prayed for me. Thank you."

Instinctively, her arm seized around him, the stone of his form abruptly becoming muscle and bone once more. Yet between her sobs and the rawness in her throat she could not form a single word.

He broke the hold of her embrace and turned toward her. He did not release her hand. "Lilavois? Say something. Please."

"I … thought you were dead."

"I tried," he said. "When your arrow went in, I felt pain. I fell. There was a darkness I did not fight. I chased it in my mind, but it only led me back to the sound of your voice. I could hear you. Even in the dark."

Lilavois looked down. The arrow that had been protruding from his chest was gone without a scar, or even a trace of fluid to prove it was ever there. Stunned, she turned around to find the arrow clean in his hand.

"Maybe next time …"

"No!" Lilavois rasped. "There won't be a next time. Not with me."

"Lilavois, you can't —"

Shaking her head, she sprang to her feet. "I won't do this again."

"But you swore, as a member of the Sisterhood. You swore an oath to be a slayer of demons."

"I never swore to be a murderer!"

"I am not *human*, Lilavois. You and I both know I shouldn't be here."

"But you are!" she shouted. "Despite everything, you are here. Maybe instead of trying to kill yourself, you should find out why. Maybe you should try."

RaZiel shook his head. "I have tried, Lilavois. I can't. I feel this emptiness almost every second of every day."

"RaZiel." Lilavois rarely addressed him by his name. The sound was new to him. Arresting. "I can't help you. I won't."

But he did not hear the thing she could not say.

"If…if I tried to attack you, would that make it easier?"

Lilavois stared at him. As fearsome as he was, she realized at that moment she had lost the ability to see anything beyond his beauty, his kindness, and the conscious way he held himself still and far apart, even now, always giving her the chance to run away.

She turned to gather her things. "If you want to die, you'll have to do it somewhere else. If that is all you seek from this place, please go."

Lilavois did not look at him. Without a glance back, she hoisted her crossbow high with one arm and shouldered her quiver with the other before bending down to grab the sack with the two remaining smoke bombs. The downward motion caused one of the arrows to shoot out. Lilavois caught it quickly, too quickly to be careful. She felt the searing burn on her fingertip before she even noticed the cut. It was a tiny nick at the tip of her rubber glove, but it was enough to bring the worst pain she'd ever experienced.

Lilavois dropped everything she carried to the ground as she held her wrist and fought not to scream. It took all her strength to bear it. She could not even spare the breath to call for help.

Instantly, RaZiel was at her side, ripping the glove from her hand. Lilavois convulsed as she saw the tip of her middle finger dissolving in a bubbly mixture of blood and smoke. Without a word, he put her finger into his mouth, holding her hand firmly, as he sucked the poison. He held her, closer than he'd ever been, close enough to pull her away from the pain of the obsidian powder into the soft warm cavern of his mouth and the hunger in his eyes.

RaZiel stared at her — into her — judging the efficacy of his efforts by the rhythm of her heartbeat, the sweat of her brow, and the trembling in her body. The burning in his throat was nothing. He barely felt the acid chewing at his gums and teeth. His only thought was to spare her what he had suffered. No one should have to endure such pain, least of all her.

He could not say when the flesh around her finger began to heal. Sometime after her blood stopped flowing and her breathing became less shallow, he lost track of time. The specifics of her recovery became clouded by her scent and the way she was looking at him. Or maybe it was the way he was seeing her? His tongue caressed the tender new skin on her finger and traced the jagged scar the poison left behind.

Her body began to tremble again, but in a wholly new way, a way that mimicked his own reaction to the powerful sensation between them and the knowledge that he had touched her and she had not pulled away. Instead, he watched her gasp as her heartbeat began to race in a new cadence. She did not smell of panic, but she was not quite at ease either.

She is still afraid, he thought. *As she should be.*

RaZiel forced himself to remove her finger from his mouth and let go of her hand.

Lilavois swayed a little as he released her, only to steady her again with a gentle hand on each shoulder. He could see the full flush of her cheeks as she withdrew her hand and backed away. Was her trembling worse than before? He had never seen the expression she wore as her eyes shot to him quickly, then looked down at her hand. Suspicion mixed with fear, and something else he could not name.

"I'm sorry," he began, taking one step back and then another. "I didn't mean to hurt you. I only meant to take the pain away."

Lilavois shook her head, trying to get ahold of herself. The pain was gone, but the vibration of him inside her brought a new trembling that felt just as dangerous, just as out of control. She had never gone through so many emotions at once — from pain to shock to relief to calm to something new bubbling up from a depth she had only just discovered. The sight of him backing away from her made her heart constrict.

He should go, shouldn't he? Didn't she tell him to go?

"You healed me," she replied flexing her hand with the same dexterity she always had with no trace of any damage beyond a tiny, raised scar at the tip of her finger.

RaZiel was struggling to focus. Despite her proximity, he could barely hear her over the rush of something impossible coming into focus. He felt the current of her touch running through him, swirling through his confusion. He looked down at her finger where the skin was slightly red.

“You have a scar.”

The fact that his response sounded like an apology would have vexed her if she was not so grateful.

“Did you know your healing abilities could be shared with another?”

“No. I’ve never tried before.”

“RaZiel, imagine what you could do. How many people you could help.”

“I didn’t help you. I caused this. You’re in this garden because of me.”

“If we had been successful tonight, you would not have been alive to save me.”

“If I had not come here, you would not need saving.”

“No!” she said, closing her eyes for clarity. “Because you came here, we discovered —” She opened her eyes, “You discovered what you’re capable of. There’s a reason — a reason for you to stay. To be here!”

“I know the reason I’m here and I cannot bear it anymore. I’m only grateful that I lived long enough to repair some of the damage I caused.”

He had uttered the same words less than an hour ago, yet somehow, the pain that Lilavois suffered from them was worse. They seeped into that deeper place she’d only just found and made a tear she knew he could not reach.

There were only so many lessons Lilavois could take in discovering all the ways she was fragile. She had had her fill for tonight.

If he refused to see any reason he should live, she could not be his ally.

Without another word, she gathered up her things and walked away.

chapter seven

CONSISTENT. VIVID. TRUE.

LILAVOIS avoided the garden for three days. When she finally returned under the premise of resuming her midnight pruning, RaZiel was gone. She did not allow herself to cry.

“You told him to go, didn’t you?” she muttered aloud.

As if in answer, the wind brought his scent to her: night jasmine, lilies, and sandalwood. She had noticed early on that no matter where he had been, sitting in a tree all day or cleaning the latrines all night, he smelled the same. Nothing but loveliness clung to him.

Was it her imagination, or did the trees seem to droop a bit lower in his absence? Beneath her feet, the ground felt a little harder. The night noises around her were strangely muted. If the inhabitants of the garden had less to say to her, she could not truly blame them. They were the only ones left who knew what she had done, and they had every right to be angry with her.

Lilavois dropped her empty basket and pressed her calloused palms to her face.

She could feel the sound her soul wanted to make pressing on her throat. She sucked her bottom lip in and bit down as the tears began to well. Realizing she would not win this fight, Lilavois leaned against the white birch tree that had served as his ballast until her grief broke free. The bark was cold and brittle against her back.

"A month is not so long a time to know a person," she reasoned. Yet the images of him came consistent, vivid, true.

The bronze tips of his locs in the sunlight.

The patient way he listened.

The way he always held her eyes when he spoke a difficult truth.

The distance he kept from her at all times, as if to always give her a choice, as if to always make her feel safe.

The wonder on his face whenever he looked up at the sky, even on a cloudy, dark, and miserable day.

The way he offered rather than wielded his strength.

Desperately, she tried to recall the cold, sickly yellow eyes of the demons that had attacked her family, almost stolen her sister, and killed her father. But the image would not hold. It dissolved into a form which nothing inside her could ever fear.

Somewhere out there was the antithesis to every book on demons ever written. RaZiel had said there were others like him. And while other demons had looked into her father's pleading eyes and showed no mercy, breaking him as easily as if he were a twig, she knew a being such as RaZiel would never do such things.

Wherever he was, she hoped he never found the solution he sought.

Lilavois gave up fighting the words she had wanted to say since he left. There was no reason not to say them aloud except for her cowardice, which was no reason at all.

Besides, the garden was her only witness now, and she knew it felt exactly as she did.

Lilavois gathered the basket and rose to her feet.

"I will miss you, too," she said softly before heading back to bed.

chapter eight

WHAT YOU WISH FOR

AS winter turned to spring, Lilavois struggled to redefine herself, to determine what, if anything, she still wanted from the Sisterhood, and, most of all, to keep her thoughts of RaZiel to a minimum.

It was a strange balance.

The experience of him awakened a new mission in her: to temper the Sisterhood's teachings with a more nuanced approach to how they understood the demon world. What if the mission was not to vanquish every demon you saw, but to subdue them and learn from them instead?

There was little tolerance among her instructors for these ideas except for Sister Agnes, who had taken over the Advanced Medicinal Remedies class after Sister Ignatia left on one of her frequent trips to visit her family. Unlike Sister Ignatia, Sister Agnes was always open to lively debate.

"And what would we do with these demons once we wrestled them into submission, Lilavois? Should we set a placement for tea?" The class chuckled, but Sister Agnes' eyes were kind and patient.

"Maybe," Lilavois ventured. "There is so much we still don't know. They have thousands of years of knowledge. Imagine what we could learn."

Sister Agnes turned thoughtfully. “It is a provocative notion. There is no disputing that they have experienced things no other being can fathom, but they have displayed no willingness to share their insights with us. Violence and manipulation are their methods.”

“There are some early accounts from when they first arrived of them sharing knowledge with us. Even helping to ease the burden of our daily lives.”

Sister Agnes looked impressed. “My! It seems we’ve done our research. You are correct, but unfortunately those records are from ancient times, when they were content to play gods here on Earth. But they’ve since turned from that path and have never returned to it. There is no disputing that for the last few centuries, their record is one of tyranny.”

“Humans have a similar legacy, but we do not assume all humans are bad because of the actions of some.”

Lilavois felt the moment the intensity in Sister Agnes’ eyes shifted from a casual gaze to a penetrating stare. From the sudden silence in the room, she was sure the class felt it, too. Lilavois shifted in her chair, replaying anything she might have said that could have revealed this was far more than a theoretical debate.

“This is hardly a comparison worth making, Lilavois. The cruelty and power wielded by The Fallen is unmatched in the history of the world.”

“That’s true, but humans have also —”

“They are *not* human.”

Though she did not raise her voice, Sister Agnes’ voice carried the full weight of her conviction. She took a deep breath, then crossed the room to stand in front of Lilavois’s desk. At just under five feet tall, Sister Agnes was a slight woman by any measure, yet her presence was overpowering. Her usually jovial eyes felt sharp enough to peel back each one of Lilavois’s layers like an onion.

Very slowly and very deliberately, Lilavois forced herself to lean back and relax in her chair.

I will not give him over to you, she thought, suddenly fearful and protective of him. She took her time, licking her lips and modulating her tone before she continued.

“We have assumed that they are capable of nothing but violence. Yet if we choose it — and we *can* choose it — why wouldn’t they be able to make different choices as well? From what we know of them, they are actually capable of many things: transformation, long life, access to infinite knowledge. It would stand to reason that they have as much, if not more, capacity for choice than we do.”

A memory of him smiling with his eyes closed against the sun scattered the focus in her thoughts. She turned from Sister Agnes’ gaze.

“They came from a place of eternal beauty and peace. What if their basic instinct is to love? What if they learned the need to dominate from us and used it to make themselves fit into our world?”

From the stunned expressions of her classmates, Lilavois didn’t have to guess; she *knew* she had said too much, but she could not find it within herself to regret it. Two things could be true at the same time. She had learned this the hard way. When Lilavois met Sister Agnes’ eyes again, they were filled with worry and a flicker of suspicion.

“These are important questions, Lilavois.” Sister Agnes’ voice was calm, but the steel had not left her gaze. “I’m glad you’ve had the courage to raise them. This is the true purpose of study, to examine all questions so that we might discern fact from fiction and carry out our mission with certainty. If they are in fact higher beings, they have failed to live up to their making. There is no evidence of what you speak, child. Perhaps in the beginning they were as you say, but the Fall twisted them away from whatever their true nature might have been. They testify to what they have chosen to be in their actions, as all creatures do.”

Sister Agnes reached for Lilavois’s chin and held it firm. “I have observed your mind ever since you came to us, and I have never known you to entertain romantic notions. All ideas are welcome and worth exploration, but I offer you this one caution if you choose to ponder this idea further.”

Sister Agnes stepped back and pulled the long black habit that shielded everything but her face from view. The tight coils of her hair were gray and cut low enough to reveal the deep scars that ran past the groove at her temple to the mangled remains of her left ear and down to the soft paper-thin skin of her neckline. As she removed her black collar, the fabric of the white robe relaxed around her thin shoulders to reveal more ravaged skin and deformed, misshapen muscle held together by an intricate network of scars.

Lilavois heard the gasp from her classmates, but she could not make a sound. She knew this horror. She had seen those wounds before with blood running from her father's lifeless body. But the memory no longer dominated her worldview. There were other factors and other things that were also true, and she held Sister Agnes' hard gaze even as she took in the pain and anguish the nun had never shared until this moment.

"Through all the documentation that exists, we know that mooncraft was gifted to the world, to humans. Our Sisterhood uses this gift because it is our only defense against their cruelty. We wield the sacred shield to protect those who cannot fight for themselves. While we may dream of exceptions, the cruelty of their power *is* the rule. One does not play with the devil, Lilavois. You are either destroyed or consumed."

Sister Agnes walked back to the front of the room slowly then laid her habit down on the surface of her tidy desk.

"That was quite dramatic," she added with a hard and bitter laugh. "I suppose now I owe you a story. I share this with you now because I knew a girl once who harbored such ideas.

"Her name was Akaliza. She was my sister. I earned these scars defending her after she walked willingly into a harem of other girls who were seduced by a demon who had come to our village seeking mates to father his child. There were eight of them. He promised the families of these women — our family — their daughter's weight in gold and more if one of them brought a child to term. We were not a poor village, but greed, like violence, seems to be one of our most basic human frailties. And so I watched as families sold their daughters for the privilege of bedding a monster.

"But do not misunderstand me. These girls were not forced. Quite the opposite. They were sure of themselves. He was wealthy with a sprawling estate and a handsome face that glowed as if lit from within. They imagined him as a suitor. He claimed that he was not like the others and that he wanted to live a simple life as a human and to know the joys of family and love."

The class held its breath as Sister Agnes paused, maintaining her control over the raw emotion that lingered from so many years ago. After another long pause, she continued.

"Only the prettiest girls were sent, and there were many pretty girls in my village. My sister was perhaps the loveliest among them. I begged her not to go, but she had romantic notions." Her eyes flashed to Lilavois. "Of 'making him love her'. He promised to marry the one who bore an 'eternal heir' as he called it. Of course, things did not go as planned. After a year with no child and no marriage, both demon and townsfolk were dissatisfied. The demon demanded more time and more women. The girls who were already there vied for control and favor.

"The families whose daughters were passed over demanded a chance to cash in on the boon of their neighbors. Some families who already had daughters living with him had spent their small fortunes in anticipation of their daughters' success and wanted more money for the pleasure of their daughters' time.

"Only a small number of parents simply wanted their children back, but over time there were enough of us to mount an attack. My family was among them. As you can see, it did not go well. The few of us who did not die were scarred beyond repair. My sister defended him to her death as did the other seven. You might think he somehow bewitched her, but I assure you he did not. Nor did she love him. I spoke to her often during her time with him. She never spoke of love. No, she was in love with who she felt herself to be with him. The idea that her child would be immortal. She fancied herself elevated above all others, wealthier, prettier, more powerful, and that is what she died for."

"Surely they were under some spell," Sabine said. It went against everything in her nature to believe that any young woman would throw away her life so easily.

"I wish that were the case, but as I spoke with my sister, I realized it was something far worse. The more time she spent with him, the needier she became. He seemed to feed on the worst parts of her: her fear of aging, her jealousy of others, her insecurities about her own worth beyond being a thing of beauty. She saw in him the cure for all these. Without him, she believed all her worst fears would come true.

"He manipulated her, amplifying her own fears to make his approval more important to her. Necessary to her. Her whole personality changed. Her doubts became her arrogance, cruelty, and vanity. It happened to every one of the girls who left with him. They did not die for him as much as the things they believed they would be nothing without."

Listening to Sister Agnes, Lilavois felt a stillness growing inside as the outer layers of her secret fear trembled and fell away. Until Sister Agnes' story, Lilavois had not realized how truly afraid she had been of somehow being bewitched by RaZiel.

It was believed that demons did not have magic, but Lilavois had witnessed the way the leaves —everything in nature — seemed to bend towards RaZiel whenever he came near. Yet in the month that she was with him, she had never experienced anything like what Sister Agnes described. Instead of manipulation, she found him accommodating to a fault. He was patient and kind and never asked her for anything in return for his help. He merely gave his word and kept it. During their time together, she had held back every feeling and every inclination of attraction. She had let her crossbow fly just to prove that though he may have touched her heart, she was still the master of her will. She had nearly killed an innocent man because she feared the softness of his touch.

The class moved on from Sister Agnes' story, leaving Lilavois behind to revel in her own relief. In his absence, she could finally allow herself to admit that she found him captivating and beautiful, not as a creature, but as a man.

Being known as a troublemaker within the convent was nothing new, so when talk of her latest "ideas" and Sister Agnes' horrifying story traveled throughout the convent, Lilavois hardly noticed. However, she did not anticipate Jhonna's and Sabine's reactions. Jhonna had always seen Lilavois's ideas as a more than a little crazy, so her looks of annoyance did not truly bother her, but Sabine was a different matter. Before RaZiel, Sabine had been her closest friend and confidant, but the more Lilavois questioned the Sisterhood's approach, the more she noticed Sabine holding herself at a distance as confusion over the expression of her new ideas turned to hurt, then skepticism.

At first it was nothing overt. Sabine simply stopped asking Lilavois for help with her studies. Their conversations became strained and the laughter between them less and farther between. But something seemed to snap after the conversation in Sister Agnes' class. By dinnertime, Sabine could no longer hold her tongue.

"What is wrong with you, Lilavois? How can you even think those things you said in class today after everything they've done to your family and mine?"

Lilavois had endured harsh whispers and hostile glances all day. By the time she reached the dining hall, even the kitchen staff seemed to scowl as they deposited stingy portions of food on her plate. She had been looking forward to the relative peace of an awkward dinner with her friends, but Sabine could not even wait for her to take her seat.

Lilavois looked across the table where Jhonna and the two other students sat, heads down, studying their plates. For a brief moment, she considered taking her tray to her room, but almost every eye was already tracking her, and she was too tired to leave.

With a sigh, she sat down. "It was just a question, Sabine. I didn't mean to upset Sister Agnes. You know she's one of the only teachers here who doesn't hate me. Why would I do something like that on purpose?"

"Then how can you talk of them as if they're even capable of love? They dominate and destroy everything they touch. Every one of us is here because we've seen the pain they've brought to the world. Did you forget that?"

"My father was killed by a demon!" Lilavois snapped. "I was there when it happened! I watched him die! I don't need you or anyone else to remind me."

Sabine shook her head and lowered her voice, but it did not matter. Anyone within earshot might as well have been sitting at their table.

"Then why do you suddenly want to believe they are capable of anything good?"

"Why are you so certain they're all evil? Why are you unable to tolerate the *idea* that there might be another possibility, another reality to consider? Why is it easier to speak in absolutes than to question? To interrogate?"

"Look at the evidence, Lilavois," Jhonna added. "Yes, there are accounts that they were good once — thousands of years ago — but how can you be so uncertain now? There are still reports of demon attacks. One came just a few months ago."

Tears of frustration squeezed Lilavois's throat. Though she'd lived it for months, she'd never allowed herself to feel how alone the secret of RaZiel made her before this moment. She couldn't explain why her ideas had changed without telling them everything, and if she'd ever thought that might be a possibility, she knew now it wasn't and would likely never be. Without the experiences she'd had, without the new world he'd shown her, they would never understand.

"I … I just don't want to be so blinded by anything that I can't see other possibilities. I want to know what I'm doing is right."

Sabine stared at her in shock for a moment before reaching out to hold Lilavois's hand. There was a new pain in Lilavois's eyes that Sabine could not place within the things they once shared. Yet some things were still true — would always be true.

"We are doing the right thing," Sabine whispered. "We are going to save people, like your father and my family. We'll save them all. You'll see."

Lilavois was about to tell her that she had already decided to discontinue her training as a member of the E'gida when a commotion at the far end of the room drew Lilavois's and Sabine's attention away from the first tender moment they had had in weeks.

"Calm yourselves," Sister Agnes shouted over the raised voices. "We will investigate the reports from the Sisterhood in due time."

"What's happened? There something about the Sisterhood in the paper?" the students around them whispered.

While in the heat of their exchange, Lilavois hadn't noticed that Jhonna had gotten up from the table until she returned holding a fresh copy of *The Daily Drum*, the local paper from Esa.

Sabine turned her full attention to Jhonna. "What's going on? Why do you look so stricken?"

Jhonna glanced at Lilavois first, before unfolding the paper in front of her.

"There's been a demon attack in Bagwahl. The paper says they were raiding villages and demanding fealty. The Sisters of the Light chapter in Meen responded to the threat, but they did not get there first. When they arrived, a small group of demons were already fighting their own kin, defending the village! They drove the demons off, then left the Sisterhood to provide aid. The report said there were four of them. They asked for nothing in return."

The whole table looked at Lilavois as her mouth fell open in shock, in joy, and in hope. But their gazes were not the ones that bothered her. From across the room, Sister Agnes was staring at her with a depth that was too wise to think their conversation and the recent story were a mere coincidence.

chapter nine

ALONE

AFTER more than 4,000 years, RaZiel thought himself acquainted with every kind of suffering. Yet the pain of yearning was a revelation.

Different from the yawning ache of loss or the desperate desire to return to the only place he had ever belonged, this emotion was gentler. It brought with it no urge to flee, no compulsion to resist. Sometimes when he thought of her, it even made him smile. The sensation was hot and precious like a tiny coal burning in his chest.

She'd asked him not to return, and he'd tried to respect her wishes. And at first it worked. Every time he felt in danger of flying back to her, he remembered the sight of her walking away and not looking back even though he could taste her tears in the air.

The memory kept him in place for a month until he remembered or rather finally heard the words she had spoken that night. Words he had been too focused on dying to truly understand.

There's a reason — a reason for you to stay. To be here.

He'd always felt unworthy of her, but since he could not die, with the benefit of time and wisdom, could he not make himself so? Perhaps he could find whatever good there might be in his existence and live for that?

The thought, like so many things she had brought to him, was utterly compelling.

At least I can try.

And as he chased his purpose, the distance between them eroded without any conscious effort or thought.

chapter ten

RUMORS

LILAVOIS was back in the garden, but not by choice. Sister Ignatia had barely been back a week before assigning Lilavois weeding duties, her latest punishment for questioning the elder's assertion that the alchemy of metal and magic could only be mastered by those with a deep practice in meditation.

Lilavois never meditated. Her brain raced with far too many silent questions and loud thoughts, yet she had no trouble crafting the arrows and dagger she had used with RaZiel. She shook her head to clear the image of her arrow piercing his skin.

Returning to the garden had not been easy. Her place of peace was now haunted with shadows that no longer hid his frame and memories too terrifying and precious to be disturbed. A flash of RaZiel's body, still on the ground, made her fingers tremble enough to loosen her grip on the ragweed. Lilavois redoubled her efforts to pull and forget. At least the garden had finally forgiven her. After weeks of entreating prayer and offerings of compost to soothe the soil, the night critters finally came out of hiding to sing their songs. The wind brushed against her skirts once more, the ground became yielding, and the leaves of the Katmon trees did not keep the moon's light from her.

Ironically, Sister Ignatia's most recent punishment also helped validate the new path she'd decided on within the convent. Having dropped out of her E'gida training, Lilavois switched her course focus to medicinal healing and alchemy with a specialty in surgery.

Though Sabine and Jhonna were not pleased, they took the news with the somber acceptance of people who had seen the outcome brewing for some time. As spring brought the beginning of their fourth year, E'gida apprentices were separated from the other students to build stronger bonds and focus on cultivating their mastery of mooncraft. It was a hard separation but one that Lilavois knew was inevitable. She had changed too much, and though she loved them dearly, their paths were no longer the same.

Her heart settled into the new applications of her skills with an unexpected peace. She no longer needed to argue against the dogmatic teachings on the Sisterhood's sworn enemies, which meant the tensions between Lilavois, Sabine, and Jhonna were somewhat lessened. Though she still had classes with Sister Ignatia, she also had far more time for independent study with teachers who were actually interested in her ideas. And though she would never be able to conjure a shield of her own, her training as a blacksmith gave her a new outlet to channel her mooncraft, one powerfully and uniquely her own.

It had once been Lilavois's dream to make the perfect poison to render demons helpless, wounded, or worse. Having accomplished that goal and having seen the horror of her success firsthand, Lilavois had no desire to do it again. She knew there were many demons who needed to be vanquished, but the thought of creating something that could harm *him* was something she could no longer do — especially now that the world knew he was not the only one worth saving.

Reports from *The Daily Drum* came in regularly, each spreading the tale of a group of four demons who protected humans and fought against the recent surge of demon attacks. What began as a single incident reported over two months ago had grown into a mix of fanciful accounts featuring winged angels with swords of gold to more subdued accounts in the papers.

Despite the wide variety of stories, they all had one thing in common: these rogue demons saved human lives. The papers began calling them the Covenant, harkening back to the days when the demons were revered as angels and protectors of the realm.

How fitting, Lilavois thought.

The descriptions of the four demons were always vague, but Lilavois did not need one to know RaZiel was among them. He had found a new purpose just as she had. The thought that she might have impacted him as profoundly as he had changed her made her smile.

Demon attacks were always a possibility but in recent months the outbreaks had escalated significantly, scattering the E'gida and straining the Sisterhood's reserves. The only small bright spot amongst the growing tragedy was that such attacks were always good for recruitment as victims and survivors sought ways to fight back. As the numbers of recruits surged, Lilavois hoped her recent switch to medicine might keep her far away from any conflict.

But it was not to be …

Three months after the first sighting of the Covenant, every apprentice in the convent was called to an evening meeting in the dining hall.

Sister Carpethianna read aloud from the latest issue of *The Daily Drum* as soon as the students were settled in their seats.

The Town of Whent Under Siege!

Women. Men. Children have been attacked by demons and held in the small town of Whent.

Local authorities have called on the Sisters of the Light for help. No signs yet of the Covenant who were most recently reported three days ago off the Ivory Coast, more than 5,000 miles away from these attacks.

In the dining hall, Lilavois could feel the buzz of tension in the room. The space which had always struck her as unnecessarily large suddenly felt crowded with chatter. Not wanting to be a part of what she knew was coming, she clung to the back corner of the room.

"We have been called to provide aid and support to our Sisters who are already in battle," Sister Carpethianna announced. Her words pierced through the noise until only silence remained.

"This is not an ideal time, but there is never an ideal time to be at war. You may tell yourself that you are not ready, and the truth is that may be so, but you will not know what you are capable of until you are tested. Sister Agnes, Sister Ignatia, Sister Zhao, and I will handle any demon confrontations we encounter. Your primary goals will be to provide aid to the townsfolk and organize any assistance that is necessary."

Sister Carpethianna did not try to mask the sadness in her eyes as she continued, "Some of us may not survive this trial. While it pains me greatly to face this possibility, we have no choice. Our Sisters have been fighting for two days; their stand will not hold without reinforcements. Though we study here, the Sisterhood exists because of the demon threat. It is time to join that fight. All third- and fourth-year apprentices leave tonight. It is a full night's journey by train to Whent. We must move quickly if we are to be of use."

From within the crowd a question emerged. "What of the Covenant?"

Lilavois held her breath. To her surprise, Sister Carpethianna took the question seriously enough to answer it.

"According to the paper, the last sighting of them was two continents away. We have no reason to believe they will be in the vicinity to offer aid."

The murmurs of disappointment escalated before Sister Carpethianna refocused the group.

"Other than your weapons, pack only what you must. We leave within the hour. You are dismissed."

Lilavois looked over the crowd, searching for Jhonna and Sabine. She found them huddled together with the other E'gida in training. She moved closer, weaving through the crowd until Sabine and Jhonna looked up and met her gaze with the same fear she felt mirrored in their eyes. They closed the distance between them in a rush, holding each other tightly.

"We'll look after each other," Lilavois whispered.

"Stay close," said Sabine.

"Sister Agnes wants us to practice our shields one last time before we leave," Jhonna whispered. "We should go."

Sabine gave a weak smile. "We'll see you on the train."

"Save us a seat," Jhonna added, before grabbing Sabine's hand and rushing out the door.

Within the hour, forty-two third- and fourth-year apprentices of the Sisterhood had boarded the 10:00 p.m. train to Whent. Sister Carpethianna urged them to get as much rest as possible, but from what Lilavois could tell, no one slept. From her own couchette, she could see Sabine, Jhonna, and the other apprentices tossing and turning in their uncomfortable beds, each trapped within a blanket of dread they all shared. After more than an hour of trying to sleep, Lilavois propped her head up against the window to watch the moon race past and wonder if she would ever make it back to their garden again.

chapter eleven

SOMETHING BURNING

LILAVOIS woke up coughing, her mouth dry and bitter with the taste of ash. Turning to the window, the dark, lush green of the hills that surrounded the convent were replaced by a landscape of twisted metal and charred wood.

Whent was a logging town with a thriving milling industry that supplied timber to all four corners of the Pangian peninsula. She had seen it a few times, first on her trip to the convent and once again on the one trip home she was allowed until her training was complete. She remembered rushing through Whent's colorful main shopping district to the post office to purchase postage stamps and silk-woven stationery before the train conductor announced their 15-minute stop was almost over.

But the charred edifices before her bore no resemblance to any living, thriving town. Roiling plumes billowed from every broken building. Firelight blazed in the distance. Pressing against the window, Lilavois strained to see the town more clearly. The view came to her as the train slowed, allowing ample time to take in the acrid death around them. A few feet away, a dozen other girls were crowded around the main car window.

"Is this Whent?" she asked. She could not imagine sleeping the whole trip, but what other explanation was there for the train slowing down.

"It can't be," Jhonna replied, stretching into a yawn. "The sky's still dark."

"It's the smoke you see. It's past dawn," another girl added, tears flowing from her eyes. "We're too late."

Lilavois peered through the window, refusing to believe her eyes. She searched the rubble for signs of green or a building still intact that might be strong enough to shelter survivors, but there was nothing that was not shattered for miles. In the desolation, she saw her family as they had been so many years ago, trapped and afraid, hoping for someone to save them. For three years, Lilavois had studied, committing herself to the rigor of the Sisterhood's training so she could have the skills to do more than watch people die as she'd done with her father. Too late? She would not accept that.

"We can't be. We have to stop the train!" Jumping from her bed, Lilavois strode down the aisle to the conductor. "There must be survivors!" By the time she reached the third car, she was running, but Sister Carpethianna's legs were longer. She caught up quickly, grabbing Lilavois's shoulder, but the girl bent her knees and shrugged away.

"Stop!" Sister Carpethianna bellowed. No one moved except Lilavois who was finally within reach of the conductor's booth. She placed her hand on the knob twisting it open just before Sister Carpethianna used one hand to slam the door shut and the other to swing Lilavois around and pin her to the door.

"We've instructed the conductor to keep the train moving no matter what. It's over, Lilavois. We have to leave here as quickly as possible."

"But ..." Lilavois stammered, tears stinging, falling. "We can help. We're supposed to stop them."

"They left none alive."

"How do you know that?"

"Because they left a sign."

Lilavois searched the open window, confused before Sister Carpethianna continued. "There was no one here to stop them. The conductor is preparing to switch tracks and turn the train around. We need to leave."

"A sign?"

Sister Carpethianna's eyes squinted to hold back her own tears. "You'll see soon enough — the reason why we have to get you and the other girls home."

With a jolt the train lurched to the left then rattled around a rail that brought them level with a large metal sign. Five figures hung from the *Welcome to Whent* sign. Their bodies swayed in the hot breeze like spent vines. The few blue patches of clothing that had escaped the carnage of the fire and the sturdy custom boots of the Sisterhood let Lilavois and every person on the train know who they were, or rather who they had been before they were hung with their own lassos.

Screams erupted throughout the train, but Lilavois was more terrified than that. Too terrified to make a sound. In her mind, she was back at the tavern with her family, helpless and at the whim of demons. She knew Sister Carpethianna still held her in place, but she could no longer feel it.

In Sister Carpethianna's eyes, Lilavois finally saw the truth. They had walked into a trap.

chapter twelve

RETURN

ANXIOUS murmurs and bursts of hysterics travelled up and down the train car like a contagion, while Sister Carpethianna and the other elder members of the E'gida huddled together. They spoke in whispers that were difficult to hear yet easy to understand between fragments of "too many" and "if they killed some of our best…"

Lilavois took her time walking back to her couchette. Though her intention was not to linger, time itself felt strapped to her feet. She could not, would not, rush what was coming.

She tried her best to memorize the distinct features of each classmate. Though somewhat distorted and blanched by fear, she could still recall the way their mouths bowed in happier times. Jhonna's distinguished height in a crowd. The lovely reddish-brown braids that piled on top of Sabine's head. Some avoided her gaze or barely noticed. Others matched her, heartbeat for fretful heartbeat, until the sound of the first high-pitched screech turned everything into a crimson blur.

Lilavois could not be sure if it was the deafening cry, the explosion of shattered windows, or the impact of two large paws buckling the copper ceiling of the train, that brought her and most of the other apprentices to their knees. Terror and bile caught in her throat as one large black claw ripped a hole in the ceiling. It came so near it would have taken Sister Carpethianna's head off if she had not crouched down in time. Lilavois watched as the woman peered up into the hole with fearless eyes, took aim, and let her crossbow loose.

The claw jerked away.

For a moment, they held their breaths as silence returned.

But it did not last.

They heard the rush of air first before the impact hit. Demons crashing into the right side of the train tilting it precariously off its tracks. Lights flickered. The train canted further, sending bodies, luggage, and weapons flying. Everyone around her screamed.

Instinctively, Lilavois pressed her body to the floor, bracing her weight against the edge of a seat. In the aisle, there was nothing else to hold on to or catch her if the train tumbled over. She looked for Jhonna and Sabine but couldn't make them out among the crowd of bodies on the floor. Unlike her classmates, Lilavois did not scream or cry. Terror still held her insides in a vise. Her only thought was that she was not ready to die and that if she made it to the Ever, RaZiel would not be there, so what was the point?

From the left, something solid hit the train with enough force to hurl Lilavois to the right side of the aisle and stop their descent. From the twisted mouths of those around her, she knew there was more screaming, but the sound was muted by the impact of her head against something cold and metal. Lilavois groaned, reaching to stop the flow of blood seeping from her scalp onto the foot of the seat.

"I'm ok," she murmured mostly to keep herself so. "It's ok."

Others moaned in pain around her, but the lights were out and Lilavois could not see anything. Vaguely, the sudden darkness struck her as strange, but she could not hold the thought long enough to ponder it. Had it not just been dawn? With nausea tightening her belly and the train car back on level ground, Lilavois tried to pull herself to her knees. She made it halfway before a furious roar shook the air.

"Why do you save those who would see us burn?" a voice snarled from the right of the train. In the second of silence that followed, there was no reply that Lilavois could make out before something or someone began battering the right side of the carriage. Lilavois sank back down on her belly, shielding her head from the spray of broken glass. Yet the train did not fall. The left of the train began to buckle inward, with the pressure of something countering the force from the right. To the conductor's credit, Lilavois noted that the train did not stop.

"We must attack," a distinctly female voice bellowed, "or Judah will crush them."

"Can you hold them?" replied a voice she felt more than heard. Despite the chaos, the glass, and the shrieks around her, Lilavois got to her knees and looked out the broken window to her left.

She saw three large, bird-like creatures with wingspans the size of bedsheets covering the length of the train windows. Given the length of the train, Lilavois guessed there might have been others, but she only needed to recognize one. In between them was a man, his clothes tattered and frayed as if torn by wind or singed by fire. She did not see his face, but she knew every other part of him by heart. The perfect cords of his arms as they held on to some fragile part of the train. The ebony of his skin. The honey-tipped locs whipping around him.

Lilavois took in her first conscious breath. "RaZiel."

Her voice was a whisper buried under the deafening crush of metal, screams, and howls of pain. There was no way he should have heard her and yet at that moment he crouched down, bringing his face to the window with a look so fierce, it pinned her in place and pierced her soul. The next moment he was gone. Springing up from the window, she heard the weight of him land atop the train like an anvil that somehow did not leave a dent. Light poured through the right window as two others leapt up to join him.

"It's the Covenant! They're here!" someone cried.

Lilavois felt the hope riding on their name. Those who were bruised and battered struggled to their feet to help those who fared far worse. Lilavois stood somewhere in the middle. Her vision was still blurred. Her head throbbed and her stomach felt sicker with every move, but she registered all these things from within a mind that had no regard for its body. She was focused on the sounds of RaZiel fighting on the roof of their train. Between the snaps and the snarls and the sound of metal bending and breaking, she could not tell who was winning. She only knew that he had come back and now he was fighting for his life and hers.

Their battle travelled the length of the train, too far a distance for her to take in everything, but she stumbled back and forth trying to follow the sounds as best she could. Every now and then she saw a claw hang over the edge of the roof as someone fell. She feared it was him but had no real way of knowing. RaZiel had told her he could take many shapes; perhaps claws were his weapon of choice.

Every cry of pain, every collision against their roof drove her a little bit mad wondering, *Is it him? Is it him?*

After a whirlwind of scuffling and the sound of nails on metal, they heard a piercing shriek followed by the sight of a werewolf plunging off the side of the train into the ravine below. Cries of fury erupted at the right side of the train before every demon still clinging to the moving train swung onto the roof. To the left, the Covenant followed suit. Underneath the almost deafening sounds of demon bodies colliding was a slow steady peeling of metal. A shaft of light broke into the car directly behind Lilavois, but with her attention fixed on the fight above her, she did not notice. Only Sister Ignatia saw the danger as two demons, one in the shape of a gryphon and the other the form of a pale, gaunt man with a bald head and four-inch claws, dropped into the car behind her.

“Get down,” Sister Ignatia commanded. She had barely raised her voice, but then again, she never had to in order to command attention. Startled, Lilavois shifted her gaze. She did not recognize the woman running toward her. Without her constant frown, Sister Ignatia looked serene, beautiful even. In her singular focus, she pushed Lilavois to the ground, then she charged forward. In her left hand, she held the lasso of E’gida high. Low on her right, she gripped a machete of well-worn iron tinged with the iridescent sheen of moon fire poison along its edge.

Sister Ignatia used her lasso first, whipping it so hard that Lilavois could hear the singe as it struck the gryphon in the face. It shrank back, gripping the angry lash across its face in pain. Enraged, the second demon tried to snare the lasso with his claws, but the rope burned the inside of his fingers before slipping deftly away. He lunged so quickly that Sister Ignatia did not have time to wield the lasso again. Her machete, however, was ready. She brought it down with powerful force across the arm that reached out to her. Though the edge of her blade did not penetrate the skin, the burn from the moon fire was evident in the red trail it left behind and the high-pitched wail that echoed through the cabin.

By then, the gryphon had regained its footing, towering over Sister Ignatia by more than two feet. It let out an ear-piercing cry and brought both forearms down over her shoulders like an anvil. Lilavois screamed, as if screaming would do anything to stop the malice in the demon's eyes, but Sister Ignatia was a tested Sister of the Light. Her shield erupted from her body, deflecting the blow. She slid back, absorbing the momentum while drawing the demon close enough to slip the lasso she'd somehow fashioned into a noose around its neck. The gryphon jumped away and inadvertently tightened the rope. It crashed to the ground, clawing desperately at the rope around its neck.

While Sister Ignatia kept her grip on the lasso tight, Sister Carpethianna, Sister Zhao, and Sister Agnes were at her side before the second demon could close in. With their shields and their lassos, they held the demons off, driving them back and blocking the path to Lilavois and the other apprentices.

Seeing their boldness, Lilavois understood two things clearly for the first time. First, she had never seen bravery like what she was witnessing now, and second, she needed to get everyone they were fighting to save off the train as quickly as possible. She looked for Jhonna and Sabine first and found them already in motion, clearing their classmates from the aisles. Together, they agreed to get the conductor to stop the train, then organized the other apprentices to provide help to the injured. With a strange clarity,

Lilavois dove in, blocking out the chaos of fighting above them and the battle the E'gida were waging in order to staunch blood and bind bone with clinical, focused urgency.

While Jhonna spoke with the conductor, Lilavois and Sabine organized the other apprentices to take everyone who was able to move to the last car. With so many injured, the task was cumbersome. They managed to get everyone who could walk out in three trips, leaving only two students remaining who needed to be carried.

When Jhonna returned with two third-year apprentices, Lilavois and Sabine had just finished tying the last of the bedsheets and blankets together into makeshift gurneys.

"The conductor will let us off at the platform in Cypress. It's coming up in ten minutes."

Sabine nodded to Jhonna as Lilavois and another apprentice lowered the first of two unconscious classmates onto the gurney. "We're ready. Grab that end." Jhonna and Sabine carried one student while the other apprentices lifted their last classmate. Lilavois trailed behind, grabbing scraps of bedsheets and anything else she thought they might need.

They had just passed the threshold to the last car when the ceiling fell between them. While Sister Zhao managed to pull Sister Agnes out of the way, the impact knocked Sister Carpethianna across the small cabin and buried Sister Ignatia under a twisted sheet of heavy metal, cutting them off from the rest of the students. Against the exposed smoke-filled sky, another pack of demons descended.

Lilavois took off running back down the aisle. She was not sure what she could do, but she knew she could not leave the reason she still lived dying on the floor. Lilavois reached for the pouch at her waist and the blade that had cut RaZiel's skin.

From a booth on her right, a strong pair of arms locked around her waist and swung her around.

"No!" Lilavois protested, but Sister Agnes had already broken her stride. The elder's eyes burned with a fear Lilavois couldn't deny.

"Go back! Now!" Sister Agnes demanded, before joining Sister Zhao to face the three demons in front of them. Sister Agnes whipped her lasso in a wide arc as if to engage them all at once.

Lilavois turned and ran back down the aisle. At the rear of the car, Jhonna carried a classmate in her arms while the other apprentices used the gurney. In front of them, Sabine conjured her shield to protect their retreat.

"Run, Lilavois!" Sabine screamed. Lilavois kept her eyes on Sabine who was looking past her with an expression of growing horror. Whatever she saw, Lilavois knew it wasn't good. Nonetheless, she pushed forward. Her legs were strong, built for sprinting, but she wasn't fast enough.

She felt the snag of a hook on her gown and twisted away to avoid being caught, but her momentum worked against her. She tripped, landing on her back with such force it knocked the wind from her. Her head was a cauldron of pain she could taste. Bile made its way up her esophagus. She opened her eyes, gasping for breath and found herself beneath the sneer of a beast who merely growled in disgust before raising his hoof to stomp her out.

Lilavois closed her eyes, but the blow never descended.

She lay on the floor frozen as the sounds of growling and cracked bones erupted around her, only to be silenced the next instant. Confused, Lilavois opened her eyes to face her attacker again, but he was not there. Instead, she saw RaZiel dragging a thrashing body down the aisle before he leapt into the gaping hole in the ceiling and out of sight. A moment later, she heard the creature's scream fade as it made its way down the ravine. When RaZiel reappeared, Lilavois had only managed to roll to her side. Cautiously, he approached Sister Agnes and Sister Zhao as they struggled to free Sister Carpethianna and Sister Ignatia from beneath layers of metal and debris.

"Please," he said softly. "I can help."

Sister Agnes looked at him with unguarded desperation but could not bring herself to answer. Beside her, Sister Zhao nodded, taking a pained step backward.

Sensing slightly less fear from Sister Zhao, RaZiel stepped forward. Easing the metal from her hands, he freed Sister Carpethianna first, then Sister Ignatia, who lay at the bottom of the pile. When he was done, he hurled the last of the metal through the open ceiling. He knelt to lift Sister Ignatia from the ground, but stopped himself when Sister Agnes drew back her lasso.

"Don't." Her eyes were filled with tears.

RaZiel stepped back. "I understand, but take heart, Sister. They are not dead." He pointed to Sister Ignatia. "Though her heart keeps an odd rhythm. You must hurry home."

Staring down through the jagged hole in the roof, three beautiful beings stood against the ashen sky, waiting for RaZiel. Each looked mournful, Lilavois thought, as if their efforts had been in vain, as if they were defeated.

"Why? Why would you help us?" Sister Agnes asked, fighting valiantly to keep her voice steady.

"Because we can," RaZiel replied. He turned, catching Lilavois's eyes for only the briefest moment, then leapt on to the roof and away.

Though the train's frame was twisted and battered, its wheels managed to stay intact, allowing the conductor to steer them slowly back to Kesar. To make the journey easier, they abandoned the most damaged cars, condensing their party into a luggage car they made into an infirmary and a passenger car with boarded up windows.

After arranging the luggage car into neat pallets made of a few suitcases and spare clothes, Lilavois organized the least injured into a triage unit. Even with her head pounding and her vision blurry, the task of coordinating their care came like second nature. The biggest challenge was Sister Ignatia, who did not regain consciousness throughout their journey back.

At the convent, Lilavois and others in the Sisterhood worked through the night to break Ignatia's fever and tend to her wounds, using every healing potion they knew. Lilavois checked her eyes every hour for any sign of her return, looking past the burst blood vessels, but there was none.

She only realized she had fallen to sleep when she woke with a shudder, startled by the gentle press of hands on her shoulder.

"Lilavois," Sister Carpethianna whispered with gentle reproach. "You are not well. To help others, you must first take care of yourself. I'm here now. Go rest."

"No, I can do it," Lilavois insisted, wiping the drool from the side of her cheek. The sun barely lit the sky, but it was already too much for her. Even the sockets around her eyes throbbed. She tried to stand, then thought better of it when a fresh wave of nausea swept her stomach.

"Do you truly imagine yourself more capable than the rest of us?" Sister Carpethianna teased. With a bandage over her head and a cane to aid what was clearly a painful gait, the woman was not well herself. Yet her eyes were bright and clearly tolerating the light better than Lilavois.

Lilavois shook her head as tears filled her eyes. The ache. The guilt was too much. "I owe her my life. I was always so much trouble ..."

Gingerly, Sister Carpethianna sat next to Lilavois on the bench where she had fallen asleep beside Sister Ignatia and slid a small vial of clear liquid towards her. "Drink. It will settle your stomach."

Lilavois looked up in surprise as the woman next to her smiled.

"You're an excellent healer, but a terrible liar. You wear your feelings brightly. We only let you stay the night because it was not safe for you to fall asleep so soon after your concussion. We decided to let your general refusal to keep still help save your life."

Lilavois shook her head at the irony.

"Do you know why Sister Ignatia is so hard on you?"

Lilavois swallowed the vial's contents quickly before answering.

"Because I always question her."

Sister Carpethianna chuckled softly. "Because she felt your arrogance would hold you back. She wanted to temper it so when you came into your own you would be as suited to serve as you are to lead."

"But she hates me."

"She dislikes your lack of reliance on others. To be a part of the Sisterhood, you must hold your talents with the utmost confidence and humility. It is a difficult balance. She felt you needed help with the latter. We are a greater power together. Like you, Sister Ignatia has little patience for people she does not respect. If she hated you, you would not have been allowed to stay in her class."

Lilavois's tears fell freely. "She risked her life for me."

"She risked her life for all of us," Sister Carpethianna corrected before handing Lilavois two tiny gelatin balls. "Now that I'm sure your stomach can handle these, take them both. They're Sister Ignatia's recipe, both a powerful sedative and a superior anti-inflammatory. When you wake, you'll feel more yourself. Now go rest, or Sister Zhao will be angry with me."

Lilavois looked at Sister Ignatia. The stillness of the woman made her tremble. Yet she could not bear the thought of this being her only chance to say thank you or goodbye.

"We'll do our best to keep her alive until you're rested enough to resume your vigil." Sister Carpethianna smiled before nodding towards the door and silently giving Lilavois her dismissal.

"Thank you," she whispered before walking slowly from the room.

chapter thirteen

SISTER IGNATIA

WHEN Lilavois woke again it was midnight. It had once been her favorite hour. She used to wander the gardens delighting in the scents and sounds, the shadows that both tempted and frightened her … before he stepped out from one of them and changed everything.

And yet he had come to save me … us, she corrected herself. He was part of the Covenant. When did that happen, and had she played some small part in his decision?

Maybe, she thought, *but you pushed him away. You tried to kill him then told him to leave.* The memory of how he had looked at her on the train flashed before her. Even with her blurred vision, she had felt it. She could feel it still.

Where is he now?

Lilavois tried to push the thoughts away, but they stayed pressed to the front of her mind all through bathing and getting dressed. When she closed her eyes, he was there staring back at her. When she was ready, Lilavois made her way to the infirmary barefoot, as was her custom while prowling the convent at night. As she entered the room, she was even more careful with her footsteps so as not to disturb Sister Ignatia while she rested.

Though the low burning candles barely gave off enough light to cast a shadow, Lilavois knew this space, with its glistening potion bottles and ever-present scent of alcohol, as if it were her home. In many ways, it was. She had certainly scrubbed the stone floors and washed the bottles enough. But tonight, those memories felt comforting. The floor was spotless underneath her feet, and even though she had not mopped it in over a week she felt pride in knowing her work helped to keep it that way. Taking a seat at the empty bench beside Sister Ignatia, Lilavois recalled all the curses she had muttered at the poor woman's expense while doing her chores and smiled despite herself.

"Is that pride or contempt behind that smirk?"

Shocked, Lilavois looked up to find Sister Ignatia staring at her. "You're awake! I mean, did I wake you? I'm so sorry."

Sister Ignatia shook her head. "I wasn't sleeping." With her face now turned toward the dim light, Lilavois could see the deep hollows under Ignatia's eyes and cheekbones. Her left eye was as red as the drop of fresh blood that clung to the corner of her mouth. She had always been a gaunt woman, but never had she resembled a living skeleton until now.

Sister Ignatia's parched lips spread into a wiry smile. "Do I look so near death?"

"Of course not! You just need rest."

"Come now, girl. You've always spoken truth to me even when I was loathe to hear it. Do not fill these ears with lies."

Chastened, Lilavois leaned closer. "Are you in pain?"

"Not anymore. My body has no use for it now. The deed is almost done."

"What can I do?"

"I saw him, the dark angel, look at you through the window on the train."

Lilavois jerked back, but Sister Ignatia's hand reached out like a viper and held her in place.

"I don't know what ..." Lilavois began before Sister Ignatia's gaze cut through her insides like a blade.

"I saw you, too," she rasped between labored breathes. "I didn't know how or why they chose to save us. I've been lying here thinking. Trying to understand, but I couldn't remember until I saw you just now."

Lilavois placed a hand on Sister Ignatia's neck then forehead, wondering if her fever had gotten worse. "It's all right, Sister. Be still. We're safe now."

"They saved us, but he came for you."

Lilavois's hand stilled. "You can't know that."

"You don't, but I do." Sister Ignatia's grip was like a brand against Lilavois's skin. "Be careful, child. You cannot live in two worlds at once without being torn apart."

When Sister Ignatia released her grip, Lilavois thought she might fall through the floor. Her legs, her whole body, shook.

"In the afterlife, I will pray for you."

"Sister, please. It's not what you think. I didn't call him."

"And yet, he came."

Guilt, shame, and relief at hearing her hopes spoken out loud warred within her until Sister Ignatia's laugh drew her attention.

"Poor thing. You've looked for trouble all your life. And now it's finally found you."

"I didn't mean ..."

"What you meant is of little consequence. He saved our convent, and you are the reason. Had you been less yourself, we might all be dead, which makes me grateful for your mischief, but —" a fit of coughing seized her. Lilavois brought a cloth to Sister Ignatia's mouth only to see it stained with blood when her body finally settled.

"Hold on," Lilavois urged. "I'll find someone to help."

Sister Ignatia shook her head. "No! This is more important. For once, listen to me! In many ways, you see what others do not. There are … things … even I have missed. Signs I'm only now starting to suspect. I've used my time away to seek answers. Though my part is over, the search continues. If my suspicions are true, they will find you."

"What answers? Sister Ignatia? What search?"

Sister Ignatia sighed, clearly exhausted from the effort it took to speak.

"I only hope you'll survive the mess you've made," she whispered. "Now go and let me die in peace."

Lilavois watched as Sister Ignatia turned her head away and with a feeble wave of her hand, dismissed her as she'd always done, without another word.

The heat of Sister Ignatia's grip still burned her skin.

You've been looking for trouble all your life.

Lilavois wandered the convent with no plan of where she was going. Stone turned to wood then earth beneath her feet and yet she took in none of her surroundings. Before her, she saw her life —the comfort of it, the defiance to her parents, the attack on her family, the years of training at the convent fighting the rules while greedily consuming their lessons, her arrogance in thinking she could push the boundaries of their collective knowledge, and her failure in forging the shield of E'gida — all of which led her to a demon in need of death.

The perfume of moon flowers told her more than any other sense that she had reached the garden. Clouds shrouded the stars, leaving her to wander in darkness. She stepped past the gate toward all the intoxicating herbs that held her confidences over the years and had been her willing accomplices in countless experiments. She remembered the comfort this place once held for her. The echo of it was still there, but she also felt the absence of light, the absence of *him* acutely.

For the first time, she did not run away from it. When the pain stopped her short, she took a seat at the bench just inside the gate and closed her eyes. Hard as she tried, the memories would not stay locked away. The poisonous gas. His surrender as she bound his hands. The look on his face when she turned away.

The tears came, and here, in the silence of friends, she could let them go. Tears turned to sobs as she let grief and exhaustion take over her body, running through her until she could no longer bear them upright. Lilavois curled up on the bench. The feeling of being utterly spent forced her mind to be calm. Shifting onto her back, she almost felt peace.

Until she heard his voice.

"I am truly sorry for your loss."

chapter fourteen

REUNION

LILAVOIS bolted up from the bench. As if unfolding from the shadows around him, RaZiel stepped from between the two white birch trees, tall and beautiful with the same deep sadness etched into his sable brow, as if he had never left.

He took another step towards her. Deliberate but tentative, as if giving her every opportunity to send him away.

Lilavois could not move. She could not speak. He came within one arm's length away, close enough for the scent of him to wash over her. It was only then that she knew he was real. He smelled of sandalwood, night jasmine, lilies, and wind. All her favorite scents. Her shaking ceased.

"You're here."

"Do you wish me to leave?"

"Never."

Her words unbound the well of emotion inside him. Softening every feature on his face and the entire frame of his body. The tension he had lived with for so long fell away. Unconsciously, he opened his arms. She moved into them willingly and unafraid.

For a long moment they stood there, being still together.

"You saved us," she whispered into him.

"Not all of you. I am sorry."

"Sister Ignatia?"

"She has returned to the Ever. She took her last breath shortly after you left."

Lilavois closed her eyes, feeling the pain of the loss more sharply than she expected. With a heavy sigh, she pulled away.

"She knew about ... us."

"Us? How?"

"She saw you look at me through the window on the train."

If RaZiel could have felt bashful, he would have, but his feelings could not be contained by so small a sentiment.

"I did not mean to expose you to ridicule, but whatever she knew is taken with her."

"She didn't ridicule me. She knew you saved us. She said…you came for me. Is that true?"

RaZiel hesitated. "It is."

"Why?"

"You challenged me to see that my existence might have a purpose beyond grief. That I, and others like me, might be helpful in some way. My sister, SeKet, has been trying to tell me this for centuries, but it took you to help me finally understand."

"How many of you are there?"

"Four. I hope one day there will be more."

"How did you know where to find me?"

"I didn't. We were tracking them from Ohn but lost them again. In Bree, we heard the rumors of a standoff with the Sisterhood. I feared we might be too late."

"But how did you know I was on the train."

"The scent of your skin. There is nothing else like it. I would know it anywhere."

Without thinking, Lilavois reached out, only to realize that he had widened the distance between them as if preparing to leave. She took a step closer.

"You came for me."

"I tried to stay away. Truly. My intention was to keep you from harm, but then I saw you were injured, and Sister Ignatia was hurt. I had to make sure you were all right."

"You're trembling," she whispered.

"It is hard to leave you. I must force myself to move."

"What if I didn't want you to leave? What if I changed my mind?"

"You should not," RaZiel rasped. "It's better if we part."

"Why?"

"Because I know this feeling and I am not worthy of it."

"Who are you to decide that?" She took another step closer. He did not back away.

"These … feelings," he said.

She was close enough to see directly into his eyes. "You don't know what I feel. You've never asked me."

RaZiel stared in silence, bewildered.

"Has it occurred to you that I might have missed you, too?"

The pain of loving her entire existence was enough. He could not bear the hope. "You should stay away from me."

"I thought that was what I wanted, but now I want you to stay."

She placed her hand on his chest and felt the frantic pulse of her own heart echo back to her. He shuddered but did not move.

"Lilavois, I am cursed because I could not trust the only thing that is true. God has forsaken me as I chose to forsake Them."

"I don't believe that. Can't you see yourself? The flowers, the trees, the grass underneath your feet, all bend to be near you. They know who you are. They love you. Nothing so connected to everything pure can be unloved."

"They remember me, perhaps, but I am only a shadow of what I was."

"Then your shadow is enough. What if . . . what if I loved you, too? Could you accept that?"

RaZiel's eyes filled with tears. The space in his chest felt tight. He needed no air, yet he struggled to breathe.

"I failed to recognize love once before and lost everything. Never did I expect its light to shine on me again. If that is truly what you offer, I could not refuse."

It had been so long since he had wanted anything other than death, freedom from the slow maddening ache of being separated from the source of true peace. But he could not deny the look in her eyes. He knew that look. He had seen it reflected back to him when he stared into the calm surface of a gentle stream thinking of her or felt his eyes glisten with the same moisture when he looked to the sky. There was wonder. There was love. A love he knew because he felt it too, regardless of whether he deserved it or not. She was a miracle.

They both stepped closer than they had ever allowed themselves to be. Her skin, her entire being was charged with anticipation.

RaZiel placed his hand on Lilavois's neck and brought their foreheads together so that he could breathe her in more deeply. "I am broken, Lilavois.

What could I offer you?"

"Your love," she answered. "That is what I want."

"That is the only part of me that is whole, and you have it. You must know that."

"It is of no use if you keep yourself from me."

"What else can I do?" He stared down at her, the confusion on his face showing that he truly did not know.

His innocence, despite the eternity of his existence, all the horror and miracles he'd witnessed and the sheer power of his being, made her smile.

"Give yourself to me," she whispered, before tilting her head up to touch her lips to his. The sensation was so soft yet electric, like dipping her hands into a pool of cool water. His lips brushed hers gently with enough pressure and rhythm to feel him everywhere. When she opened her eyes, RaZiel was looking back at her with all the awe and surprise she felt. They shared a slow smile as their lips parted and their breaths mingled in the same slow exhale.

"Does it always feel like this?"

Lilavois thought about all the suitors she'd had back home. She'd hardly liked any and only kissed a few. She could not recall a single one being worth the effort, but then again, she had never felt anything like this.

"I don't know," she replied thoughtfully. "I've never kissed someone I loved before."

"Neither have I," RaZiel said, pulling her close to bring her lips to his once more.

They stayed that way for a very long time.

chapter fifteen

SOMETHING NEW

FOR two people with very little experience kissing, RaZiel and Lilavois were determined to spend the rest of the evening perfecting their newfound skills.

"It's almost dawn," Lilavois whispered into RaZiel's neck as she ran her lips over the smooth edge of his jaw. Reflexively, he squeezed her more tightly against his chest.

"I should have let you sleep. You could sleep here. I'll be very still."

Lilavois glanced up to catch him smiling down at her.

"And what will you do? Watch me?" she teased.

"No. I'll do this," he replied before lifting her entire body close to his nose and inhaling deeply. The sensation of being carried so easily was jarring.

"Stop that!" she laughed, trying to wiggle away despite knowing he would not let her go.

"I can't." His lips trailed kisses from her shoulder to the hollow of her neck, watching in awe at the way it made her shiver with pleasure. "You are my favorite scent."

Lilavois stared back at the love in his eyes, so open and immense she could barely breathe. She leaned forward and kissed him back, trying with all her heart to give him everything he had given her.

An hour later they were nestled together under the Katmon trees as the pale blue light of morning peeked through the leaves. Lilavois had drifted off for only a moment, but he wanted to make it last as long as he could. Yet if she did not wake up soon, she would risk getting in trouble.

"Sister Zhao is up," RaZiel whispered reluctantly. "I can carry you back to your room, but we'll need to hurry."

"No, I can make it," she yawned. Lilavois went to stand and almost stumbled over before RaZiel caught her.

"Are you certain?" His face was so etched with concern it made Lilavois smile.

"You've been holding me all night. My legs have forgotten how to support themselves."

Lilavois's second attempt was more successful than her efforts to beat the wrinkles from her gown. She gave up after a moment in favor of a more pressing matter.

"How will I find you?"

"I'll wait for you here as always."

"All day?"

"Of course."

Lilavois frowned, shocked she did not already know the answer to the question she was about to ask.

"Where do you go when you're not here? Do you have a home?"

"I . . . wander," RaZiel replied. "I don't usually stay in any one place very long. I've not needed to before."

"Well, that's not going to work. I have one more year of school. You can't stay in this garden the whole time, and I can't take you into the convent with me. You need a place to be."

Lilavois looked him over with eyes that were determined to sort out a very obvious but never before tackled problem. "You probably don't have any money," she muttered more to herself than him. "I have some, but I doubt it would be enough for more than a room at the Raven Inn, and that's really too public. People will talk. I could send for more, but then I'd have to give an explanation. My sister, Charmaine, is so nosy. She'll tell Mother, then I'll never have a moment's peace ..."

RaZiel watched Lilavois as she began to pace, contemplating what she was offering. Permanence, companionship, things he had never thought to have, but wanted now with an urgency that was thrilling.

"You want a home," he asked, still stunned by the notion. "A place for us."

"It would be nice," Lilavois responded shyly. "Someplace we can be together."

RaZiel beamed. "Like a house."

Lilavois smiled back, amused by his excitement. "Or a shack or anything that won't let in the rain. It doesn't have to be fancy. My father left me money. I could post a letter to my bank for funds today."

RaZiel nodded, ideas he had never contended with rushed to the forefront of his mind. "Give me three days to return."

"Return from where? I thought you didn't have anywhere to go."

RaZiel's answering kiss was as deep as it was quick.

"Three days," he said. "You'll see."

chapter sixteen

EVERLAN

THREE days later, RaZiel placed a heavy polished metal key in her hand and Lilavois had her first inkling that he'd gone too far.

"You found a place?"

"A home," he corrected. "For us."

The implications of 'us' made her heart race.

"I hope you like it. I've never had a home. I wasn't sure what it should have."

"Before, there wasn't a place for you to keep your things?"

RaZiel smiled, taking in her pressed apron and lace trimmed shirt. The delicate pink pearl earrings she wore and the fine leather boots that peaked out from underneath her skirt.

"I didn't have any *things*, Lilavois. I rarely ever took form. There was no one place that I belonged. The Ever was my home."

Lilavois hesitated, looking at the key in her hand. "A home is not just where you belong, it's also where you keep what you love." She took his hand, happy to see some of the pain in his eyes subside. "Where is it?"

"Not far. I picked a place you could get to easily by horse."

"Horse?" Lilavois questioned, running over in her mind all the structures that were near to the convent. There weren't many. The church, a small abandoned castle past the northern edge of the convent's border, and a few houses scattered across the countryside. She had no idea what he could be referring to.

"The convent stables are off limits to us. Only the E'gida ride. Did you build a house?"

RaZiel hesitated. "No. I found something suitable. I hope." Lilavois tracked the anxiousness in his brow to the key he'd placed in her hand.

"All right. How do we get there? "

"I can fly there."

Lilavois stared at him. "I thought you lost your wings."

"My angel wings, yes, but I can transform into any creature I choose. I can turn into a bird and carry you."

Lilavois's eyes went wide. She had seen him transform before but could not imagine what kind of a bird could bear a fully grown human's weight. After pondering for a second, she decided she didn't want to know.

"Ah, I don't think I'm ready for that."

"It would be quick. You can close your eyes if you're afraid."

"No, I don't think I want to see the bird that could carry a whole human in flight."

"It's quite beautiful," RaZiel smiled. "They haven't evolved here, but in the Sukili Galaxy, they are spectacular beings."

"The Sukili Galaxy? Where is that exactly?"

RaZiel realized with a start that she had no reference for what he was referring to. Worse, she would never see the creatures with translucent feathers that reflected the many suns of the galaxy he could picture so clearly.

"It's two thousand of your lifetimes away," he said quietly. "I wish you could see it. I wish we could travel there one day together."

Lilavois stepped close, placing her hands on his cheeks. "Then you can draw it for me. We can decorate the house with drawings of all the creatures from all the places you've seen."

RaZiel turned and kissed the palm of her left hand. "Would that please you?"

"It might," she teased. "But first I have to see what we're working with."

Her smile pulled him back from his sadness. "OK, I'll bring around the horses."

He was already walking toward the barn when she whispered, "The stables are closed."

"Not for me."

"You bought a castle!"

"For us." The fact that she had said it four times was beginning to make RaZiel feel like perhaps this was not the thing he should have done. "Do you not like it?" SeKet had sworn to him that women liked grand gestures.

Lilavois shook her head and smiled, circling the large foyer that led to an even grander dining room. Beyond a large, round table and chairs enough for eight people, the rooms were completely bare. Lilavois did note that somehow, he had managed to clean and dust every surface.

"It's not that I don't like it. I was just expecting something smaller. Like a cottage."

"There weren't any cottages that were close to the convent for sale," he explained apologetically. "And I thought building a cottage would attract too much attention. I also wanted to make sure that it would be easy for you to travel the distance between here and school safely."

"And where did you get the money for all of this?" she asked, looking at his coarse pants and simple tunic. "You said you didn't have any money."

"I said I didn't have any *things*. *You* said I didn't have any money."

"And *you* didn't correct me."

"I didn't want to interrupt. I enjoy watching you walk around in circles."

Lilavois closed her eyes and shook her head. "Go on."

"My sister SeKet keeps track of money and those types of things. Just in case we need something," he said simply.

"Like a castle."

"Like a home." RaZiel corrected.

Lilavois extended her hand. "All right then," she said with a grin. "Show me the rest."

"You like it?" he asked, gently pulling her close as they walked up the stairs.

"How could I not?"

They took their time winding through each room, taking in the views and the way the moonlight made each space glow with the same dewy peace that Lilavois felt vibrating between them. Even though the castle had been abandoned for many years, it was in good condition. And as she passed through each doorway, she began to understand the enormity of what he was offering. While she had only been thinking of a place to stay, he brought back a place that could truly be a home. A place that could hold an eternity of love shared by two.

As they moved from the library and drawing rooms to the living quarters and bedrooms, RaZiel let go of her hand, dropping back to watch her as she roamed. He paced his steps to the sound of her heartbeat for no other reason than he didn't know what else to do.

This experience was completely new to him. The thought made him dizzy with excitement. Behind her, RaZiel smiled quietly at the very source of his joy, in awe of the sweet tension that grew and expanded with every step she took away from him. Her thorough inspection tickled him as he took note of her tastes and things that must be changed, making a list that would keep him busy for months. When Lilavois reached the master suite, he waited in the hall and listened to her soft gasps of approval and the click of her heels as she moved from the wood of the floor to the tile of the bathroom and back. She returned to settle in the doorway. Her eyes were calm but heavy, and her scent had changed to something utterly provocative. He inhaled deeply.

"What are you smiling about?" Lilavois asked leaning against the door frame.

"You. You like it here."

"How do you know? Maybe I haven't decided yet."

RaZiel shook his head, but there was something deeper than humor in his eyes.

"I can smell your pleasure."

For a second, Lilavois held her breath, startled by how the soft tone of his voice hit her so profoundly, and she wondered just how deeply his sense of her could go.

"Can you?"

"Yes. Does that bother you? Your heart is racing."

"You do that to me a lot."

"Is that a good thing?"

"What does it smell like?"

RaZiel closed the distance between them so quickly he was almost a blur, but his kisses landed softly before they consumed her wholly. They kissed and planned and kissed some more in an empty house with no bed until dawn.

In between RaZiel's trips to fight with the Covenant, he worked to bring the plans they made for their home to life. While Lilavois attended classes, RaZiel spent his time planting seeds for their own garden, making sketches of galaxies and creatures from other universes, painting and ordering carpets to cut the chill in the air he never would have noticed if she had not said anything. And when he was done, he waited for night to come, so that he could send the steed he had brought to carry her back to him.

In two months, almost every room was finished to her specifications, which suited him fine because all he wanted was to be surrounded by her. When she was not there, he felt satisfied that her favorite patterns and colors kept him company until she returned. The new bed they designed together was now finished and would arrive by afternoon.

His thoughts raced with the realization that they might finally sleep in a real bed through the night and perhaps more. She had spent most of the last month asleep in his arms while he drank in the sounds of her soft breathing, memorizing the feel of her body against him, and letting the warmth of her skin penetrate every part of his being. While he did not need as much sleep as she did, he often let himself drift off with her, finding peace for the first time in his life on Earth.

Each night RaZiel waited by the castle bell tower because he liked to close his eyes and hear her approach. From his perch, RaZiel counted the seconds, never quite getting used to the thrill he felt, the rightness that overwhelmed him. As her horse, Enod, galloped through the gates, RaZiel jumped down from the tower and landed outside the front door to greet her a moment before she arrived.

"Were you on the top of the tower a minute ago?" she asked while peppering his lips with kisses.

RaZiel's smile was shy, but earnest, in between returning her kisses.

"Are you hungry? I made beef stew just the way you showed me."

Lilavois took his hand and led them inside. "Always!" she laughed. "They served lamb in the dining hall tonight. Jhonna told me it was good, but no one could truly enjoy it over Sister Zhao's speech. She spent the entire dinner admonishing us for our lack of discipline. Every afternoon between classes and dinner, she intends to take us out for chores and exercises to sharpen our fortitude. Luckily, I'm already in trouble with Sister Agnes so I think I'll be excused."

Lilavois walked into the kitchen first and stopped at the small table RaZiel had built while she was away. It was set with two bowls of stew and a cluster of lit candles. It was not an unusual sight. He made their dinner almost every night of the week. On the weekend, she used her fourth-year weekend privileges to pretend to be visiting nearby relatives. Saturdays and Sundays, she cooked, teaching him new recipes that he would perfect then feed back to her during the week. It was a routine that touched her deeply every single time.

"Thank you," she said quietly, settling down into the seat he pulled out for her.

RaZiel kissed the top of her head and smiled. "You are welcome." As before every meal, RaZiel took her hands and offered a blessing over the meal. During their prayer, Lilavois took a moment to marvel at the faint glow that emanated from his being whenever he prayed. She had told him about it their first meal together, but the observation seemed to make him sad and so she didn't bring it up again.

"Did you pray like this before?" she asked before taking the first spoonful of stew. "Oh! This is delicious."

"We did not eat," he explained. "So we did not offer blessings for food as many of you do here."

Lilavois began sopping up the stew with bread. "You never wanted to taste anything? Even for reference? I can't imagine that."

RaZiel took a helping of his own bowl then sat back, sifting through words to explain a way of being that was completely foreign to anything mortal.

"Our sense of smell is very strong. I always knew how something might taste. It just never produced a need to eat. And prayer is a constant thing in the Ever. Every thought is prayer. Every word we speak to God directly, within ourselves and through each other."

"But no stew?" she teased. This made RaZiel laugh as she knew it would.

"No stew," he agreed.

They had spoken of this before, but as Lilavois scooped up the last of the broth with her last crust of bread (how did he always know the perfect portions for each serving?), she knew she could not truly fathom an existence without need or desire for pleasure in any form.

The last thought made her blush. They had spent every night together since he had rescued their convent on the train two months ago, and in that time, they had gotten close. She relished their kisses and falling asleep in his arms after long talks, but she had never been with a man. Before RaZiel, she'd never particularly wanted to. At first, she was nervous, but his gentleness and his patience eased those feelings away until only curiosity and desire were left — that and want of a bed. She could see it in his eyes when he looked at her and feel in his touch that he felt the same way, but he never pressed.

Over the last month, Lilavois realized that with the patience of an angel, he most likely never would. She was not that patient. The question was how to begin.

“Are you satisfied?”

“What?” Lilavois’s blush deepened. “I mean, yes. I’m not hungry anymore.”

RaZiel watched her pensively before taking her hand.

“Is everything all right? You seem so on edge.”

Lilavois closed her eyes and took a deep breath, trying to calm all the nerves that sprang to life in her body whenever he touched her.

“Lilavois?” Something in his voice made her open her eyes. “Is this because your bedroom is ready?”

She looked away, overwhelmed by her desire and the fact that he could see it so plainly.

“I don’t expect anything from you, Lilavois.” His calm acceptance suddenly infuriated her.

“But what if I do?”

They stared at each other in silence until his gaze grew so intense she had to look away. RaZiel leaned across the table and took her other hand in his.

“I will give you whatever you want.”

Something deep inside her fluttered. There was a certainty in his voice that spoke of confidence and experience. She was both jealous and relieved. At least one of them would know what they were doing.

"You've done this before?"

He nodded. "When we first came here. Many, many years ago. Have you?"

Lilavois thought about the boy she had kissed and fondled in her brief but adventurous days before the Sisterhood. She might have if the boy had been able to get out of his own trousers before succumbing to the most cursory of explorations.

"No, I've never had this experience."

"Neither have I. I've shared my body, but never myself, my love. Nothing like this has ever happened to me."

Lilavois reached out to caress the smile that blossomed on his face as he said the words.

"But I don't want you to be anxious. You are safe with me."

"I don't know what to do." Her laugh was thin and unsure.

"Why don't I draw you a bath?"

Lilavois watched the water drip through her trembling fingers, enjoying the luxury of doing nothing. Still, the anxious excitement that bubbled through her belly made gentle tremors in the water. Soaking in the washroom that he had painstakingly rebuilt for her with pearl white tiles and blue accents to remind her of the beaches of her homeland, she was grateful for the peace of her surroundings. But more than that, she was surrounded by his love.

Somewhere outside the door, she could feel her tremor connecting with the energy of his presence.

Did she want him to come to her?

Lilavois licked her lips. She would only need to whisper his name.

"Lilavois, are you all right?"

She let out a shuddering breath and smiled. Apparently, she would not even need to do that much.

"I'm fine. Why do you ask?

"Your heart." His fingers brushed against the door lightly. "It races. I thought perhaps I drew the water too hot. I brought you a glass of water. I could leave it by the door."

"Thank you."

"Of course."

"RaZiel?"

"Yes."

"Would you like to take a bath with me?"

"Are you sure?"

"Would you like to?"

"I would like that very much."

He stepped into the bathroom with bare feet and a glass of cool water in his hand.

Her chest broke out in a rash of sweat at the sight of him. He was still clothed, but the thought that he soon would not be made her heart race with an anticipation that felt slightly less than courage, yet very far from fear.

"Are you sure the water isn't too hot? You're sweating."

"It's fine," she said, taking the glass he offered and pressing it to her cheek before taking a sip.

"Your heart is still racing ..." His voice trailed off watching the mound of bubbles break over the surface of the water. There were thousands of them, but each would eventually dissolve revealing the length of her body submerged underneath. His eyes returned to hers. "If I had a heart, it would be racing, too," he whispered.

Lilavois smiled, his shyness giving her courage. "Come in before the water gets cold."

She watched as RaZiel reached for the loose muslin shirt he washed and wore almost every day, and slipped it off, letting it fall to the floor softly.

He was always beautiful. There was no ignoring the obviousness of his perfection, but in the dim candlelight, glowing in the moist air of the bathroom he made for her, he was more than that. He was hers.

His slim fingers flicked the buttons of his trousers. In one efficient motion they were off, revealing something she did not realize until this moment: RaZiel wore no underwear.

With a subtle elegance that was unhurried yet sure, she watched his long powerful limbs climb over the edge of the tub and descend beneath the water until she felt his feet come to rest at either side of her hips. The shock of being this close seemed to reset all her senses. Her breathing, along with her sense of time, slowed. Outside this room, there was no one. Nothing. Under the water, he reached for her foot and brought it to his lips, kissing her toes one after the other.

Her whimper was tiny, but in the world they made together, it ricocheted off the walls and set something in RaZiel's eyes ablaze. Embarrassed and aroused beyond her senses, Lilavois moved to pull away, but he held her firm by the arch of her foot.

"Does it tickle?"

"No."

"Should I stop? Do you not like it?"

"I think I like it too much," she laughed. "You make me tremble."

"You do the same to me," he replied while massaging the arch of her foot. "I like the way it feels."

"Me, too, but it feels a little out of control."

"I don't want you to be afraid." He lifted her leg higher to knead her heel. "Touching you like this calms me, and at the same time, I feel overwhelmed. Tell me if you want me to stop. I will do whatever you ask."

He placed her foot on his chest, where she could feel his muscle shifting as he leaned forward. His touch traveled from her ankle to her calf to her knee. The core of her was a pulsing river almost completely open to him now and it felt exactly right.

"Don't stop."

RaZiel responded by raising her leg and pressing a kiss into the tendon just above her ankle. He took his time caressing and sometimes licking her skin, behind her knee, just inside her thigh, always letting out varying octaves of the same satisfied hum.

In contrast, Lilavois had become this panting, gasping thing, holding on to the edge of the tub as if it were the last tether to her sanity. She was about to lose her grip when RaZiel suddenly shifted his position, kneeling before her with her legs hung over each of his elbows as if they were merely strips of brown satin. Next, he gripped her hips firmly and pushed her up so that her back was once again fully braced against the tub.

“God help me!” she gasped. The look in his eyes took the strength from her arms as they slipped underneath the water.

“God has made you perfect, Lilavois. I mean to honor Their creation.”

RaZiel disappeared below the water as he shifted her legs onto his shoulders and settled between her thighs. The first swipe of his tongue over her was light, tentative compared to the almost violent reaction her nerves made in response. She arched her torso almost completely out of the tub spilling water everywhere, but she no longer cared. Her cry was only louder than his because it was not muffled by the water, but she felt it through her entire body unlocking the last hold of her restraint.

With one hand he held her in place, kneading her breasts and belly while the other gripped her waist, molding to her body until she was incoherent with desire. Her body came undone with a current that traveled through her to a pinpoint of ecstasy that exploded then released itself in a heavy rush that brought tears to her eyes and a bliss that she had never known. But he did not stop, holding her together by the slow sucking of his mouth as he cared for her and loved her over and over again until her heart rate returned to a slow pounding in her chest. There was only one thing missing, a yearning deep inside that would not be satisfied without him.

When he rose from the water, his locs were drenched and his eyes dazzled. She reached for him with a desperate strength she did not know she had, sucking at his tongue, tasting the essence of them both. It was her turn to devour him. Her body still shook as she pressed forward, but he yielded to her effortlessly, as if he knew and understood what was happening inside her.

Still limp from her orgasms, RaZiel helped her move her legs above his so that she sat astride with the evidence of his unfulfilled pleasure between them.

"My heart," he gasped. "I love you." She took him in her hands and guided him to where they both needed him to be.

"As I love you," she answered, taking him inside. The feeling of fullness was overwhelming in the way it felt not just good, but right. She held him tightly as she sank down onto him. RaZiel shook in her arms, silent tears falling as he kissed her own tears from each cheek.

"I know this feeling," he whispered in awe of something he never thought he would find again. "I am whole."

The fullness, the newness, the beauty of what their bodies could do together stole her breath so that all she could do was hold him tightly and cry with joy and relief. Despite all the perfection he had known, he could feel it, too, as she did — the perfect miracle they were creating together.

Their bodies came together slowly, driven by awe and a love that grew deeper the more they surrendered to it, until finally RaZiel threw his head back and gave into his own release.

"You belong here with me," she whispered, holding him through his tears.

"How can this be?" he whispered in prayer.

"Because I love you," Lilavois answered, before nuzzling into his arms and drifting back to sleep.

chapter seventeen

HUMAN RITUALS

AFTER their first night together, RaZiel and Lilavois found it almost intolerable to be apart, deciding that Lilavois would move out of the convent and into their castle, unofficially. Though all apprentices were required to live, eat, and sleep at the convent, Lilavois had two things working in her favor. Fourth-year apprentices who were not studying to join the E'gida were not held to as strict a curfew as their more junior peers, and ever since Sabine and Jhonna moved into the dorm rooms reserved for the E'gida, there was no one in the dorm room who noticed or cared about her comings and goings.

Aside from Lilavois's lessons, they barely left each other's side. Sometimes, RaZiel would attend her classes in secret to help her study at night from the home they shared. After class, she had taken to sleeping through dinner so that she could wake up refreshed at night and spend their precious midnight hours together. They ate and studied together with RaZiel supplementing the class lectures he attended with his vast knowledge of everything in the natural world. Sometimes he helped her experiment with new salves and healing potions that she would brew in the lab they had created for her.

When RaZiel went away to defend a town from the demons that still plagued the world, Lilavois used the time to catch up with Jhonna and Sabine, who were more than a little suspicious of Lilavois's erratic schedule.

"Are you going to at least tell us about him?" Jhonna teased. "You used to tell us everything. Now you're so secretive! It's bad enough we barely have any classes together anymore since you decided not to complete E'gida training."

"He can't be that bad looking," chided Dawnetta, a new E'gida apprentice who had joined their group without Lilavois noticing. "Tell us something."

"There's nothing to tell," Lilavois lied while keeping her eyes on the gruel the nuns passed around as dinner. RaZiel was a much better cook, she thought with a smile.

"See!" Sabine yelled. "There it is again. That smile! We're not stupid, you know. We know you're not riding off into the night just to hunt for herbs."

Jhonna's eyes twinkled with mischief and knowing. "Although she has been bringing in some amazing varieties of medicinal herbs," Jhonna added. "I think even Sister Agnes is a bit jealous of . . . Wait! Are you having sex?"

For some reason, Jhonna saved her highest octave for the last word which echoed across the dining hall like a boomerang.

All eyes turned to their table, while Lilavois silently thanked God for the stroke of luck that made her sit with her back to the room.

"Jhonna, lower your voice!"

"Yes," Sabine agreed. "The last thing we need is the whole school thinking we're having an orgy at our table!"

Jhonna had the good sense to look embarrassed enough for all of them, but not enough to stop her line of questioning. "Well, are you? You know Sister Carpethianna frowns on romantic entanglements."

"That's because she isn't getting any," Dawnetta quipped.

Well, of course I am! Most definitely, every day, as often as I can! is what Lilavois thought. What she said, however, was a carefully constructed tool of misdirection.

"Please." She made sure to meet Jhonna's gaze with equal measure of incredulity and sarcasm. "And where would I find this late-night lover? Everyone knows the Sisterhood picked this location for the convent because there is no one to date within a hundred miles."

Jhonna sighed in resignation. "It's true. All the boys in town are idiots. And all the girls here are too mean to date, except for you all, of course. We need better options."

Dawnetta sucked her teeth. "We'll all just have to get our fix on our one trip home."

Sabine, who had been suspiciously quiet through most of the conversation, leaned in. "I heard there is a new resident at the old mill castle. No one has seen the new owners, but rumor has it they've been quietly fixing up the place for months. The postman said that they get deliveries of new carpets, tiles, and furniture almost every day, and all the best linens from Criseth and Dojen. He also said they were installing copper pipes for indoor plumbing in all the bathrooms like they do in Kemet. But he hasn't been able to take a peek at the renovations because their groundskeeper — an old wizened man with a slight hitch in his gait, I'm told — meets him at the gate and carries all their packages up to the house in a wheel barrel! Isn't that strange?"

Lilavois had never been more grateful that RaZiel had chosen such an appropriate groundkeeper disguise. "How do you know all this?" Lilavois blurted out before she could catch herself.

"Well," Sabine began haughtily. "If you'd come with us when we go into town on the weekend, then you'd know the latest gossip. It's important to keep abreast of what's happening around you, Lilavois. If you weren't so busy digging in the dirt all night, you'd know more about what's happening under your very nose!"

Lilavois settled back in her chair as the conversation moved past suspicion of her to rumors of a pop quiz in Advanced Astrology. Thanks to RaZiel, Lilavois already knew more about what could be seen in the sky and what lay beyond than any of their textbooks could offer. In fact, she had been thinking of requesting more independent study courses for her last semester so that she could finish her studies earlier and move to a safer, more remote, and less gossip-prone part of the world.

He would not be home before midday tomorrow, but Lilavois still rode Enod over to their castle after her roommates fell asleep. With the castle empty, Lilavois missed him terribly, spoiled beyond repair by the sound of his voice sharing incredible stories of distant worlds, the all-encompassing warmth of his arms around her, and the feel of him inside her filling places she had never known were empty until his touch brought them to life.

He woke her up the way he always did, with his hand caressing her belly and his lips tracing the curve of her shoulder. Barely conscious, she still clutched his arm and pulled him closer.

"You're not supposed to be here."

"I missed you."

"Were you able to help?"

"Yes, we drove them back. There were fewer than we expected. I came home as soon as I was no longer needed."

"You missed your castle," she smiled shifting in his arms to face him and touch the skin she craved.

"This place is not my home. You are."

The teasing smile faded from her cheeks as she took in the seriousness of his words. How could she doubt a man that looked at her the way he did? With eyes that had seen the universe, every universe but only truly ever settled on her?

Her sleepiness burned away as her desire took hold, linking her legs over his to pull him on top of her, to join with each other in the way they both craved.

"Be with me, RaZiel." She kissed him then, tasting the sweetness of his mouth and chasing away the hours they spent apart.

"Always," he murmured as his fingers shifted, pulling up the bottom of her nightdress while she unlaced his pants. Normally they were less hurried, but normally they were only apart for a few hours. Now they were ravenous, not truly at rest until they were joined, as if with each coupling they became more intertwined, more a part of each other.

Hours later they lay together, Lilavois too sated to move any more than was necessary to cradle him against her chest so that he could listen to her heartbeat. She had been about to drift off when he suddenly raised his head.

"Do you want to get married?"

"You mean now that we've made love?" she teased. It wasn't that she had never thought about it, but the circumstances between them did not quite seem to fit. She was definitely not planning to bring him home to her mother, and marriage had never been in her plan anyway.

RaZiel lifted himself up on his elbows to see her more clearly and to show her how serious he was.

"I know there are rituals for this. I don't want us to forego them if it's important to you because of me …"

"It is only because of you that I would even entertain the notion," she corrected him. "What do you want?"

RaZiel's fingers wrapped around the end of her braided hair. "What I want is to spend eternity loving you. Human rituals for love have always seemed strange to me. I am not interested in proclaiming my love in a church today, then seeking the pleasure of another tomorrow, or taking you for granted or resenting you years later for the person you have always been. For many, this seems to be what marriage is, but that is not what I feel for you.

"In other worlds, many species, even animals here, mate for life. There is no other. That is what I want with you. To be with you and love you for as long as you live." He paused, swallowing down the thing he could not say, the thing they never talked about, before continuing. "I want to keep loving you for as long as I live. I don't know what ritual that is, but that is what I want."

Lilavois had not realized she was crying until RaZiel began wiping her tears away. When he was done, she drew his hand to her heart.

"Then that is what we shall be."

Things began to go wrong on a Wednesday.

Lilavois had been feeling queasy for three days, with none of her usual remedies working to settle her stomach. She didn't think much of it until she threw up in the middle of her power cycles of the moon presentation in Sister Carpethianna's Astrology class.

That was the first time Lilavois thought she might truly be sick.

It was later still when she realized that her period was seven weeks late that she began to entertain the possibility that she might be pregnant ... Except she could not be. In all the research and records, it was clear that demons were cursed with infertility. How many morbid tales had been cataloged of demons' countless efforts to produce offspring? How many countless girls had been seduced by dreams of being the one to give birth to the elusive "Eternal Heir"? While the tales were almost always sordid, the endings were always the same. No one. No one had ever succeeded. Lilavois always thought the mere pursuit was nonsense. She had never even really considered whether she wanted children. She had been so focused on becoming the greatest demon slayer that ever lived until she fell in love with one.

Sister Carpethianna insisted that Lilavois go to the infirmary, where Sister Zhoa — knowing Lilavois was a capable herbalist — wasted no time on the usual remedies. She insisted that Lilavois lay on the gurney for a full energy reading. After a few moments of channeling the mooncraft in her hands to examine the flow and strength of her chakras, Sister Zhao looked at Lilavois with a curious expression.

"Your chi is strong but disturbed by a strange force of uncommon energy. Perhaps it is a surge of mooncraft, gathering to help you summon the shield, if you ever decide to resume your E'gida training."

"I doubt that, but thank you, Sister. I have been spending more time in the garden."

"Hmm," Sister Zhao mused. "You've taken ginger root and elder sap I presume?"

"And essence of mauby, too," Lilavois added. "I've been sipping on my own brew for two days now, but it hasn't helped."

"Well, all your vitals are strong. No sign of waning chi. But there's a strange energy I've never felt before within you."

Her hands hovered over Lilavois's torso, concentrating so deeply her eyes were crinkled shut. Lilavois watched Sister Zhao with equal parts fascination and terror, wondering whether her secret would be named. "It's not a human source. It feels more divine," she muttered finally.

That is exactly what it is, Lilavois thought.

"You must be deep in your meditation practice," Sister Zhao concluded. "The ancestors are heavily upon you. Drink more mauby root tea to help balance your chakras and get plenty of rest. You will need it for whatever they are preparing you for."

Lilavois could not remember climbing the steps from the infirmary to her room. In her hand, she held a note that excused her from classes for the rest of the day. She would be expected to be in class or in bed when Sister Zhao checked on her every few hours until nightfall to monitor her progress. If she was not in either place, Lilavois would get detention.

Before RaZiel, this would hardly have been a deterrent, but now Lilavois studiously avoided putting herself in any position that risked her access to him. While RaZiel would find a way to visit her and help with whatever ghastly chores she might be forced to endure, Lilavois treasured their time alone too much to put it in danger.

But if she'd had her way, she would already be racing Enod to tell RaZiel the impossible news. She couldn't fathom his reaction, given that she had barely formed her own. With Sister Zhao's root potion keeping her constant nausea at bay, she thought she would have the luxury of feeling something, but instead her mind could not get past the shock.

What would RaZiel say? Unable to lie still in her dorm room, Lilavois chose her lessons.

The thought consumed her as she drifted from class to class, drowning out the sound of any information that hoped to seep in. Before RaZiel, her only thought was to become a member of the E'gida, a demon slayer. Now it was possible that she would become the mother of a demon. That anyone would see her child, her baby, as something to destroy was ludicrous — yet she knew many around her would. Would people be able to tell that her child wasn't fully human?

Lilavois did not know, but she was certain of this — she would use every skill the Sisters of the Light ever taught her to protect her child from anyone who meant them harm. While they insisted that she join them for dinner to make sure she was feeling better, Sabine and Jhonna didn't press when she was silent on the latest gossip and idle chatter about the impending convent renovations that surrounded their evening meal. It was a struggle to keep up the pretense of interest long enough to excuse herself and retire early for the evening. Once the first round of night patrols was complete, Lilavois scaled the descent from her bedroom window with her usual ease and found Enod waiting for her outside the stable.

RaZiel stood on the edge of the bell tower, listening to the pounding of Enod's powerful yet light hooves and, as she brought Lilavois near, the short quick breaths that told him Lilavois was just as anxious to be with him as he was to be with her. Next, he listened to her heartbeat, studying the pounding that deepened as she grew closer, but tonight, he did not smile at her approach.

Tonight, he forgot he had no wings. He nearly fell from the rooftop because as she broke through the tree line, while he waited for her to come into the full range of his senses, when she was still half a mile away, instead of one heartbeat, he heard two. Enod had not crossed the gate before RaZiel lifted her off the horse.

"Are you all right?" he whispered cradling her close in his arms. "Your heart has an echo I've never heard before."

Lilavois pulled back and searched his eyes for any understanding of what was happening, but she found nothing but confusion and worry staring back at her.

Of course, she thought. *How could he know? This is supposed to be impossible.*

"You can hear it already?"

"Hear what?"

"The baby," she replied with a growing smile.

RaZiel looked around genuinely confused until Lilavois cupped his beautiful face in both her hands. "Our baby," she said softly. "That echo you hear is our baby inside me."

If he were not among the strongest beings on Earth, RaZiel would have fainted. Instead, he dropped to his knees with hands at each side of her hips and stared at her belly. Lilavois had worked over a million possibilities in her mind on the ride to him. She had imagined shock, disbelief, even anger, but never had she considered reverence. All her life, Lilavois had taken for granted the possibility of a child as inherent in her being, like a doorway always open should one choose to walk through. But for him, there had never been a door.

Every baby was a miracle, but this child — their child — was something more than that. She had no words for something that was more than a miracle. She only knew how it felt to have it, to know that it was growing inside her, to be a vessel for the impossible. The enormity of it made her tremble.

"I don't understand." RaZiel shook his head. "My kin. We're supposed to protect life. We don't. We can't . . ." The doubt, the shame, and the disbelief pooled in his eyes.

Lilavois took his face in her hands. "But we did," she whispered, wiping the first of his tears away.

A faint sob broke from him as more tears fell. "But how? I am not worthy of this gift. I am nothing."

She had known it was there, this feeling, this self-loathing, but she had never seen it so naked before, not even in the garden when she tried to take his life.

"You are not nothing," she replied fiercely. "You are mine!"

He looked up from her stomach to meet her gaze as if he were lost, but Lilavois knew better.

"You belong to me. You belong to this child, and the family we will create. You are not what you were, but you are mine now, and that is worth everything to me, to us! Do you understand?"

He felt her words deep inside him, and even though he was not sure of himself at all, her heartbeat was true like a promise he was bound to keep, a promise to her and someone else yet to come.

chapter eighteen

UNEXPECTED

BEYOND the nausea, which they managed with a daily regimen of ginger root and licorice tea, the first four months of their pregnancy went by without incident or detection. Lilavois went to her classes as usual and tried to focus on her schoolwork and the lessons being taught by people who knew less about the demon world than she did.

Once, this knowledge would have made her want to speak up. She had always been someone who enjoyed displaying her superiority. Now the instinct was gone, buried under a far greater urge to protect the life growing inside her and the love that created it.

In the last six months, RaZiel had taught her more about astrology, botany, and history than any human had access to. She taught him in turn the magic of alchemy and metal using the forge they built for her work.

Lilavois was on schedule to graduate as an apothecary and surgeon from the Sisters of the Light several months before the baby was due. She had no idea what they would do once they found out about her condition, but in truth, it didn't matter. She already knew enough to pass any test she would need to be certified as an apothecary and surgeon, but she wanted to finish what she had begun four years and a lifetime ago.

RaZiel sent word to SeKet that he could no longer join the Covenant on their raids, insisting that since Lilavois could not go to a doctor, he would monitor her health while she was pregnant. And he did an excellent job, pressing his head to her belly and chest every night until he knew the rhythm of their heartbeats as if they were his own.

At school, her sudden agreeability did not go unnoticed. In Advanced Botany, Jhonna was the first to bring it up.

"It's almost as if you're trying to be the teacher's pet now," she teased one afternoon on their way from what used to be the most contentious time of the day.

"Yeah," Sabine agreed. "Your debates with Sister Agnes were the only thing keeping me awake in class. Now your notes are the only thing keeping me from failing."

"I just decided to stop minoring in scrubbing latrines," Lilavois joked. "I only have a few months left."

"Can't blame you there," Sabine agreed before she turned down the hall to shielding class. This is where they parted ways as Lilavois headed in the opposite direction to alchemy class. "See you at dinner," Sabine called wistfully.

For several weeks after Lilavois first made the decision to change her course of studies, she tried to feign disappointment when her friends continued to class, just to mask the sudden shift in what had been, up to that point, a singular pursuit. Having dropped the pretense completely, Lilavois caught the frown on Sabine's face as she no doubt noticed her lack of interest.

Lilavois couldn't blame her. She had changed a lot in the last year, and, for the most part, they had no idea why. Sometimes Lilavois would catch

Sabine watching her curiously and want to assuage the hurt and questions in her gaze, but Lilavois was never sure if the depth of their friendship would outweigh Sabine's hate for the demons who killed her family. And so, she let the silence between them grow.

By the beginning of their winter break, Lilavois was well into her second trimester, and the effort to hide her pregnancy would soon become pointless. Tired of hiding it any longer, she marched into the head administrator's office, threw off her winter coat, and declared, "I'm pregnant!"

Sister Angustella recoiled as if Lilavois had just dropped a pile of dung on her desk. Nevertheless, Lilavois waited for the nun to take the full measure of her, watching as her expression shifted from shock to disgust to a calculating scrutiny.

"Why did you wait so long?" she asked. "It would have been easier to get rid of it earlier."

Lilavois was not surprised by the assumption as much as the bluntness with which it was leveled.

"I'm going to keep my child. I just wanted you to know that I will not be hiding my pregnancy any longer."

Sister Angustella scoffed. "Keep it? You can't be that stupid. You don't expect us to let you waddle your way around the halls in such a state, do you?"

"I do," Lilavois replied. "I've only got one term left. I'll be out of here before the baby's due."

Spurred by Lilavois's casually insolent tone, Sister Angustella's thimble of patience tipped over. "I forbid it! You will not distract from our business with the evidence of your misconduct. You will leave immediately."

The sting of tears was immediate, though she struggled not to let them fall. After all, this was one of the reasons that Lilavois had chosen to hide her pregnancy in the first place. She had prepared for this moment, although she had hoped it would not come. Still, the reality of it threatened to close her throat. Her mission had altered completely since she first joined the convent, but she still believed in the Sisters of the Light and the value of what they taught. Her goals had changed, but she was no less committed to learning everything they had to offer. The thought of not being able to complete what she began filled her stomach with the sour taste of failure, a conclusion she knew she did not deserve.

"My family has already paid for the year. You can't do that."

"Oh, believe that I can, and I will. Our policies are clear regarding the aesthetic nature of our order. You are the one responsible for being a waste of their investment."

Lilavois took a deep breath and tried reason one last time. "There is no rule against pregnancy in the admissions policy or the code of conduct."

"Read between the lines, Lilavois. Even you can't be that obtuse."

Lilavois didn't want to play her next card, but Sister Angustella's rudeness made it easier.

"That's an unfortunate position, especially since it threatens the large endowment pledge you just received. It would be a pity to see the plans for the new laboratory and E'gida quarter abandoned just as they were getting underway. Such a needed expansion of this facility."

The flicker of alarm on Sister Angustella's face was quickly masked behind an indulgent smile.

"Child, you know nothing of our business. Your desperation is most unbecoming."

Lilavois leaned forward, placing her hands on the back of the one chair in Sister Angustella's office. "Oh, but I do. My sister, Charmaine St. James, is a very generous woman. When I wrote to her of our need, she was only too willing to pledge half the cost of the renovations. You haven't received the money yet though, have you?"

"Those pledges are anonymous. You can't prove your family is involved."

"The pledges are anonymous, but the money is not. My sister transferred the gold to our account in Bonn just yesterday – all 100,000 pieces of it. You received notice of it being deposited into an escrow account on the convent's behalf yesterday, did you not? I believe the pledge specifies that the funds are to be transferred to your account only after all other financing is secured and you have broken ground on construction. Is that not correct, Sister Angustella?"

Lilavois watched the color drain from the woman's face.

"I'll take your silence as a sign that you're familiar with the terms to which I refer. As the person closest to the business at hand, my sister appointed me as the authorizing signatory on the account, which means no funds of any kind can be released without my approval."

"You are a treacherous young woman," Sister Angustella seethed.

"But not obtuse," Lilavois replied.

"You may complete your studies off-premises and take your exams at the end of the term, but otherwise I want you out of my sight." Sister Angustella returned her attention to the correspondence that cluttered her desk, her mouth etched into a thin, angry line.

Recognizing the dismissive tactic, Lilavois grabbed her coat. She was almost at the door, when Sister Angustella added, "I wonder if the man you've wasted your talent on is worth it? I hardly think so. He isn't even here to share in your disgrace." Sister Angustella let out a bitter laugh. "Don't expect this young cad to be around once the –"

Lilavois turned around without thinking, rage like fire in her mouth.

"Don't you dare speak of him!" Lilavois roared. "He is closer than you imagine, and you know nothing of him."

The cold certainty in Lilavois's voice made Sister Angustella look up from her paperwork, sensing danger.

"Pack your things now and leave at once. I hope he's close enough to help you carry your things. I want you gone by the dinner bell. You have one hour."

Lilavois left the office unconcerned with packing. Anything of real value had been moved piece by piece months ago. Instead, she raced to the girl who had been her best friend for three years, a girl who had no idea that Lilavois was being forced to leave or why.

RaZiel had wanted to be with her when she confronted the convent administrator, but Lilavois had insisted on meeting with her alone. He insisted, however, on waiting for her in the garden, and given how hard a day it was turning out to be, Lilavois could not deny she was glad to know that he was close by.

Standing in front of her best friend's door, Lilavois felt her body welded in place. Yet, she had less than an hour to say what she had come to say. Even if she did not get to see anyone else, she had to tell Sabine. Sabine answered the first timid knock on her door.

"Who is it?"

"Sabine, it's me."

There was a brief pause, before she heard Sabine's voice. "Come in."

Her room was a disaster, as it always was before Lilavois came and tidied up while chastising Sabine for her poor hygiene. It had been a while since Lilavois had tidied up, and the room testified to her absence. When she entered the room, Sabine was sitting at her desk.

"I'm almost finished with my mooncraft homework. Give me a second."

"Oh, do you need help?" Lilavois had already finished Jhonna's just to keep herself from falling asleep in Advanced Botany. Sabine scribbled down the last incantation and closed her notebook.

"No. I'm all right." Her smile did not reach the crinkles at the corner of her eyes as she turned to face Lilavois. "I can figure it out on my own now."

"Right," Lilavois sighed. "I guess I haven't been around much to help you at night lately."

"No, you haven't." Sabine turned away, rearranging the notebooks on her desk. "Did you need something?" They were less than five feet apart, yet it was only in this small space that Lilavois finally felt the true distance that had grown between them. Sadness simmered and sunk in her belly as she realized she would not have the time to fix what had been broken between them.

"Yes. I want to . . . I need to tell you something."

Though her hands abandoned their busy work, Sabine did not turn around. After a moment, Lilavois wondered if perhaps Sabine had not heard her.

"I wanted to tell you, I'm..."

"I know," Sabine said softly.

"You do?"

"Of course I do. I figured it out when you stopped eating and started wearing your cloak everywhere a month ago." Something about Sabine's admission made Lilavois smile. All this time, she had felt terrible keeping this secret from her dearest friend. It eased her spirit to know that they'd shared the secret anyway.

"Why didn't you say something?"

"Why didn't you?"

"I was . . ."

"We used to tell each other everything." Lilavois heard the crack in Sabine's voice. "Then you fell for that boy and suddenly you weren't around anymore."

Lilavois stepped closer. "I've been here every day."

"No, you haven't. Not really. You don't argue with the teachers anymore. You don't make jokes and pass notes in class. You barely say anything. You're like a ghost."

Lilavois couldn't deny it. The richer her life became with RaZiel, the less she shared with anyone else. She could not count the number of times she had been ready to contradict a teacher with an answer she should not know — could not know — had RaZiel not taught her. Over time, the urge to be right felt far less important than protecting him, so she did her work, got better grades, and avoided detention. She thought she was slipping into the background unnoticed. She should have known Sabine was watching.

Lilavois placed a careful hand on Sabine's shoulder. "I'm sorry. Please forgive me. I didn't want to be distant from you."

Sabine turned then, breaking Lilavois's heart with her puffy eyes. Lilavois pulled Sabine into a crushing hug and exhaled when she did not resist.

"Oh!" Sabine said pulling back in surprise. "Did that hurt?"

"No! We're held together pretty well."

They smiled at each other, friends for just a moment.

"So what are you going to do? Sister Angustella is going to grow a third eye," Sabine joked.

Lilavois stepped back, but gripped Sabine's hands more firmly. "I wish. She did worse than that."

"You told her!"

Lilavois nodded, regretting what would come next. "And she kicked me out of the convent."

"You're expelled!" Sabine shrieked.

"Ssshhh. Almost. She told me I could come back for my final exams, but she wants me off the premises. I have to be gone by dinner, but I had to see you. I wanted to tell you in person."

"No!" Sabine said through fresh tears. "You're almost done. You've only been pregnant for a couple months, right? You'd be finished before you have the baby."

Lilavois felt so comfortable, so safe in this moment that she let the truth slip through her lips. "If it's a normal pregnancy," she replied.

Sabine frowned. "Are you sick? Why wouldn't it be?"

Lilavois tried to laugh off her strange admission. "Well, it's my first. You never know how things will go."

"You'll be fine," Sabine said, squeezing Lilavois's hand. "You'll have the smartest most beautiful baby ever."

"Thank you," Lilavois said, pulling Sabine back into a hug. She needed her assurance, the assurance of a woman, more than she realized.

"They should let you stay," Sabine whispered into her ear.

"I wish they would, but Sister Angustella said she refused to have me 'waddling around the convent halls' since I insisted on having the baby and wasting my talent."

Sabine pulled back. "She said that!"

"And more. Let's just say there's no love lost between us."

Sabine stared at Lilavois until the dinner bell startled them both.

"I have to go, but I promise to write you when I can."

"Wait," Sabine said looking around the room desperately for a reason to keep the friend she had just gotten back from leaving. "How will you study if you can't get to the library? Do you want my books?"

"I've already stolen all the books I need from the library," Lilavois winked.

"Of course you have," Sabine laughed. "Where will you go? Back home?"

Lilavois blinked, realizing for the first time that the thought had not occurred to her of any other alternative. "No. I'm staying with him."

"We were supposed to kill demons together."

Lilavois felt the edges of their conversation close in like it always did these days, reaffirming the reason, the necessity of them growing apart. "We were," was all Lilavois could say.

"I hope he's worth it."

Lilavois pulled Sabine into a hug. "He is. Please tell the others. I'll write when I can."

By the time Lilavois slipped past the dinner procession into the garden, tears were running freely down her face. RaZiel did not make her wait for her comfort, flying down from his raven's perch to transform before her and wrap her in his arms.

"Sabine is right to ask her questions. Are you sure I am worth this?" He did not loosen his grip but stared down into her eyes with painful earnestness. If she said no, she knew he would release her and without a question he would break his own heart as he had done again and again to keep her safe. He would do it, if she asked.

"How much would you give to be with me?" Lilavois asked.

"Everything I am. Everything I have."

"Why?"

"Because I love you, and for me, there is no greater truth."

"Then we are the same. Take us home."

chapter nineteen

HOME

THEY spent their days leading up to the birth of their child in a frenzy, preparing the baby's room, growing her garden, and spending time together on Lilavois's studies.

Their isolation suited them well. Lilavois had never really liked being around a lot of people, and RaZiel, after centuries of solitude, found a peace he thought he would never experience again simply listening to the sound of two heartbeats murmuring in tandem inside her.

A month before she gave birth, Lilavois passed her certification exams with high honors. A few days later, she watched with pride as Sabine and Jhonna were inducted into the E'gida. They were both assigned to the Sisterhood station in Bonne and would begin their duties in one month so that they could travel and spend time with their families. As they hugged goodbye at the graduation ceremony that Lilavois was allowed to attend, but not participate in, she marveled at how much their paths had diverged. As they walked away from each other that day, Lilavois knew it was for the best. Though she was proud of their accomplishments, their goals were no longer compatible. With any luck, she would never see them again.

Managing the distance with her family would prove more difficult. For the time being, she had told her mother and sister that she was doing a prestigious internship that would require her constant travel for the next twelve months or more. By their letters, it seemed they had bought her explanation. By now, they were used to Lilavois taking off to far corners of the Earth. At some point, she knew that she would have to tell her sister the truth, but she would cross that bridge when she got to it. For now, she wanted to focus on the life she had in front of her.

In the days leading up to the birth, they pored over every resource they could find on childbirth, but nothing truly prepared her for the experience of it. Their daughter, Ada, was born on a Tuesday at 4:44 in the afternoon. The late spring day was fragrant with lilacs, tea roses, and the sound of Lilavois as she brought their child into the world. Lilavois used her mooncraft to pull strength from the trees that braced her back and carried her arms when she felt in danger of collapsing on her birthing bricks. She had insisted on having their child outside in the garden, surrounded by the testimonies of God's creations. And every living thing in their vicinity seemed to gather to watch the miracle they created. More than anything, the sound of RaZiel's steady voice pulled her through the most challenging thing she'd ever had to do.

With no reference for what their child would be, RaZiel cried with delight as he watched his daughter emerge with the human features and deep brown skin of her mother. Her eyes were his though, pitch black and wide with a depth that made him wonder if Ada was born with everything he knew already within her. He carried them both inside, bathing them with the herbs that Lilavois had prepared to help her body heal. He then lay down beside them as his family slept, singing his prayer in a pitch no human ear could hear for the first time in a millennium.

In the early months after Ada was born, RaZiel would not let Lilavois do anything if it was not related to caring for Ada or herself. But as they both grew comfortable in their new roles, RaZiel and Lilavois discovered a surprising new rhythm to their lives. Away from the structure of the convent, they built a life together that was full of love, harmony, and magic.

Lilavois continued her studies, creating and selling new medicines, and honing her mastery as a blacksmith and wielder of mooncraft, until she could imbue the objects she created with magical properties that would do everything from enhance the potency of any medicine to offer protection to her daughter.

Ironically, it was RaZiel who finally helped Lilavois unlock her ability to conjure her shield, insisting that she continue to work on her defensive skills. Though he never planned to be parted from her, he knew that what they had in each other and Ada was rare and therefore must be protected with every available measure. It was this notion, not only of her own defense but her need to protect those she loved, that finally gave Lilavois the focus to understand how to pull the mooncraft through her body and activate her shield. For most of the E'gida, their energy flowed through their extremities, but Lilavois learned that her shield burst straight from her heart. This revelation, which Lilavois had never heard of within the Sisterhood, was unusual in itself. What made it shocking was the way her two-year-old daughter, who had been watching her on newly steady legs clapped and giggled before walking right through her mother's shield, which was supposed to be, like so many things with Ada, impossible.

Even though she looked like a normal human, both RaZiel and Lilavois knew Ada was different. It began the moment she was born as she stared up at RaZiel as if she was actually aware of the miracle of her existence and was as surprised as anyone to be here. She slept between them soundly from the first night she arrived and woke to the sound of her father singing songs with words older than time itself. By the end of her second month, she began to mimic her father's voice in tones only they could hear so that they could sing to each other all morning while Lilavois worked.

While her physical development followed the general phases of a human child, Ada displayed an uncanny awareness that Lilavois and RaZiel nurtured to the best of their ability. Lilavois also noticed that when Ada began crawling, any surface scratches she received from around the garden would be healed by the next morning.

“Maybe it’s just your ointments,” RaZiel offered as they bathed their daughter in the sink. “You heal quickly too.”

“I didn’t put any ointment on her last night. I just cleaned the wounds. No human heals this fast, RaZiel.”

“But she is human,” he said, placing his hand over heart as if to prove it to himself. “She has a soul. She is not like me. At the end of her life, she will make it back to the Ever.”

Lilavois’s heart felt heavy as she reached for him, cradling his cheek in her hand. “She is like you. She has all your best qualities. You are so much more than what you lack.”

Ada had Lilavois’s keen intelligence and curiosity and RaZiel’s deep connection with the natural world. But, more than anything, they were happy just taking walks and discovering the world again through their daughter’s eyes.

On the eve of Ada’s third birthday, Lilavois went in town to buy a set of paints and the ingredients to make their daughter a very special birthday cake.

“Can me and Papa come?” Ada asked with open, eager eyes.

“Not this time, my love, then it won’t be a surprise.”

Ada’s eyes widened in anticipation as her mouth formed the tiniest little “o”.

“It’s *my* surprise,” she whispered, full understanding blooming on her tiny, round face.

“Yes,” RaZiel replied lifting her gently from Lilavois’s arms with a chuckle. “That’s why you have to stay here with me. Besides you’re supposed to help me pick your birthday flowers.”

With a burst of newfound purpose, Ada wiggled free of her father's grip, landing on her two plump legs with all desire to head to the market forgotten.

"Can we play hide and seek?"

"I think we must," RaZiel replied, but she was already making her way out the back door.

"I'll see you soon," Lilavois called, leaving them to their chase.

For RaZiel and Ada, playing hide and seek was an all-day affair. With acres of land to explore and his keen senses attuned to her, no place was off limits. With Lilavois gone for the better part of two hours, RaZiel was looking forward to following the laughter of his beloved daughter as she hid beneath the raspberry bushes or scrambled up a low tree branch, which is why, perhaps, he did not hear them coming.

chapter twenty

THE LAST SONG

IF he were human, RaZiel would never have heard the sound of gravel shifting under padded feet or the low rumble of menace over peels of innocent laughter.

It took him longer than it should have that day, longer than they could afford.

He approached Ada with care so that she would not know her hiding place was found. He, of course, had known where she was the moment she climbed up the wheels of the wooden barrel he'd placed, *just* so, to create a space for Ada to hide. Ada never guessed how, despite its years, the barrel was sanded so smoothly it was almost shiny, nor figured out how the barrel was always filled with enough soft blankets to lie down on comfortably and pull over her head.

The hem of her dress was still peeking out of the side of the barrel blowing in the breeze as if to say, "I'm here, Daddy."

Every sense was focused on her happiness until the gentle pitter patter of her heart was interrupted by the jagged sound of earth moving quickly. RaZiel smelled them next. The distinct odor of his four brethren was foul on his tongue, their natural fresh scent made putrid with grime, sweat, and blood.

Any second, the demons would be upon them. If he went to Ada now, they would find her first, and without knowing what their intentions were, he decided that she was safer where she was. With only a second to spare, RaZiel stood before the barrel, blocking their view.

"RaZiel." Ilhan's tone was soft yet mocking as he stepped from the bushes surrounding their castle and onto the main path. "Imagine our surprise to find you here of all places, after all these millennia."

Given that Ilhan's affinity with God was power and RaZiel's was kindness, they had never been the closest angels in the Ever, but RaZiel could still feel the yearning for the spirit kin they had been.

"Your scent is everywhere. I can't imagine you going through all these lengths just to get away from us," Nephycil added. He looked around the area in disgust.

Both wore the torsos of a human with the legs of a bear. Vitus and Saisho emerged last, saying nothing but looking around with a similar air of disdain.

Nephycil laughed at RaZiel's tense expression. "Have you no embrace for us, brother? Even now?"

RaZiel's every thought willed Ada to be quiet. Her heartbeat had picked up only a little, he imagined out of curiosity for the new voices suddenly all around. He tried to keep the fear from his voice. When Ilhan drew closer, RaZiel held up his hand.

"You smell of blood."

"Still pious like SeKet," Vitus spat. "There was a time when you were with us!"

"Never like that."

"True," Saisho admitted. "You never let yourself have too much fun."

"It is forbidden to take life." RaZiel replied. "Leave. You are not welcome here."

Nephycil laughed. "You don't order us around! We are gods here. We do what we want. Anything!"

RaZiel shook his head and tried to keep calm so Ada's heartbeat would slow down. If he could hear it, eventually they would too.

"A being with only the power to destroy is no god. Leave. Now."

"We know you have a woman here. We can smell her. Do not fear," Ilhan cooed. "We would not dream of sampling that which you have clearly claimed."

"But if she prefers us," Saisho joked. "Who could blame her?"

"I will not tell you again." RaZiel let danger seep into his voice.

"So territorial," Vitus said tilting his auburn head to one side. "Do you imagine we can't hear the child's heartbeat behind you? Why don't you let us meet the little human?"

"She is none of your concern."

"Papa? Are you going to find me now?"

RaZiel's heart sank, but he did not dare turn around. "Not right now, sweetheart. Stay where you are."

"Oh, how sweet! The poor thing thinks you're her father. You've been here for too long, RaZiel. It's not like you to be so deceptive," Vitus smiled. "Maybe you've acquired a sense of fun after all."

"We should tell her now before her heart gets broken," Saisho added, attempting to step around RaZiel toward Ada. And in that brief moment, something stirred in RaZiel that had never stirred before. Without thinking he grabbed Saisho by the neck and threw him across the field.

Enraged, Vitus lunged forward, but RaZiel met him head-on with an arm to the chest that connected with such force that the impact shook the ground beneath them. Nephycil and Ilhan attacked together, overpowering him and wrestling RaZiel to the ground.

Ilhan held RaZiel's wrists behind his back as he pressed against him, while Nephycil crouched down to hiss in his face. "You dare attack us over this human!" With his head pressed to the ground, RaZiel looked up to find Ada standing up inside the barrel looking down at her father in horror.

"Don't hurt my Papa," she cried.

He wanted to tell her it would be all right.

He wanted to tell her that he wouldn't let them hurt her, but he couldn't promise that.

All he knew for sure was that for the first time in his life he discovered something worth killing for.

I'm sorry you have to see this, Ada, RaZiel thought as he twisted his wrists until they were flush against Ilhan's belly and extended his claws piercing clear through Ilhan's body.

"Ilhan!" Vitus screamed as his corpse began to darken and crumble into shadow.

The birds went silent. Around him, RaZiel saw every blade of grass and tree branch shrinking back from what he had done. The sky veiled itself in dark clouds that began to sprinkle then rain to wash away the sorrow of God's most divine destroyed forever, never to return. Nephycil shifted away, scrambling to gather the ashes of his brother in his hands. RaZiel turned from the ground to see what he had done, his eyes wide with shock.

Yet as he watched Nephycil tremble with grief, RaZiel felt only relief, knowing the price had been worth it. He found Ada staring at the puddle of ash that was dissolving into the earth with eyes that were full of sorrow, but her heart rate was steady, as if even in her fear, she understood that she was in a little less danger.

RaZiel sprang to his feet. "I'm sorry you had to see that, my love. Close your eyes now and hide. You will be safe," he whispered. Without a word, Ada sank back into her blankets.

"Never!" Nephycil hissed behind him. "She will never again know safety or comfort."

RaZiel shifted away from the blow that swept out over his head from above. When RaZiel turned to face Nephycil, he found him transformed into a beast with the head of a snake and the body of a bear.

"You have traded Ilhan's life for hers, and I will take it slowly, until she is old enough to beg for de—"

There was a chance that Ada might understand his words, so he could not let Nephycil finish. RaZiel lunged, aiming his claws at his neck but Nephycil evaded him, dropping down on all fours. Using the new position to his advantage, RaZiel kicked him hard in the jaw, sending him spiraling on his back. With a roar Nephycil righted himself, but pain made him slower than he needed to be to evade RaZiel's next attack. But Vitus was faster than either of them, knocking RaZiel to the ground before he could reach Nephycil. They tumbled, lancing and clawing at each other until Vitus was able to gain the upper hand, wrapping his arms around RaZiel's neck and forcing him to the ground so that while RaZiel struggled, he could not move.

"Now you will watch as we have," Vitus declared.

RaZiel could not escape. Terror closed around his thoughts as he watched Nephycil walk towards Ada. He couldn't speak. He couldn't cry out for mercy, yet RaZiel also couldn't look away as Nephycil pulled back the blanket with his claws and peered down at Ada.

"What a precious little thing, RaZiel."

Through the sliver of air he could breathe, RaZiel rasped, "Please. Don't!"

If I tell them what she is, would it save her? His mind and body were on fire with desperation, but he already knew the answer. They would kill her, just as he had killed. Over his many years, RaZiel had seen death and cruelty yield surrender, but never mercy.

"Oh! Look how she watches me, as if she understands she's about to die."

From the ground, RaZiel saw his daughter stretch out her tiny hand.

"Is she reaching for me," Nephycil laughed incredulously. "They really are the most foolish species in all the galaxies."

RaZiel ignored the insult, his eyes transfixed.

She's trying to make the shield, he realized. Could she? Even though he knew it was unlikely, hope sparked. But there was no glow, no flickering of the blue light that might have protected her. Her heartbeat spiked as her fingers closed. Nephycil grabbed her by the leg and lifted her from the barrel.

Ada made no sound as she wriggled and writhed to free herself, at least none that RaZiel could hear. His body and consciousness had entered into a place of complete silence, as if he were back in the Ever floating among the cosmos and time did not exist. The only thing that was real was the look of terror on Ada's face. He did not recall when his arms broke free, or how he managed to reach up, hook his claws onto Vitus's neck, and rip it from his body. If Nephycil made a sound, RaZiel didn't hear that either, but the evidence of his labor lay beside him in a pile of ash and the look of rage in Nephycil's eyes. RaZiel knew there would only be a second between the moment of realization and the exacting of retribution. In this realm where time was the true measure between life and death, there was not enough of it to have Ada firmly in his grasp, but he could try.

That was his right.

He was her father.

RaZiel grabbed a handful of Vitus' ashes, threw it at Nephycil and began running to catch her. Startled, disgusted, and grieved, Nephycil fell back just as RaZiel had intended. But it was not enough. It was less than a second, but it was still a moment too long. Sound came back to him in the form of Ada's scream as Nephycil's claw pierced her leg.

chapter twenty-one

A BIRTHDAY WISH

LILAVOIS ran in from the strange downpour, soaked but happy. Her cloak had done its job keeping the flour and sugar she had bought for Ada's cake safe.

With a sense of supreme satisfaction, she entered the side door of the castle, only to dump the contents of her shopping pouch on the floor at the sound of RaZiel's cries. Lilavois responded with her feet, taking the stairs two at a time in an effort to get to him quickly. Though she hated to hear the agony in his voice, instinctively she knew that only one thing could cause such pain. Ada. Something terrible had happened to Ada.

With growing dread, she followed the droplets of blood on the steps. She followed them to the bathroom or more specifically to the bathroom tub, which was surrounded by a mangled bloody mess of bandages, potions and ointments. Every healing potion, salve, powder, and ointment she made was turned over and drained dry. In his arms, RaZiel, ragged and torn, held their daughter gently to his chest swaddled like the baby she used to be with one or two feet peeking out from the blanket, one brown as a warm chestnut and the other black and cold as ash.

Demon poison.

On the floor, she saw her old blue jade dagger, which only meant one thing. He'd cut himself hoping the fluid that leaked from his wound would heal her, but it hadn't worked. Lilavois rushed forward looking between a swaddled Ada, asleep as her body shut down to fight the poison, and a nearly catatonic RaZiel. The color of her skin and the heat of her body told Lilavois that her daughter was alive. But one look at the ash, gray-black veins that crept up Ada's leg from her foot to her ankle, told her there was no guarantee of how much longer she would be. She had studied the effects of demon poison many times at the convent as she trained to be a surgeon. She knew her daughter should already be dead. Demon poison could kill in an instant. But she wasn't dead, which meant if they acted quickly, Lilavois could save her. Lilavois would put her sorrow, her grief, and her anger aside to do so. Carefully, she began lifting Ada from RaZiel's hands, but they locked around Ada like a vice. Lilavois understood.

"RaZiel! Listen to me. I need to take her. We have to seal the poison off. How long has it been since the attack?"

"I tried everything. I can't make it stop."

"Give her to me."

RaZiel loosened his grip, bloodshot eyes searching her clear steady gaze. She felt the question he could not say.

"I'm going to amputate her leg."

His face crumpled. "No! It's my fault. It's ruined. It's ruined. What if... No!" he moaned.

"She will live! That is all that matters. Help me, RaZiel. Help me save our daughter!"

There was no light in his eyes as he followed her, but she would deal with that later. With Ada in her arms, she raced to her lab. She laid Ada on the large wooden table in the center of the room and went to work.

"Get me the vial of poppy seed potion and the boiled bandages from the cabinet while I set the fire."

Though his countenance gave no sign he had heard her, Lilavois did not have to ask him twice. Because they had spent so much time here, so many nights teaching each other, RaZiel knew where everything was. He was a blur, moving faster than she had ever seen him before. He placed what she needed beside her and lit the fire before she was halfway to the knives. Lilavois was grateful for his speed because her legs felt like lead with the realization of what she was about to do. She swallowed tears she could not afford. Sorrow poured down her throat to burn her heart. She had taken her first steps barely a year ago, and now . . . *No!* Lilavois grabbed the bone saw and wiped her face with shaking hands. She would grieve later. She needed all her focus to save her child. When she turned back to the table, RaZiel had the gauze, the alcohol, and a small bowl of boiling water ready. The droplet vial was poised at Ada's lips.

"How much?" he whispered.

"Three drops under the tongue." He frowned but did not voice his question; again, Lilavois knew.

"I concentrated the formula. It will be enough. You can monitor her heart rate while I . . ." Lilavois watched him administer the dose as she set the timer. The poison was almost to Ada's knee. Lilavois had hoped to save the joint, but now that would not be possible if she wanted to get ahead of the poison. She took the bonesaw with hands that were capable but less steady than she would have liked them to be.

RaZiel placed his hand over hers. "I'll do it. It's my fault this has happened."

Lilavois shook her head violently. "No." She did not know what happened, but she knew one thing with certainty. Whatever guilt he carried, RaZiel was the only reason Ada was still alive.

"I can be quick. She'll be in less pain. Just tell me what to do."

Lilavois could not deny this, and because she could not, she handed RaZiel the saw.

Though the amputation took only a few seconds, they worked through the night mending their daughter as best they could. The poppy potion kept Ada pain-free and heavily sedated as they laid her down in her crib and returned to the lab. If she stirred, RaZiel would hear.

After multiple rounds of testing, Lilavois verified that the tissue above the knee was free of the poison that caused the necrosis in her lower leg. When RaZiel returned from the garden with a clean pair of clothes and a cup of Lilavois's favorite lavender tea, she was happy to have some good news to share.

"Thank you for the tea," she said gently. "It won't spread. We got it in time."

RaZiel shook his head, with fresh tears welling in his eyes. "Because of me, our life, our family, is ruined."

Lilavois frowned. "She'll recover. I know it's hard for you to understand, but her body will heal from this. She'll adapt."

Somehow, her words made RaZiel feel even more defeated.

"I didn't mean Ada. She's our child, and I could never see her as anything less than a miracle, but I couldn't save her, Lilavois. I couldn't save us."

"I don't understand. Tell me what happened?"

RaZiel looked down at his hands, unable to hold her gaze. "They tracked my scent. I led them right to our home."

Fear lanced through Lilavois. “They saw her, but do they know?”

“I don’t think so. We were playing hide and seek in the field. I should have heard their approach, but I didn’t until it was too late. They heard her heartbeat.”

Lilavois leaned forward and traced the angry scar that was still healing across his cheek.

“And then they attacked?”

“No. I did. Saisho threatened Ada.” RaZiel lifted his gaze from his hands. “I drew my claws and killed them.”

Lilavois put down her tea which would be of no use and stared back in shock. If it had been for anyone or anything else besides herself or Ada, she would never have believed him. But it was for Ada, and Lilavois needed no other explanation. The fear in her heart spread like acid throughout her body.

“How many others were there?”

“Four.”

“Did you get them all?”

“No. Saisho got away. After Nephycil pierced her leg, I killed him, but Ada was hurt. I couldn’t leave her to chase after Saisho. I thought she would die in my arms any second. I could see the poison spreading, but somehow, she survived long enough for us to get back to the house. I gave her every medicine I could think of, but I couldn’t stop the spreading.” RaZiel’s face crumbled just as Lilavois rose to embrace him.

“Saisho saw you kill the others.”

RaZiel nodded, holding her tighter as the realization he had already been carrying slowly came to her.

"They will kill you for this."

"It is what I deserve." RaZiel raised his head to look at her. "But I have no regrets, Lilavois. You and our daughter are alive. That is all I care about."

"We need to leave. How long will it take Saisho to reach the Council?"

RaZiel held her gaze with hopeless eyes. His palms reached up to caress her cheek.

"He is likely already there."

Lilavois's eyes shifted, calculating risks. "So we leave tonight. It will be difficult with Ada in such a delicate state, but we'll manage."

"My heart, you know Ada is too weak to travel."

"It's a risk we have to take. We can't stay here for them to find us." Lilavois tried to pull away to begin preparations, but RaZiel held her close.

"I have to go alone."

Lilavois shook her head. "They know our scent, too!"

"But it is me they seek to punish, not you. Unless you are with me."

"No. We are a family. I won't let them separate us. We can hide together."

"That is not a life, Lilavois. Please. You must see." Slowly he released his grip so she could pace.

"No!" she screamed. "No! We can make it work."

"Even with the entire Covenant behind me, it would not be enough. They will never stop hunting me, Lilavois. You know that is no life for a child. The longer I stay, the longer she is in danger. The longer you are in danger."

"Stop saying that! You kept her safe. She's alive because of us. You and me, together!"

RaZiel closed the distance between them and brought his heart back into his arms. He did not offer comfort. There was none. Everything they planned, everything they wanted, was burning away. All he could offer her was the truth.

"Don't leave," Lilavois sobbed. "We'll find a way."

"My love will always be with you. Every good thing that I am I leave with you. Every good thing."

Their kisses were soaked in tears and all the passion they would have only one night left to savor. They loved each other until dawn, until grief and love and exhaustion finally lulled Lilavois's eyes to sleep.

RaZiel sang his morning song to Ada one last time in a pitch only she could hear and cried. Wearing only the clothes on his back and the necklace Lilavois made for him, RaZiel left with a kiss to each of his loves and a bundle at the end of the bed with a note that read:

I buried the ashes of my kin last night. This bundle contains Nephycil's claws. They are the only thing strong enough to kill a demon. Use them, my heart, to protect your own.

Ada rose on her third birthday without a song on her lips because somehow she knew her Papa was no longer there to hear it.

PART II
ADA

chapter one

A WAYWARD PLAN

ADA'S eyes popped open with the quick awareness that her plans to wake up early had gone awry.

"Ada Marie St. James! Did you hear me? You're about to be late for school — again!"

"Umm. I'm almost ready!" Ada kicked her leg in a hurried effort to untangle herself from the plush linens of her bed. On her nightstand, the clock read 7:42 a.m. With a roll of her eyes, she stood with a satisfied grin.

I've got eighteen whole minutes. That's plenty of time.

At fifteen years old, she was adept at pushing the boundaries between maximizing sleep and being on time for school to the breaking point. Ada hopped from her bed to her closet to her drawer to her dressing table with ease. Despite the crutches by the headboard or the collection of handmade prosthetics lining the left side of her dresser, Ada preferred to hop in the morning to get her blood pumping and soothe the stiffness and phantom pains that sometimes plagued her when the temperature dropped during the night.

By 7:54 a.m., she was nearly dressed and making her way to her private bathroom, which was small but efficient. While indoor plumbing was common throughout the town of Liren, a private bathroom was a luxury in any home. Fortunately for her, Ada's mother, Lilavois, was the best surgeon and apothecary in the entire province — and the whole world as far as Ada was concerned — so they could afford the kind of luxuries that made staying in bed as long as possible a viable option. It also made her mother extra particular about hygiene.

"Make sure you brush your teeth well! Don't come down here with troll breath."

"I am!" Ada mumbled through a mouthful of toothpaste. *Who even says 'troll breath'?*

She rinsed quickly, then pulled off her night scarf, releasing a lustrous tangle of dark curls that floated above her head and shoulders. With no time to braid it, Ada grabbed her favorite green and brown silk headband and slid it into place. Her hair was too thick for the headband to do more than keep her hair off her face, but for today, that would be enough. After settling onto her dressing table bench, Ada reached over to grab Samantha — her mother-of-pearl-encrusted prosthetic of choice for the day — and slide her into place. With the mooncraft that Lilavois imbued into the soft cotton and thin rubber sleeve embedded in the leg, it fit as easily as her own skin and stayed on all day without irritation.

It was her second favorite after Esha, the copper molded leg with the moonflower petals etched into the front and side panels. Atholas, the prosthetic she used for sports, came last, but only because she had the least decoration. But what Atholas lacked in ornamentation, she more than made up for in speed and agility.

Almost all of Ada's skirts were fashioned with a split on her left side to accommodate putting on and taking off her leg with ease. It also allowed

Ada to show off her chosen prosthetic's hand-crafted beauty. She had a presentation today on renowned astrophysicist Thaddeus Medupe's latest theories on life outside the known galaxy, and while Esha was her favorite, Ada wore that prosthetic most of the time. Though slightly heavier, Samantha would add a bit of pizazz and confidence as she spoke in front of the class. Plus, the opalescent color of the prosthetic was a perfect contrast with the dark blue ruffles of her shirt.

Professor Medupe's careful preservation of mankind's earliest depictions of space and recorded uses of astronomy was one of the things she was looking forward to seeing firsthand on her class field trip to Bonne in one month — *if* her mother let her go. Ada was supposed to have woken up early enough this morning to spend some extra time convincing her. With that plan derailed by her own love of sleep, Ada would need to shift strategies to a dinnertime ambush.

With three minutes to spare, Ada rounded the second-floor hallway and began moving down the staircase with a distinct air of victory.

"Did you make your bed?" Lilavois called from the kitchen.

"Mom!"

"Hurry up! Simon shouldn't be late for school just because his walking partner can't get up on time!"

Certain her mother was being difficult on purpose, but smart enough not to say so out loud, Ada ran back to her room. With less than a minute to prove her mother wrong, Ada yanked her duvet cover straight to hide the mess of sheets below, fluffed her pillows, and made it back to the second-floor landing just as Simon tapped gently on the pane of stained glass that graced their front door.

"I'm ready!" Ada called, a little moist in the petticoat but no less triumphant.

Lilavois met her daughter at the bottom of the steps with a peck on the cheek and a wedge of toast smothered in peach preserves.

"Barely," Lilavois teased, shoving the toast in her daughter's mouth. Peach jam was Ada's favorite. She swallowed her protest with the first delicious bite.

"Thank you," she mumbled.

Lilavois let out a knowing chuckle. "Open the door. I'll get your bag."

Ada reached for the doorknob after snatching another piece of toast from her mother's tray.

"Good morning," Simon Abara greeted, stepping into the foyer. "Still eating breakfast. Must have gotten up . . ."

"I am not late," Ada insisted around another bite.

"She would have been if not for me," Lilavois teased as she walked back from the kitchen. She set Ada's bag on the floor then leaned forward to give Simon a warm, one-armed hug. "Good morning, Simon, would you like a piece of toast?"

"Yes, please." With the metabolism of a sixteen-year-old, he could not afford to turn down food even with a belly that was already full of his father's breakfast.

"How's your father, Simon? Please tell him I used the spices he brought back from the Maroons just last night. They added just the right flavor to my stew."

Simon licked the crumbs and jam from his fingers hastily. "I'll tell him when he gets back. He left for Keffar this morning."

"So soon?" Lilavois asked.

Simon shrugged. "He was home a whole month between trips this time, so I guess he was overdue. At least now I don't have to stay at my aunt's while he's away. He said I'm old enough to be on my own now."

Lilavois smiled, trying to keep the concern from showing on her face. "Well, I will expect you for dinner then, often, until he returns. But for now, you two had better get to school before Ada makes you both late."

Ada picked up her bookbag from the floor with an exaggerated sigh. "You know, Mom, for such a stickler about time, it's hard to believe you almost got kicked out of school."

"You —" Simon gaped.

Lilavois narrowed her eyes. "Who told you that?"

Ada smiled sweetly before taking the last piece of toast from the tray. "Aunt Charmaine."

"Your aunt talks too much," Lilavois muttered.

Knowing that Ada and her mother could keep this playful banter going well past the school bell, Simon thought it wise to change the subject.

"Do you have everything you need for the presentation?" he asked Ada.

"I packed last night."

"Excellent. Let's go."

Ada cleared her throat and looked at him expectantly. Simon squinted back in confusion before she gave him a quick pinch to jolt his memory.

"I mean I *think* I have everything," Ada added pointedly.

"Oh . . . oh! What about your permission slip for the Bonne field trip? Do you have that?"

Lilavois fought the urge to roll her eyes as both teenagers looked in her direction.

"No, she doesn't have her permission slip signed because her mother hasn't decided if she's allowed to go."

"Mom, please! Everyone else—"

"Is already on their way to school," Lilavois finished, with a slight pucker on her lips that let Ada know that the conversation was over — for now.

She headed toward the door in defeat before her mother caught her by the arm. Lilavois took Ada's face between the palms of her hands and placed a gentle kiss on her cheek. "I love you," she said, all trace of annoyance gone from her expression.

"I love you, too. See you later."

Not wanting to interrupt, Simon stepped outside. No matter how early or how late they were, Ada and her mother never parted without this ritual. Ada joined him on the street when they were done, still smiling with the remnants of her mother's love and peach jam on her cheeks. Simon's first instinct was to lick the lucky dollop clean off. Instead, he handed Ada his handkerchief, gestured toward her face, and tried to quell the irrational jealousy that he would not be the one to get the job done.

"You know, if you were trying to get her to let you go on the field trip, you probably should have tried getting to school on time."

"Simon, you've known me since I was six. If getting up early is going to be the deciding factor of anything, I might as well give up now."

"True," he laughed. "But didn't your mother say you used to get up early as a baby? What happened?"

"Who knows. I'm allowed to outgrow bad habits, aren't I?" Ada quipped, trying to recall a memory that was just out of reach. Ada's grin slipped just a little as she quickened her stride and stepped out into the street, weaving through the rush of streetcars and buggies that bustled by in the early morning traffic.

Jaywalking with Ada always made Simon a little nervous. He knew Ada was capable, more capable than he was in many ways, but his protective side tended to rise up in her presence. A younger Simon had been foolish enough to say so and got a sound tongue-lashing for his trouble, but now he was older and wiser. Rather than take her hand as his palm itched to do, he hung back as she made her way across the street, just a step behind to pull her back or push her out of the way if necessary, not because she needed him to but because that was who he wanted to be to her since he first laid eyes on Ada in their schoolyard playground. With Ada's panache for risk-taking, he was always glad that their school, the Phule Academy of Higher Learning, was only a few blocks from Ada's house.

"Come on, slowpoke! We've got bigger problems to solve than me getting out of bed!" She waited for him to reach the sidewalk before continuing. "We need to solve the *real* reason my mother won't let me go. Have you heard anything more about the Stone Murders?"

"There was another one reported in The Crimson Herald this morning."

"Crap! Where?"

"Uh," Simon began searching the stuffed pockets of his overcoat. "Pra … Prakesh," he remembered finally, pulling the piece of newspaper he saved for her. Ada slowed down to read it carefully.

Third Victim In The Mysterious Stone Killer Murders Found!
Demon Poison Confirmed!

The latest victim appears to be a farmer from the remote village of Lilm who had travelled to Prakesh to buy supplies. He was reported missing five days ago by his family when he did not return home from what should have been a four-day journey. The village sent out a search party. The victim was found two miles from his home in the Red Pine Forest with a single puncture wound to the chest. Like the other victims in these disturbing cases, his body was petrified and ashen. The Lilm police department, along with the local chapter of the Sisters of the Light, have no leads on these seemingly random attacks that have come without warning across the globe. However, the morgue has confirmed that the attacks are demonic in origin.

"How far is Prakesh from here?"

"Three thousand miles at least," Simon guessed. Ada frowned. "It's farther away than some of the other attacks," he added.

"True, but still too close for my mother."

"But why now?" Simon wondered. "There haven't been any attacks since the Covenant and the Sisters of the Light put an end to them almost fifteen years ago."

"Excuse me!" A stern voice called from across the street. "Do either of you plan on joining us today? Or will you be gleaning all your learning from that tiny piece of newsprint in your hand?"

Even from across the street, Headmistress Ngozi Mwaso's tone was cold enough to make them shiver. Simon and Ada hurried across the street and managed to slip past the Headmistress without quite meeting her scathing glare. With their first classes in opposite directions, Ada stuffed the news clipping in her skirt pocket and waved Simon goodbye just before the first school bell rang signaling that they had in fact made it to school on time.

Ada and Simon weren't the only ones abuzz about the Stone Murders. During Ada's presentation in her Elements of Science class, the discussion quickly turned to the demons in the news.

"What if demons are really aliens? What if they flew here from another galaxy?" Erik Gallister, one of Ada's least favorite classmates, blurted out just as Ada reached the part in her presentation where she broke down the various possibilities for non-carbon-based lifeforms.

"Demons can't fly unless they transform," Ada replied.

"I'd like to see that," he snickered.

"You wouldn't see anything!" Malini Pratchett huffed in her usual know-it-all tone. "You'd be turned to stone."

Undeterred, Eric kept talking. "So back to my alien idea. They're technically from a different realm than ours, so I think I'm right about that."

Miles Kipling put down his Jetstream penny novel, deciding that the conversation was finally worth contributing his uniquely macabre perspective. "Aliens, demons, who cares! If they start picking us off one by one, maybe this time even the Sisters of the Light and the Covenant put together won't be able to save us. They can't be everywhere at once."

"But why would they start attacking us now," Liesel Odu asked. "It's been years since the last demon scourge. I almost forgot they existed. I thought maybe the Covenant had killed them all."

Not one to miss an opportunity to darken the mood, Miles leaned in. "Maybe that's what they *wanted* us to think. You assume the Covenant were a group of 'good' demons, but what if they weren't? What if they just pretended to fight each other so we would let our guard down? Besides, demons don't kill other demons. Everybody knows that."

Though Ada could admit that Miles favored Simon in some ways, it never failed to surprise her how two people who looked similar could be completely different in every way that mattered. Simon was fun and curious, while Miles was simply annoying. Ada looked to Professor Quinlen, hoping he would guide the discussion in a more productive direction, but he was apparently too enthralled with the speculation to intervene.

"My mother said that during the scourge, demons would block out the sun with their wings," the normally very quiet Cassidy Fine added from the back of the class.

Ada was always cautious about what she said regarding demons. Given her mother's extensive training as an apothecary and the uncanny effectiveness of her medicines, some in Liren suspected that Lilavois was once a member of the Sisterhood. Still, Ada was not sure how everyone felt about that association. While most were grateful when the Sisterhood intervened, some were suspicious of the secrecy of their methods and their mastery of mooncraft. Unwilling to expose her mother to any ridicule, Ada's first inclination was usually to say nothing in the face of absurd demon conjecture. She had already failed once with Erik and his demon-flying comment and could feel herself losing the battle again.

"That's ridiculous," she said. "No group of demons is big enough to block out the sun."

"How do you know?" Erik asked. "Have you ever seen one?"

Ada's first instinct was to say yes, even though she never had. "My mother told me," she replied.

Erik's eyes lit up. "Did she ever fight a demon?"

Ada hesitated. If her mother had ever fought a demon, would she have told Ada? Outside of the few tidbits Aunt Charmaine shared, Ada knew very little about her mother's life before she was born. "I don't think so," she admitted. Disappointed, Erik turned away.

"Do you think they'll institute the curfews again?" Cassidy asked. "My father said that during the last scourge, it wasn't safe to go outside, even in the daytime."

"If the Covenant or the Sisterhood are so powerful, why don't they stop the killings?" Malini asked.

"No one knows why the Covenant decided to fight in the first place," Professor Quinlen added, foregoing his lesson and Ada's presentation completely. "Some say that God sent them down to defend us. Others say they just got tired of the treachery of their kin. There has never been any coordination between their kind and ours. Even the Sisters of the Light didn't consider them allies, though there are accounts of them fighting side by side. No one really knows what their motivations were."

"Well, I don't care which one solves the problem," Malini replied. "But if they're fighting for us, one of them should do something."

"That's a good point," Professor Quinlen added. "Does anyone have a theory as to why they haven't been able to?"

Ada lowered the carefully constructed poster she had made and sat down. While she had worked hard on her assignment, she was not about to pass up the chance to discuss her latest obsession. Ada waited a minute to see if anyone else would volunteer a theory before she raised her hand.

"Yes, Ada," Professor Quinlen nodded.

"With the scourge, it was easier for the Covenant and the Sisters of the Light to intervene. The demons didn't hide. They roamed from village to village, burning and looting. With the Stone Murders, there's no discernible pattern, at least not yet. It makes it hard to predict, so you can't intervene. I think that's the intention of the murderer."

"That's a scary thought," Liesel whispered. "That means they could be anywhere."

"What if there's more than one killer?" Miles added. "They could all be working together from different locations."

A rumble of fear rose throughout the classroom.

"Now Miles, let's not start a panic," Professor Quinlen cautioned. "The authorities are doing everything they can, and so is the school. Regarding our upcoming field trip, we've decided to ask parents for additional money to secure an entire airbus for our trip. Only authorized personnel will be on the flight, and we've also decided to visit the museum in Kemet instead of Bonne so that we're closer to home."

Ada's mouth fell open. This might be the news that would finally get her mother to say yes. "Really?! When will you tell our parents about the new security measures?"

"We won't. You will," Professor Quinlen smiled handing out the updated permission slips. "We need all the funds by next Friday, so make sure you give these to your parents as soon as possible."

Ada took the permission slip and tucked it carefully between the pages of her notebook, already plotting out her dinnertime strategy.

chapter two

UNDERNEATH

THINGS were not quite going as planned. Ada had done everything she could think of to get her mother in the best mood possible. She had come home and done her homework in between greeting customers and helping in the apothecary. After, she had weeded their garden, checked on the chickens, and even offered to make dinner — all without prompt or complaint.

In retrospect, Ada realized it was likely the dinner offer that tipped Lilavois off to her ulterior motive. Her mother knew how much Ada hated cooking. Nonetheless, Ada forced a smile while muscling past the weird slimy grit that comes from peeling potatoes then dicing them small enough to cook quickly with the curry chicken her mother was making. Every once in a while, Ada thought she saw Lilavois watching her with a knowing smirk, but she couldn't be sure. The woman could be as stoic as a statue.

Halfway through dinner, Ada made one too many a compliment on the curry. Lilavois put down her spoon and levelled a no-nonsense gaze at her daughter.

"OK. What's all this about, Ada?"

"What? The curry is really good. Browned just right." When her mother sighed in exasperation, Ada decided to give up the pretense.

"Have you thought about the school trip anymore?" She had the permission slip in her pocket but wanted to feel her mother out before presenting it.

"No, Ada. I told you, with the Stone Killer on the loose, I just don't feel comfortable with you going so far away." Something about the caution in Lilavois's words grated on Ada's nerves. Lately her mother's protectiveness was beginning to feel stifling.

"Everyone else is going," Ada mumbled sorely.

"You're not everyone else, Ada. You're my child."

Ada could feel the anger and doubt bubbling up inside her. Before she could tame it, her worst fears came rushing out. "It is because of my leg? That why you won't let me go, isn't it?"

Lilavois jerked back in her chair as if her own daughter had just slapped her in the face. Ada had been teased as a child for her artificial leg. At the time, most of the prosthetic makers were not used to designing for a child so young and they didn't always fit well with her growing and awkward little body. Sometimes she fell. Sometimes they came loose. Lilavois would never forget the day she picked Ada up from school to find that some little boy had pushed her down, pulled her prosthetic off, and ran around the schoolyard with it yelling, "Come and get it, Stumpy." This went on for several minutes before a teacher finally got a hold of him. Ada was six years old.

Three things happened that day. First, she met Simon, who was sitting outside the principal's office with a bloody nose and a shell-shocked expression from trying and failing to get back Ada's prosthetic. Second, as Lilavois carried her sobbing daughter home, she decided then and there that she would begin making Ada's prosthetics herself. Third, she began teaching her daughter how to defend herself if only as an alternative to Lilavois harming any child who dared to bully her daughter again. Though that incident — and others like it — was nine years ago, the emotional wound clearly had not healed.

"How could you think that? You're as capable as most adults. More so. You know that. I hope you know that I know it too."

Seeing the hurt in her mother's face, Ada's anger petered out. "I'm sorry, Mama. I know. It's just . . . you're always so protective, much more than other parents. Sometimes, I can't help but wonder if it's just about me."

Lilavois sighed, absently fingering the gold locket with a lock of Ada's, RaZiel's, and her own hair intertwined that she never took off. "It is about you. I lost your . . . Djimon, your father. I won't lose you. Your grandmother is no longer with us. Besides Aunt Charmaine, you're the only family I have left."

Lilavois rarely spoke about RaZiel. Twelve years later, it was still too painful. She felt his presence everywhere, and yet, for Ada's sake, she never reached out.

"We didn't lose Papa. He died." Ada corrected.

"All the more reason. When you've seen how quickly people can take everything from you — it changes you. I won't apologize for trying to hold on to the family I have left."

Ada frowned in that way she had since she was a baby trying hard to figure out the answer to a problem. "I know you want to keep me safe, but safety isn't life. Eventually I'm gonna grow up. I can't stay in this house with you forever. I want to go on my own adventures, like you did. See the world. I love you, but someday you're going to have to let me go."

Lilavois looked down at her plate as Ada got up quietly and cleaned her place. She could not meet her daughter's gaze. The potent mix of guilt, fear, and shame was not one she planned to share. All her life, Ada had been patient with Lilavois's rules and restrictions. She had trusted Lilavois to guide her. Now her daughter merely asked that Lilavois give a little bit of that trust in return. It was nothing less than she deserved. Ada was rambunctious, but she was also reasonable and smart. She more than deserved the little bit of freedom she was asking for, the freedom Lilavois was terrified to give her.

By the time Lilavois got up from the table, Ada had finished washing the dishes and retired to her room. The impact of her daughter's frustration was like a weight over her entire body, but now she knew she could no longer hide behind her fear. On the table, Ada had left a new permission slip detailing greater security measures and a closer location for the class trip.

At least now they were taking the Stone Killer threat seriously, Lilavois thought. Plus, if Ada needed anything, her sister Charmaine lived in Kemet and would be there to help. There really weren't any more good reasons why Ada couldn't go on the field trip except fear, which was not a good enough excuse for anything.

Eventually Ada would go out into the world, and if Lilavois did not prepare her, she would not have done her job as a mother who was uniquely qualified to arm her daughter with the things she needed to protect herself from any danger that arose — be it human or otherwise.

On the way to her workshop, Lilavois took some comfort in the realization that some part of her was ready for this moment. She had been working for six months on a present for Ada's birthday in two months. It would be ready sooner than that, and now there was no reason to wait.

chapter three

THE IRON STOCKING

ADA glanced at the clock on her nightstand. It was early. 6:30 in the morning in fact. School would not start for another two hours. She never woke this early on purpose; or more precisely, she woke up every day this early to the sound of her mother making breakfast at which point she turned over and let the commotion lull her back to sleep.

This morning, there was nothing.

Ada sat up, instinctively extending her hearing past the unhurried hum of early morning insects to find her mother. The stillness in the house was almost absolute.

"Mama!"

Unable to shake the prickle of worry at the back of her mind, Ada rose from the bed and hopped to the window that overlooked their garden. Glancing over the rows of lilacs, collards, and squash, her mother was nowhere to be found. However, there was a steady stream of smoke billowing up from the workshop where Lilavois did all her blacksmithing and built her potions.

Ada knew her mother had been working on a project there for months, but that was not unusual. Her mother was always making, brewing, or fixing something. As a sought-after apothecary and surgeon, that was to be expected. But 6:30 A.M. was a little early, even for Lilavois. Ada grabbed her robe and crutches and headed toward the back door, following the well-worn limestone path in search of her mother. The fact that she could feel the heat twenty feet from the door told her that the forge had been burning most of the night.

Had she even slept?

Ada opened the door and stepped into a sweltering heat. Lilavois's workshop was of decent size, large enough for a well-appointed two-bedroom flat. If she had the mind to rent it out, they would have gotten a pretty price for it. The two lots Lilavois bought were larger than any other on their block with enough backyard space to accommodate her workshop, the garden, and her training area. When Ada was small, she also had a playground built right next to a little pond. The pond was still there, but Lilavois replaced the playground when Ada was ten years old, extending the training grounds to include an archery practice area that Ada used almost every day.

Lilavois's back was to the door, consumed with buffing a molded piece of burnished copper on the polishing wheel at the right corner of the room. Intricate designs were cut and etched into the surface of the metal with such fine detail that Ada could see it from the front door. Intertwined with the carved symbols and smooth edges of the metal was the faintest blue shimmer of mooncraft. It was only when she stepped closer that Ada realized that what Lilavois was holding was actually part of a prosthetic leg. Ada looked toward the large table at the center of the room and saw the full leg on display.

The copper leg looked like a piece of fine filigreed sculpture, delicate as a piece of jewelry, yet sturdy enough to support her weight. She had never seen anything so beautiful.

"Mama, you made this?"

Lilavois smiled, not at all surprised to hear her daughter. The fresh morning air announced her quiet entrance before she had said a word. But she did not turn. Not yet. The protection spell she imbued into the metal had to be said without ceasing throughout the polishing process to make sure it penetrated every inch of the metal.

Ada was about to call her mother again before she noticed the slight movement of Lilavois's lips as she pumped the polishing wheel. With every pass of the spinning brush a subtle blue light would appear just above the copper surface only to fade into the metal as if the buffing brush was pushing the light deeper into the grain until the glow lit the metal from within.

Ada had always struggled to access mooncraft. She could walk through her mother's shield with no effort, but she was never able to conjure one on her own. She could feel the energy flowing through every living thing, but she just couldn't access it. As she stepped closer to the center table, she knew her mother had solved that problem for her by putting her own magic into this new prosthetic.

Ada suspected Lilavois had done this before. Ever since she began making Ada's prosthetics, they fit more comfortably than she ever remembered, molding to her body in a way Ada suspected was a bit too natural, and no matter what, they never fell off. Yet looking between the metal glowing in her mother's hands and the prosthetic on the table, Ada knew this was something different — something truly extraordinary. She was so transfixed with the beauty of what her mother had created that she barely noticed when the polishing brush stopped spinning or when her mother came to stand beside her with the latest attachment, a copper molded foot with a thick layer of rubber on the bottom to absorb the impact of walking on the ground.

"Do you like it?" Lilavois asked.

"Mama, it's gorgeous. Is this…?"

"…your new leg."

"You put mooncraft in it . . . for me!"

Lilavois smiled, pleased by her daughter's quick understanding. "I always put a little mooncraft into all your prosthetics, but yes. For this one, I put a bit more. I was planning to give it to you on your birthday, but since you're going to go out into the world on this field trip, I figured you could use it now."

"You're letting me go on the field trip?" Ada's eyes were wide with disbelief.

"Yes," Lilavois chuckled. "As long as you have this leg for protection, you can go."

Ada's eyes narrowed. "What kind of protection?"

Lilavois's smile widened. "Take the poker by the forge and strike it." Ada looked at her mother doubtfully, not wanting to damage something she had put so much time into, but the confidence in her mother's eyes silenced her questions.

Ada retrieved the poker which still held a dim glow from the fire and tapped it along the side of the metal calf. A blue sheen that had not been visible before rose up to meet the blow and propel it away.

Lilavois nodded. "Harder."

Raising the poker higher, Ada brought it down with more force. This time at the knee where she was usually most vulnerable. The blue light radiated from the point of contact up through the thigh and down to the calf, but to Ada's surprise, it also set off a tiny thread of electricity that travelled up the poker to shock her hand. With a pained gasp, she dropped it.

"Are you all right?" Lilavois asked, concern in her voice but not in her expression.

Ada shook out her hand gingerly. "That hurt."

"It's supposed to. That's an extra deterrent for anyone who tries to hit you at your most vulnerable spot. The mooncraft in the leg will travel up and down the prosthetic to help stabilize you, while sending a shock to your attacker."

Ada swallowed hard, less from the pain in her hand and more from the deadly calm in her mother's voice. Lilavois had taught her how to defend herself, but Ada was beginning to realize this was something more.

"Is it powerful enough to kill someone?" she asked, fear and morbid curiosity warring within her.

"The force of the shock will equal the force of the attack. If the assailant means to strike a deadly blow, it will be their own death they receive."

Ada's jaw dropped.

Lilavois waited for the full understanding of the weapon she'd created for her child to sink in.

"How long have you been working on this?" Ada asked after a moment. Lilavois did not miss the wariness in her voice.

"Six months."

Ada nodded. "What else can it do?"

Lilavois stepped closer, attaching the foot to the base of the calf with a ball and socket mechanism that seemed to both click and float in place.

"Let me show you." Lilavois traced a set of delicate etchings that Ada had assumed were for decoration. "At the inside of the thigh as well as the calf, you have a pair of throwing stars." With a quick tap, she released the first, then the second before handing them to Ada.

"Be careful," Lilavois warned.

The metal pieces in her hand felt unexpectedly heavy, despite their delicate appearance. The edges were razor sharp.

"I see," Ada replied, inspecting the micro cuts in her fingertips. Lilavois's fingers hovered over another Adinkra symbol etched into the leg that resembled something Ada had seen before but could not quite place.

"The knee, the toe, and the heel have been infused with an electrical charge that you can activate by pressing this button at the top of the thigh plate if you should ever be in close combat."

It did not escape Ada that her mother had based each of the defensive features on Ada's sparring strengths. Even so, all of this seemed a bit excessive.

"I can't believe you did all this for me. It's beautiful, but how much close combat are you expecting me to have? I'm just going to the museum."

Lilavois took a deep breath to keep the dread from seeping out into her voice.

"I don't expect any, Ada. I want you to enjoy yourself and have a good time, but the Stone Killer is out there along with the rest of the world, and I will not trust your safety to any of it."

"OK . . . But if we run into the Stone Killer, we're going to have bigger problems? I mean, none of this stuff will work on a demon, right?"

Lilavois nodded, proud that her daughter remembered the lesson she taught her well. "Most of these defenses would barely slow them down, but this," Lilavois grabbed a piece of thick cloth from the edge of the table and pulled it back. "This will."

Ada looked down into her mother's hands and found a dagger with a handle made of the same burnished copper as her leg, but with a six-inch curved edge that looked more like a dark stone than a blade.

“I thought nothing could kill a demon. I thought they were too strong.”

“Yes, as far as we know, only a demon can kill another of its kind. But this will help increase your chances.”

“What is it?”

“It’s a demon claw.”

Ada’s eyes went wide. She had heard the legend that only a demon claw could pierce demon skin, but no one had ever had access to a claw to test the theory.

“I thought the demon claw legend was just a myth! Where did you get this? How did you get this?”

“Your father gave it to me as a gift. A long time ago.”

“Mom, this . . . If anyone knew … It’s priceless.”

“Which is why I’m giving it to you. Take it.”

Ada reached for the handle and lifted it carefully. It glowed blue at her touch.

“How does it feel? I modeled it after your favorite blades.”

“I can tell. The grip and balance are perfect. I’ll have to get a new satchel to carry this.”

“No,” Lilavois answered. “If the need arises, you’ll need it closer than that. Place it on the outside of the thigh.” Ada did what she was told and watched it vanish.

“How?”

"I devised a cloaking spell, so that you can be prepared, but inconspicuous."

"I didn't know mooncraft could do that!"

Lilavois winked. "I didn't either, but I've been working on a project that provided the motivation for me to figure it out."

"Will you teach me?" Ada glanced at the shelf above the tool case to the grimoire where she knew her mother recorded all her spells.

"Maybe, if you keep your room clean."

Ada feigned shock. "It's been clean for two days!"

Lilavois rolled her eyes and lifted the prosthetic from the table.

"Try it on and see how it feels." Given the beating it endured earlier, Ada had expected it to be heavy, but the weight of it was surprising.

"It's so light. Like Atholas."

Lilavois smiled. "Well, I learned a lot in making the prosthetic you use for running. But this one is much more fortified."

Ada set the prosthetic on the ground with her left hand while balancing on her right crutch. Slowly, she leaned into the thigh socket which was lined with a material that felt like silk against her skin, though it had no shine.

As with all the prosthetics her mother made for her, as soon as she pressed her weight onto the leg, it molded around her so that it felt not like an appendage, but a part of her very being. She rested her crutch on the table and stepped out. The movement felt soft, seamless as if her left and right legs were perfectly balanced. This was not in itself unusual; her mother's craftsmanship was always impeccable, but the hydraulic improvements in the knee and ankle joint made her feel as if her steps were lighter, more natural.

Ada took two quick steps towards her mother and hugged her tightly. She was overwhelmed but grateful that Lilavois had gone through all this trouble to keep her safe.

“It’s magnificent. Thank you! I know just what to call her.”

Lilavois chuckled, wondering what name Ada might come up with for her latest accessory. Enjoying the feel of her daughter in her arms once again, she did not let go as she asked, “And what is this new name, pray tell?”

Ada leaned back to look down at the most extraordinary work of art she had ever witnessed.

“I’m calling her the Iron Stocking.”

chapter four

COINCIDENCE

ADA had never seen anything like the Cypher. The only airship she had ever been on was *the Piper Maru* when her Aunt Charmaine took her on a day trip to Cairo to see the pyramids. Her aunt fed her caramel popcorn the whole way there with the promise of lollipops and a milkshake on the way back as long as Ada promised not to tell Lilavois. Aunt Charmaine was the best! She had stayed with them a whole month that summer. It was one of the few times Ada ever remembered Lilavois fully letting her guard down.

But even with its candy and milkshake stands, brown leather seats, and polished pine benches, *the Piper Maru* had nothing on the Cypher. The mahogany wood planks were polished so finely they shined like onyx with mother-of-pearl inlay along the banisters and railings. The main cabin was even more luxurious with round, red-leather seats that curved into black, lacquer tables that looked like marble. With so much dark wood, the interior could have been cavernous except for the enormous bubble windows that flanked both sides of the vessel. The brocade carpet was brand new. And if she did not know it before, the bar which spanned the entire length of the main cabin with its brass fixtures confirmed what Ada already knew — this was a grown-up establishment.

“Do you think they’ll let us sit at the bar?” Simon asked with a gleam of excitement in his eyes. Ada shrugged, still rendered speechless by their opulent surroundings. All around, their classmates shared the same dazzled expressions as if collectively they had all successfully entered into a place they were definitely not supposed to be.

“All right, everyone!” Professor Quinlen shouted. “Quickly now. Take your seats and don’t touch anything! Our conductor, Captain Claybourne, has graciously allowed us to accompany the Cypher on her maiden voyage. Everything is brand new, so we want to pay his airship the utmost respect. Don’t we?”

Professor Quinlen’s smile was tight and shiny as he clasped his hands together.

“Yes, Professor Quinlen,” the students replied in unison, a little deflated as the message sank in that they were not going to have the run of the ship on this voyage.

Once they were seated, Captain Finneas Claybourne stepped forward wearing a dashiki from Swaziland, a worn pair of oil-skin pants, and a long, yellow scarf that hung to the floor and almost concealed the katana at his waist. His rust-colored boots laced up to just below his knees. With a warm smile and a thin scar that ran from one side of his face to the other, he began.

“Welcome to *the Cypher!* As Professor Quinlen mentioned, this is her first trip, which makes you her very first passengers. Due to the security measures requested by Headmistress Mwaso, we’ll be working with a skeleton crew today, which means I can’t offer you anything to eat or drink.” A grumble of disappointment rippled through the cavern.

“I know,” he laughed. “You’ll just have to visit us again someday. In the meantime, you can enjoy the view. The trip should take us about an hour and fifteen minutes.” Catching the murmurs of surprise around the room, he nodded. “Yes, the trip usually takes close to three hours, but we’ve made some modifications to *the Cypher* that make her faster than any airship you're likely to have been on. So, your bellies should be able to hold on until we land. Enjoy the trip."

Once Captain Claybourne left to join his crew in the control room, Ada and Simon, along with all the other students, began looking around for clues to the design. Although *the Cypher* was longer than most airships that Ada had seen, it was narrower and only one level. Most of the other airships were made of metal, but *the Cypher* appeared to be more of a blend of different materials woven together. As the engine began to vibrate, a blue glow flashed through the seams of the wooden side panels illuminating Adinkra symbols that had been carved, burned, then polished into the wood so that they were almost invisible to the eye. But Ada knew them well. She had grown up with them all around her house. They were etched into the prosthetics she wore. Simon met her eyes.

"Those symbols look familiar, like the ones..."

"At my house," Ada finished.

"That's a weird coincidence, right?"

"Uh huh," Ada mumbled as the ship rose off the ground smoothly. Except, she was fairly certain that it wasn't a coincidence at all.

chapter five

ANGELS AND DEMONS

THE Royal Museum in Kemet was among the largest and most spectacular in the world, with the most extensive collection of antiquities outside of Kush. Scholars came from all over to study artifacts of the first human civilizations. If the beginning of mankind was what you wanted to learn about, there was really no better place. Ada had longed to visit it for years, but while her mother had promised to take her "one day," it was hard to convince Lilavois to stray too far from home.

Yet here Ada was on her first solo field trip, away from her mother's protective gaze.

"Ms. St. James, don't fall behind. We have a lot more to see today!"

Ada was so entranced by the beautiful stained-glass ceilings that graced each room that she had not noticed her class had almost left the exhibit hall.

Just behind Professor Quinlen, Simon shook his head mimicking his teacher's expression perfectly. Ada rushed ahead as Professor Quinlen watched them both in silent disapproval. Once they were out of ear range, Simon leaned in close enough for Ada to feel his breath against her earlobe.

"Yes! Please, try not to fall behind, Ms. St. James," he whispered. The sensation sent a shiver down her spine that was impossible to ignore. Still, she turned and tried to match his carefree grin. Simon was beautiful, tall, and lanky with cinnamon skin and a smile that was both bright and sly. A lot of girls liked him, but they had been friends since they were kids and she had always seen him as such. Whether she was starting to join the ranks of his admirers was something she was not prepared to think about just now.

"Whatever," she laughed.

Simon threw his arm over her shoulder the way he had always done, and Ada could not help but relax into the comfort of it. "I thought you couldn't wait to explore every nook and cranny of this place."

"There's so much to take in. I just don't want to rush through it."

"I get it," he sighed. "We really need a week. There's no way to take it all in in one day."

Ada smiled, grateful that he always knew exactly how she felt.

"It doesn't hurt that we've already passed through the ancient astrology section. I was so worried I wouldn't get to see Dr. Medupe's exhibit in Bonne, but his permanent collection of artifacts here is even better! I got everything I needed for my research paper, so I guess I can just relax," she added.

Every student on the trip had an assignment that was linked to some section of the museum. Ada's was on early innovations in astronomy and how those discoveries changed life and drove progress for the earliest humans.

"Yeah, well now we're getting to the good part. ART! I'm tired of looking at chipped bowls and rusted tools," Simon joked.

"You have no respect for your ancestors. You would think with all your news clippings, historical and travel guides, you'd have more respect for the journey. Did you pack them all with you?"

"Only a few," Simon replied. "I've got plenty of respect. I just need some intentional beauty in my life."

As they stepped into the ancient art section of the museum, Ada had to agree. Despite the difficulties of early life, it was a marvel that people found time to indulge their creativity — from masks to animal-skin paintings to entire walls from caves that had been carefully excavated and hung in the museum. Early humanity, with limited language and tools, took the time to tell the story of their lives with astounding ingenuity. From the patterns woven into carpets to intricate paintings, they documented their world, their families, and most of all their first encounters with The Fallen.

Even if the exhibit was not called Angels and Demons Among Us, from the minute you passed from the Early Art exhibit into the hall, you knew. The images were grand, as powerful, mythical, and terrible as the beings who inspired them. Some images took up entire walls brimming with the majesty and awe The Fallen first inspired; others were more intimate yet no less striking portraits.

Of course, Ada had seen some of the images before in textbooks, but up close, the reverence with which The Fallen were once regarded was palpable. Seeing them so faithfully depicted, she could not really blame them. It was hard to imagine how anyone could be as beautiful as they were shown to be, and yet it was widely accepted that the images did not do them justice.

"They could have ruled forever," Ada mused as Simon stood beside her.

"They almost did, but they weren't content with that."

The descriptions that accompanied each image grew chilling as the subject matter shifted from depictions of sublime grace to grotesque nightmares. Tears captured in pastel oils turned from joy to pain and despair right before her eyes. Ada hardly noticed when Simon drifted away, moving back and forth between images, taking notes and jotting down references, while Ada was transfixed by the story the images told.

"It's almost like they descended into madness," Ada whispered once she had caught up to him a few halls down.

"I think it was," Simon replied. "For both the demons and us. Look at their eyes." Simon gestured to a painting of a radiant angel standing tall above a crowd of adoring villagers.

"You see the calm, the focus in her gaze?" Simon asked pointing to the angel in the painting.

"I see it."

Simon began walking to another painting. "Now look at the eyes in this picture. They look bored, don't they?"

Ada had passed the painting Simon was referencing before. She had taken in the debauchery, the drinking, and the wild abandonment of the scene, but had not noticed their eyes. Looking at them now, she could see the lack of focus, the dead stare.

"Now look here," Simon said, taking her hand to lead her deeper into the hall. "What do you see?"

The painting was of a village burning to the ground with a church in the background. Broken bodies were everywhere, but even these were not the most disturbing images. Lurking in every shadow was a demon. Some were in human form. Others in the form of beasts, werewolves, centaurs, or vampires. But whatever form they took, their eyes were all the same — swollen with rage and red-rimmed with a terror that came from deep within.

"They all went mad," Ada gasped.

"Not all. Here. It looks like they saved a boy from being murdered."

Following Simon's gaze, she found them. In the corner of the painting, a spark of light shimmered within the chaos — an angel, haunted and beautiful, standing between a man and a boy and a demon.

"Maybe they were fighting each other. This was well before the Covenant, wasn't it?"

"Yes, centuries before, but look at the difference in their eyes. One is clear, focused, and defiant. The other has that red-rage stare, like the others."

Ada looked closer at the angel who stood alone. His locs hung down low across his bare shoulders, his hands were balled up into fists. The sadness was clear in his eyes as he faced his kin, but there was also determination. Ada had no idea how an expression from so many centuries ago could take her breath away. She reached out to him, before Simon caught her hand.

"Ada, what's wrong? Why are you crying?" She looked at him in confusion, until she felt the tears she had not realized she'd been crying cool on her cheeks.

His face. His face. Why did she feel so certain she knew him?

"I don't know," she stammered, wiping her face with her sleeve. "He just looks so sad, I guess. One man against all of them."

"He wasn't a man." Simon pointed to the name of the painting: *RaZiel, The Savior of Ethyne.* "He was an Angel. According to what the caption says. The painter was apparently the little boy he saved."

Then I couldn't know him, she thought, despite the familiar pull.

"What happened to him? The angel."

"He probably died. He was surrounded," Simon replied before a thought occurred to him. "Ada, have you seen him before?" There was something bright, almost hopeful in his eyes.

"Of course not," she replied with a watery smile. "I've never seen a demon in real life. Almost no one has."

"Except your mother."

"I suppose, but she never talks about it, so …" Ada's voice trailed off as they stood side by side viewing RaZiel and his last stand until their teacher announced that the museum was closing and it was time to go.

chapter six

MIDNIGHT MARAUDERS

PROFESSOR Quinlen and the other chaperones on the fieldtrip to Kemet kept a tight grip on their class. Yet despite a mandatory group dinner and a tightly enforced 8 p.m. bedtime, Ada and Simon had no trouble sneaking out. With only one night in the famed City of Three Rivers, there was no way that they were going to be caught sleeping.

On the ride over, they used Simon's travel guides to map out the places they wanted to visit during their all-night excursion. Ada could not wait to shake off the strange melancholy that lingered after their trip to the museum and enjoy the excitement that was bubbling up all around them.

Kemet was the largest and the oldest city in Asfar. Each of the three rivers that ran through the city and back to the Osen Sea made Kemet a place where explorers and tradespeople from all over the world came to exchange customs, languages, spices, textiles, and ideas. The most exciting innovations almost always began in Kemet, from donuts to the first motion pictures to the first steamboats and airships. For all these reasons, Kemet maintained a reputation across the world as *the* place to cherish the old while ushering in the new.

After slipping past the hotel bellman who eyed them with enough indifference to ensure they would not be exposed, they put their plan in motion. Ada and Simon headed toward the row of cafés with the purple awnings that lined the shore of the Afrit River, the widest and most powerful of the three, in search of Mustafa's Dough of Wonders Emporium. Despite the late hour, the streets were just as busy and well-lit as if it were midday. According to Simon's travel guides, Mustafa's made everything from beignets to cakes to doubles with tamarind sauce every hour on the hour until three o'clock in the morning. Simon insisted that they stop there first to buy as many powdered doughnuts, his personal favorites, as he could fit in his satchel before they headed to the oldest cinema in existence to watch the midnight showing of the silent motion picture, *The Brothers Jetstream.*

At home, the closest cinema was a good twenty miles away, so they had only seen the swashbuckling adventure once, but it was Simon's favorite, and when they heard it was showing, they could not resist the chance to see it again at the Grande Uptown Theater. By the time the movie was over, it was almost 2 a.m., but the streets of Kemet were still alive with the smells of savory meats, sugary temptations, music, and laughter. Even though it was well past their bedtimes, Ada and Simon tried their best to match the energy of the city.

"You sleepy?" Simon asked, suppressing a yawn.

"Only a little," Ada replied, her voice as soft as a pillow.

"I saw a woman selling wasabi almonds by the river," he added. "Wanna get some and go sit down?" Simon knew Ada could not resist the delicacy. As expected, she perked up immediately.

"Race you?" Ada replied, already extending her stride. Simon knew better than to waste time with a response. Ada was off before he could think it. Instead, he followed her peals of laughter down the slope of the promenade to the food stands that lined the river's edge. With a good four inches of leg length to his advance, he could have beaten her easily, but it was never as much fun beating Ada as it was watching her win. She ran as if running were merely the precursor to her imminent flight — wild and carefree as a bird — arms flapping, chest heaving, hair bouncing like a dark cloud behind her, and legs propelling forward, yet somehow kicking back and sideways with layers of cotton and crinolines fluttering about to hide the softer movements of her body underneath.

Sometimes he wondered if the prosthetic was the reason for her odd gait, but he had seen others with prosthetics run and none of those other examples explained the unbound conundrum of speed and conflicting activity that was Ada's run. Simon caught up with her at the wasabi stand, sweaty and joyfully out of breath.

"You're getting slow in your old age," Ada chided, warm almonds already in hand.

Simon shook his head. "I'm barely a year older than you."

"Yeah, but it's starting to show."

"If you say so," he grinned, taking two of the almonds she offered and looking her over. Sometimes after a sprint like that Ada would have a limp in her stride depending on how much walking they'd already done, but her gait looked smooth.

"You want to sit down?"

With someone she didn't know, Ada might have taken offense. A childhood full of teasing had taught her never to appear less than capable in any circumstance, but Simon knew her better than almost anyone. He was only looking out for her as he tried to do every day since they were kids.

"Not really. I feel good, actually. This new leg is really something."

"No soreness?"

"None."

"WOW!"

"I know! Even though it's metal, somehow it feels as light as my real leg. Mom put these springs in the joints that absorb most of the impact. It's pretty stellar."

Simon nodded approvingly as he knelt to take in the details of the design. But somewhere between her leg and her thigh, the curiosity in Simon's eyes shifted to something different. Ada's breath stopped as she watched his attention travel from the intricacies of her leg to her thigh, torso, and finally her face where he held her gaze for a moment that felt longer than it should have, yet not nearly long enough. The effect was electric.

Abruptly, Simon stood, cleared his throat, and turned intently toward the river. "Outstanding," he said. "Your mom is a craftswoman like no other."

Stunned by the new energy swirling between them, Ada couldn't find a reply worth making. Instead, she sat beside the one person she knew could handle the uncertainty of all her emotions. But the quiet between them only seemed to give the feelings inside her more room to grow into things she was not ready to face, and so Ada did something she'd never done before: break the comfortable silence between them.

"So — was *The Brothers Jetstream* as good the second time around?"

Simon turned to her with a sly grin, fully recovered, and himself again. "Rameses Jetstream is a god among men."

"I think he'd object to that description."

"That's only because he's too humble. I want to be him when I grow up," Simon declared.

"Really? You want to run around killing demon vampires and werewolves all day?"

"That'd be cool. Don't you think? To live a life of adventure like that?"

"I don't know. Maybe for a little while, but after so many years, I think I'd get tired of it. I'd want peace."

Simon smiled. "You sound like your mother."

Ada cringed. "Oh my God, I do! It must be time to go to bed. I'm going senile."

Simon threw his arm over her shoulder and laughed, untying the anxious knot in her stomach with his simple touch. "The sun will be up soon. We should probably get some sleep before Professor Quinlen starts pounding on our doors."

Ada looked back at the city that was only just starting to quiet down from when they first headed out more than six hours ago. "Do you remember the way back?" she teased.

Simon scoffed. "Me? What do you think you're here for? I'm the tour guide. You're the compass." He squeezed her shoulder. "Lead the way."

They walked back at a leisurely pace. With less people on the street and all the shops closed, they could browse the lavish gowns, men's attire, and jewelry on display in the store windows without the angst of knowing they had no money to buy. Though the streets were not familiar, Ada had taken note of various landmarks along the way which would make finding their path home fairly easy.

But as they got closer to the hotel, the path home took on a more ominous look with narrower streets and deeper shadows. Ada and Simon stuck close together as they chatted with pauses that allowed them to listen out for following footsteps. Although they didn't hear anything, the closer they got to the hotel, the more Ada felt certain they were not alone.

"Do you smell that? Like flowers," Ada asked as they neared a deli at the corner, which meant that their hotel was less than ten minutes away.

Simon stopped walking and inhaled deeply. "Flowers? I don't smell anything."

Before she could reply, a tall figure swept down from somewhere high above them, somewhere no human would perch.

"Simon!" Ada yelled, pushing him away from her a moment before the demon landed between them. Though its frame suggested a large man, its body shifted between an amorphous shape and a being of smoke and shadow with red, glowing eyes.

The demon leveled its crimson gaze on Ada. "You should not be here." Its voice scraped against her mind like sharp metal. It paused, then drew closer. "But I *know* your scent after all these many years. How did you survive?"

For a moment, Ada struggled to comprehend the insinuation that this creature knew her. She had never seen anything like it before, not even in Lilavois's textbooks from her apprenticeship with the Sisterhood. Ada had stumbled upon them years ago and read them all in secret, but the mystery of his existence was another matter.

First, they had to survive.

The demon was focused on her, and that was a good thing. Ada hoped it would leave Simon enough time to escape. She took a step back, flicked her skirt open to reveal her prosthetic fully and reached for the blade that lay hidden at the outside of her metallic thigh. The creature hissed at the blue light that began to glow as soon as the blade detached.

That's right, she thought with some small satisfaction. *The magic of my mother comes with me.* Ada held her blade firmly in her hand.

"I don't know you," she said in a voice low enough to mask her fear. "I've done nothing to you or your kind. Leave us alone."

"Lies!" it cried in a pitch that pierced her ears but left no echo — as if snatched from the air the moment it was released. "All your kind lies. The evidence of what you've done is in your hands! My kin died for *you*, and now you mean to use their claws against me!"

Who had died for her? How? Ada had no idea what he was talking about until her mother's words came back to her. *It's a demon claw*, she'd said. At the time, Ada had not considered who it might belong to or what her father had to do to get it. It never occurred to her that to have this weapon likely meant that someone else had made the ultimate sacrifice.

"RaZiel is not here to pay the price of our kin's death, but you will."

Its next move was almost imperceptible, a flash of movement that stole her breath. Before she could flinch, it grabbed her, the force of the demon's movements propelling them across the street and up against a brick wall. It caught her wrist in a vise her own grip could not withstand. She heard the blade drop to the ground somewhere close, but with the demon's other hand closing around her neck and its massive frame crushing her, she had no time to look for it.

The pain in her lungs as they struggled for air had almost become unbearable when she saw Simon's arm snake around the creature's neck. Simon's legs came up next pushing against the wall, leveraging his entire body to pull the creature off her. He bought her only a moment, but it was enough for her to breathe — to escape.

"Go!" Simon panted as he strained to maintain his grip while the creature flailed for purchase. She could have run away as Simon could have. But he had not, and neither would she. Instead, Ada dropped to the ground and searched for the blade. Her mother told her it was the only thing hard enough to pierce demon skin. Ada hoped Lilavois was speaking from experience as she grabbed the handle, then slashed the blade across the creature's calf. Smoke and a thin, clear liquid poured from the wound as it screamed, still fighting against Simon, who had wrapped his legs around the creature's torso. It staggered, spinning across the street as it tried to shake Simon loose.

Ada got to her feet and followed, trying to figure out the best means of attack. Blood trickled down from a wound on Simon's forehead, and while his expression was fierce with determination, Ada knew if she didn't act quickly, he would not last. The cut to the creature's calf slowed it down but it had not done enough damage to weaken it. She needed to strike again.

As if hearing her thoughts, the demon locked eyes with Ada. He moved backwards so quickly, she only registered what happened when she heard the crack of Simon's head against a wooden door at the other side of the road. His arms, neck, and legs suddenly went slack as he fell to the ground in a heap.

"Simon!"

The demon turned, grabbed him by the neck and raised him high. Simon's eyes blinked open, unfocused and unseeing as he gasped for breath. The creature drew back a hand, claws protruding from its smoky fingers — but Ada struck first, plunging her blade into its back. She cut through the substance of him as if moving through a thin slice of bread, then pulled the dagger out. Simon fell to the ground, shielding his eyes as the creature released him then whirled toward Ada.

It moved toward her, half-lurch and half-lunge, but this time it was slow enough for Ada to act, plunging the blade into its chest before stepping away. The creature stumbled a few more feet before buckling to its knees. Ada raced towards Simon, slumped on the ground listless but still alive. She grabbed his head in her hands.

"Simon, look at me. Please! Can you hear me?"

For a moment, he took her in as if surprised to see her, but he could not hold her gaze. Simon closed his eyes against the pain in his head and the nausea in his stomach.

"Changing," he whispered. "Like you." It was only then that Ada noticed the faint glow emanating from inside her hands, as if a bright yellow orb of light was tucked just beneath the skin of her palm. She had seen mooncraft wielded before by her mother, but the magic of the Sisters of the Light was always blue. Ada had never been able to summon it. As she turned and twisted her hand, watching the yellow light flow and contract from her fingers, she was certain this was something different. But Simon's attention was not on her as he pointed towards the middle of the street.

"Ada," he wheezed. She followed his gaze and saw the demon that had once been shadow and smoke shifted from a werewolf to a centaur to a winged creature to finally a man gasping for air with his hands held to his chest.

"I'm bleeding," he whispered, his voice so beautiful it sounded like song. He turned to Ada and Simon with tears of wonder in his eyes. "I'm bleeding."

Ada looked in shock from the blood seeping through his fingers to the dagger that she left discarded on the ground that was also covered in blood.

"How?" Tears ran freely down the seraphic features of his face. Gently he laid himself on his side watching the blood pulse from a heart that had just begun to learn its rhythm.

"Abba, thank you," he whispered before casting two unseeing eyes toward the coming dawn.

chapter seven

SOMETHING ELSE...

"HE'S dead?" Ada shook her head, before turning back to her best friend, hoping he could make sense of what she was seeing. She was grateful to find his eyes open and fixed on the body lying in the middle of the street.

"I thought they couldn't die," he rasped.

Ada turned to her discarded blade on the ground. "I think … I killed it."

"I didn't think one of us could do that."

"Me neither," Ada agreed.

"We need to hide the body."

"What?"

It took Ada a moment to get past her own disbelief and see what Simon had already put together. Two kids. A bloody dagger. A dead man/demon in the middle of the street and dawn quickly approaching. They needed to get out of sight. The blood had stopped running down the side of Simon's head, but that was little comfort as she watched his shallow breathing.

"Can you move?"

"Not yet, but I'm working on it. I just need my stomach to calm down so when I try to stand, I won't immediately throw up."

"I'll hold your locs back," Ada smiled gently, running her hand over the tight coils of hair that had just begun to hang over his forehead and cheek.

Simon grimaced. "Don't make me laugh. My head hurts too much."

"Sorry. I think you have a concussion."

He nodded, closing his eyes. "I'm more worried about you. Are you OK?" Simon did not need to look at her to discern the truth. He would hear it in her voice.

"I don't know. Let's get out of here first. You stay put. I'll try to drag the body into the alley."

"Don't touch it!" Captain Claybourne's voice rang out from the end of the street.

"What are you doing here?" Ada asked, both relieved and surprised to see him.

He hesitated. "Your mother asked me to look after you. I was guarding the hotel until I realized two hours ago that you'd snuck out. I've been looking for you ever since."

Ada wanted to be angry at her mother's lack of trust, but in that moment, she could not deny she was in desperate need of adult supervision.

"The body doesn't matter," Captain Claybourne continued. "We need to get you two out of here now. Take this." He picked up her blade, wiping it off on the corner of his red caftan before handing it to her with reverence. Ada thanked him, tucked the knife back into the invisible pocket at her thigh, and turned her attention back to Simon.

"He can't move yet," Ada said, watching him struggle to control his breathing.

"He'll have to. We don't have much time. The people of Kemet go to bed late and rise early."

Simon did his best to shift his torso upright. "OK, let me just —" Before he could finish, Captain Claybourne lifted Simon off his feet and into his arms.

"Don't throw up on me," he ordered, moving quickly into the shadows.

"Yes, Sir," Simon mumbled, both humiliated and deeply grateful to be carried.

"If there's time, I'll come back for the body."

Behind them, Ada watched their rear as they made their way back to the hotel.

Thankful that each student had a private room, Captain Claybourne snuck Simon back into his bed without incident, cleaning him up and tending to his wounds. As they worked, Ada noted the Captain's proficiency in tending to Simon's injuries as well as his use of the teal vials of medicine that were a signature of her mother's apothecary. She held her tongue until Simon was resting soundly.

"You're pretty good at that," Ada motioned to the pouch of medicines he was tucking back into his satchel. "Where did you learn all that?"

Captain Claybourne flashed her a knowing glance. "Your mother, of course. I'm the captain of a ship. I have to know how to tend to my crew. Your mother taught me the basics and, of course, anyone with any sense keeps her medicines on hand."

Ada nodded as she cleaned up the bloody bandages and soiled clothes. Everything about Captain Claybourne said danger and mystery, the opposite of her mother's quiet and completely predictable existence. For as long as she could remember, Lilavois had lived an unassuming life with few friends and nothing remotely resembling adventure. It also didn't escape her notice that Captain Claybourne was very tall and very handsome. So where had her mother met him?

"How do you know my mother? She must trust you a great deal to send you to look after me, yet I've never met you."

"We actually have met before, once, but I imagine you were too young to remember."

Captain Claybourne's smile was small, patiently waiting for her to assuage all her thinly veiled suspicions. "I used to bring your mother medicinal supplies that she needed. Plants and herbs that were difficult to find, and in return, she helped me and my crew with some of their ailments. After a while, we became friends.

Ada eyed him skeptically. Lilavois St. James was *very* choosy with her friends, but still, how could he be anything less if she'd imbued his ship with her own magic and sent him to protect her child.

Captain Claybourne's gentle voice broke through her silent wanderings. "Do you take me for a liar?" he asked.

"No," Ada admitted. "Your ship was made with my mother's magic. She would not have done that if you could not be trusted." Captain Claybourne nodded in agreement, his forthright open gaze burning away the last of her suspicions.

With her doubts settled, Ada broached the subject she had been waiting to talk about. "Do you know what happened back there?"

"No. I'm only glad your mother prepared you so well. I wasn't expecting you to sneak off in the middle of the night. If not for your training, I would have found you dead."

"It was a demon. Demons don't die. There have been accounts of them being wounded from the Sisterhood, but there isn't a single credible account of a human ever killing one."

Claybourne tilted his head, regarding Ada with a restrained intensity. "And yet you have done so. But what lies in the street is no demon. Somehow you, your blade, made him human."

Ada's thoughts turned to the glow within her hands, now gone. "Did you see any of the struggle between us?"

"When I arrived, you had just stabbed him in the chest."

Ada hesitated. "What else did you see?"

"I saw a bright flash of golden light in the darkness. Following it was how I found you until I saw you stab him and realized it *was* you. The light came from inside your chest."

Ada stepped back, looking at her hands, her chest. There was no light, no evidence at all of what he described or what she had seen. "How long did it last?"

"Only a moment. By the time he fell, the light was very faint, but it was there."

Ada shook her head. "It must have something to do with the leg mother made me. I've never been able to conjure mooncraft on my own."

"Did you see the light?" Captain Claybourne asked.

Ada nodded. "In my hands, after it was over."

"The magic of the Sisters of the Light is always blue." Captain Claybourne's voice was steady and certain as he gathered the last of his supplies. "You know that. And it's never been able to kill a demon, much less turn a demon human. I saw him change. What you did, what you can do, is something else."

He left without another word, leaving Ada standing at the foot of Simon's bed, staring at her hands in the dark.

chapter eight

AUNT CHARMAINE

THE *Cypher* departed for Liren at 3 p.m., which left Ada very little time to get to her Aunt Charmaine's house and make it back to the hotel to catch the trolley to the airship.

Luckily waking up early was not hard. She hadn't slept. Between watching over Simon and running through everything that had happened, from the picture in the museum that made her weep to the dagger that had somehow made a demon human and killed him, she needed to talk to someone. Someone who might know why the demon that attacked them would claim to know her. Ada knew her mother had answers. The question was, would she share them?

Ada could recall almost nothing about her childhood. She had been born with both legs but lost one due to an infection. Her father died shortly after her leg was amputated. They moved to Liren where her mother became the town surgeon and apothecary. Beyond a vague scent or fragment of memory, that was all she could recall.

When it came to anyone outside their home, her mother would deliberately obfuscate any details about their life before Liren unless it was necessary. Though there were many suspicions, very few could say they knew Lilavois St. James had been trained as a Sister of the Light. Exactly why she kept this a secret, Ada never quite understood. Her mother claimed it was to protect them from the curiosity and ignorance of others. Despite her doubts about this explanation, Ada tried to respect the code of silence around their past. The grief over the loss of her father was something Ada knew her mother still felt deeply. Against her most valiant efforts to mask it, it still leaked out in the way her mother isolated herself from others and the sometimes smothering love Lilavois displayed for her.

But now Ada needed answers, and the only other adult who might give them to her happened to be a short trolley ride away.

Her mother always said Aunt Charmaine talked too much, which, as Ada paid the trolley fare and sat down, was exactly what she was hoping for. Aunt Charmaine lived just outside Kemet's commercial district in a home Ada had visited only once but never forgot. She had been riding on the trolley for ten minutes when the conductor announced, "Next stop! The Ziryab House!" Exalted for its extraordinary example of Moorish ingenuity and the architect who designed it, her aunt's house was so famous it had been displayed in numerous periodicals. It even had a trolley stop named after it.

"I guess no one else could forget it, either." Ada smiled as she stepped off the tram.

Separated from the sidewalk by a waist-high wrought iron fence, the Ziryab House began with a garden that could only be described as a blushing oasis, filled with pale pink roses, lilacs, lilies, honeysuckle bushes, and flowering trees that perfumed the entire block.

At the center of the oasis was a pale diamond-shaped limestone walkway that matched the cream archways, horseshoe exterior, and intricate stone lattice that made up the entrance of the house. Ada had just crossed the street and put her hand on the gate when a tawny Pomeranian came racing out from under a bench, barking and baring his tiny little teeth as if ready to pounce. Fearful for her ankle, Ada froze. From somewhere deep in the garden, her aunt's voice rang out.

"Honestly, Hannibal! Stop that! You can't attack everyone who admires the beauty of our home." Ada could hear the light chuckle in her aunt's voice, which was blessedly close by. "Well, I suppose you could, but I can't spend my whole day apologizing for your lack of decorum. It's unlady-like."

Hannibal lowered his bark to a low growl which ceased the moment Aunt Charmaine emerged from behind a lilac tree. She wore a low-cut nightgown and matching robe made of silk lavender and white feathers. The ensemble fluttered and clung to her enviable curves while she held a basket of fresh cut roses in one arm and a pair of cutting shears in the other.

"Oh, my goodness, it's you!" Aunt Charmaine broke into a wide grin, her dark skin luminous and glowing without a trace of powder. "My Ada! Why didn't you tell me you were coming?"

To Ada's surprise, Charmaine ran over. Balancing on matching wedge heel slippers, she shooed Hannibal to the side before opening the gate and pulling Ada into an embrace that was soft and fragrant. Ada hugged her back fiercely, remembering in a rush how good Aunt Charmaine's hugs always felt.

Charmaine pulled back and looked at Ada's decidedly less lavender attire, balancing her disapproval and affection well.

"You didn't take the trolley here?"

"I did," Ada smiled.

"Honestly, you're too much like your mother. I could have sent a car to fetch you."

"I wanted to surprise you."

Aunt Charmaine smiled then and brought her into another warm embrace. “And that you have, my dear. I do love surprises. Come inside and we’ll have some breakfast.”

They walked through Aunt Charmaine’s grand foyer hand in hand, greeted by servants who hurried to take Charmaine’s flower basket and shears then offer her a tray with two warm wet towels to wipe her hands. Charmaine took one for herself and handed the other to Ada, who was not surprised to find them perfumed with lavender oil.

“Thank you ever so much, Eldar,” Charmaine said, placing the towel on the silver tray that was offered before Ada quickly did the same.

“I found my niece in the garden. Would you mind telling Gertrude to set another place at the table for breakfast?”

“Right away, Ms. Charmaine,” the man nodded before exiting towards the kitchen with haste.

“Now dear. Let me get a good look at you. You’ve grown at least three feet since last summer.”

Ada giggled like a child despite herself.

“Ah, but that pretty smile remains the same!” Cupping her niece’s face, she looked at Ada intently as if reading her mind at a glance. Satisfied in her silent assessment, Charmaine stepped back and clasped her hands in front of her.

“Now, tell me why didn’t you come yesterday after your visit to the museum? Your field trip is over in just a few hours, isn’t it?”

Ada stared in shock. “How do you know?”

“My dear, I know *everything*,” she said with a wink. “I’m a benefactor of your school, of course, which makes me privy to the student calendar of yearly activities, and I've been pestering your mother to let you go on this field trip longer than you have. If your trip hadn't been cut short because of this string of murders, I would have picked you up from the airship dock myself." She pursed her lips in consternation. "But your mother said you wouldn't have time."

Ada was at a loss for words. "Wow."

"But you did make time, didn't you, clever girl," Charmaine said with a sly smile. "Come have breakfast with me and tell me why."

Ada followed her aunt to the morning terrace, which was fashioned as an enclosed gazebo with grape vines growing on a trellis along the walls and above the table. With her secret agenda already suspected, Ada got to the point as soon as their breakfast was placed on the table.

"I wanted to ask you a question about something that happened last night."

Charmaine leaned forward and raised a curious brow. "Last night? I thought you were all supposed to be in bed by eight. Please tell me you've been out making mischief. Your auntie would be so proud."

"Not exactly. I mean sort of, but then," Ada hesitated. "We were attacked."

Aunt Charmaine turned to the butler who was standing quietly at the gazebo entrance.

"Alastair, would you mind giving us some privacy. We'll serve ourselves." With a nod, he left the gazebo and closed the glass door behind him. When Aunt Charmaine turned back to Ada, her expression was so stern, she almost looked like her mother's twin.

"Who is 'we'?"

"My friend, Simon, and me."

"Start from the beginning."

Ada did as she was told, recounting the ordeal in as much detail as she could bear while Aunt Charmaine settled back in her chair listening. Charmaine's expression was grave, but also strangely guarded. When Ada finished, her aunt was not looking at her. Instead, Charmaine held her hands tightly in her lap.

"It's a miracle you survived. This … it … could have been so much worse." She grabbed her niece's hands across the table and held them tightly, but Ada eased hers away.

"Aunt Charmaine, I wouldn't have survived if I didn't have this." Ada detached the blade from her leg and set it on the table.

"The demon, he said he knew me. He said someone named RaZiel killed his kin to save me. That's a demon name, but I've never met one, so why would he kill someone for me? If he's alive. I need to find him. I need to know how he killed them . . . to understand if he can do what I can."

Aunt Charmaine still had not looked at her, instead staring past the point where their hands had been joined to some far-off place only she could see.

"Aunt Charmaine? Do you know who this RaZiel is?"

Charmaine closed her eyes for a long moment before opening them and picking up the blade in front of her.

"Only a demon can kill another demon," she said. "It is said to be a rare thing, forbidden among their kind because to kill one of them means not just death, but the end of their existence. Can you imagine living for millions of years, from before the beginning of time, and then ceasing to exist with no hope of rebirth? To just be erased completely?"

"How do you know all this? Did you know the demon that attacked us?"

"Not truly. We've never met. But his name is Saisho. He's the only one of the four demons that got away. That RaZiel left alive."

"You know him? RaZiel?"

"No. Unfortunately. Though I owe him a deep gratitude for giving me a most precious gift."

"What gift?"

Aunt Charmaine's eyes were sharp and clear as they met Ada's.

"You, my dear. Your father's name is not Djimon, as your mother has told you. It's RaZiel. It is time your mother told you the story — the true story — of who you are and how you came to be before it kills you as it almost did last night."

chapter nine

THE TRUTH

ADA had the foresight to pack her things before she left for her aunt's house, and she was grateful to have one less thing to think about as she rushed into the hotel lobby and right into Professor Quinlen.

"Cutting it close, Ms. St. James. The trolley to the air dock leaves in fifteen minutes. I do hope you plan to be on it."

"Yes, Professor," Ada muttered before racing past him to the elevator. Aunt Charmaine had insisted that she take a car back to the hotel, but Ada refused. She needed the time to process what she had learned — that everything she believed her whole life was a lie.

In a daze, she stepped off the elevator and right into Simon's chest. "Hey!" he cautioned before taking one look at her face and dropping their bags. "What happened?"

Unable to speak, Ada shook her head, swallowing the tears that threatened to fall. Panic rose in his chest. Simon had never seen her like this. Of their own volition, his arms rose to hug Ada tightly.

"Ada, tell me. Please."

"I can't. We have to go. I . . . thought you would be on the trolley already."

Simon pulled back to see her face, but only a little. "When I didn't see you in the lobby, I came back up to use the room key you left me to get your bags just in case you had to meet us at the dock. It's a good thing, too. You forgot to pack your toothbrush." He pulled the brush from the inside pocket of his jacket and wiggled it in front of her. That earned him a watery smile.

"Thank you," she said blinking back new tears.

"Always," he whispered. "The trolley leaves in ten minutes. What do you need? Is there a short version you can tell me, or do you just need a minute?"

Ada buried her face in his chest as his arms tightened around her once more, overwhelmed by her grief and how well Simon knew her.

"My father didn't die when I was a child, and his name wasn't Djimon; it was RaZiel, and he killed three demons to save my life."

Slowly, Simon pulled back. "RaZiel, like the painting?" Their gazes met, holding the same impossible thought between them.

"Yes."

They held on to each other in silence for a moment longer before Simon glanced at his pocket watch and sighed. Their time for contemplation had run out.

"Ada, I don't know what to say, but we have three minutes to get to the trolley."

Ada stepped away feeling noticeably calmer. "It's OK," she sniffed. "I'm better." Ada turned around and pushed the button to send the elevator back up to their floor. Beside her, Simon frowned, doubtful but accepting that whatever stability she felt would have to be enough.

"What are you going to do?" He reached down to pick up their bags before the lift arrived and they stepped inside.

"I need to talk to my mother."

For most students, the trip home was filled with excitement to share the experiences of their field trip with their families. But Ada and Simon sat in silence, both watching her trembling hands and pondering the same path towards the impossible.

Her father killed a demon to save her.

His name was RaZiel.

Only demons can kill demons, but he did.

So what did that make him?

And she killed a demon.

So what did that make her?

"We'll figure it out," Simon whispered, covering her hands with his own. "No matter what this is, we'll figure it out.

At Liren's landing dock, parents crowded together to watch as *the Cypher* glided onto the air dock with expert ease. Lilavois stood apart. She already knew that Captain Claybourne was an exceptional aviator. She would not have called in a favor and volunteered the ship to the school if he were anything less.

Normally, her purse would be full of Ada's favorite treats, a tradition they had carried on from when Ada was a little girl. At the end of the school day, Lilavois would allow Ada to rummage through her pocket for buried treasure. A caramel, a tamarind ball, or a square of wrapped fudge could always be found. Lilavois's grandma had started the tradition when she was a girl. It was something Lilavois had looked forward to doing the moment she found out she was pregnant. But there was no candy today.

Instead, her fingers traced the edges of the two telegraphs she'd received, one late last night and the other early this morning. Each one felt like stones in her pocket. In the last 24 hours, Lilavois had gone through every emotion. As the town surgeon, she was used to being awakened in the middle of the night by urgent messages. But, when her bell rang, she was not prepared for Captain Claybourne's message and the harrowing tale of how her daughter, in spite of all the precautions she had taken to keep her safe, had almost been killed by a demon. But there was no context for what he told her next — that her daughter had done the impossible, what no human in the history of the world had done. She had killed it.

More than that, she transformed it, through some source of magic that Lilavois was sure Ada had no knowledge of. Lilavois stayed up all night vacillating between relief and fascination. She had been prepared to help Ada solve a mystery. Charmaine's telegraph, which arrived only a few hours later, let her know much more would be required of her. Ada knew about RaZiel.

Despite what now seemed like a bewildering lack of foresight, Lilavois had never planned to tell Ada the truth about her father. She had left that story in her will to be discovered after her death. It had been less of a cowardly choice than a practical one, thinking that while Lilavois was alive and well, there was no need to burden her with the truth.

"Tell her everything. Or I will. It's time," Charmaine had written.

Ada stepped out of *the Cypher* just as Lilavois knew she would, with eyes that were full of questions and more than a little hurt. They found hers, wary, yet needing. Immediately, Lilavois missed the openness of her daughter's gaze. The distrust that now took its place broke Lilavois's heart because, for now at least, she had earned it.

Though they greeted each other with a long hug, they rode their carriage in silence. Ada stepped through the door of their home and went to the kitchen to wash her hands. Lilavois found her there standing over the sink, waiting in silence.

"Am I a demon?" Ada finally asked, arms shaking despite her iron grip on the counter.

Lilavois took in a sharp breath, immediately understanding her daughter's fear. "No, but your father is."

chapter ten

AND NOW FORWARD

"WHY did you keep all this from me?"

Lilavois had been up all-night answering Ada's questions as she promised, as she was bound to do after so many years and so many lies.

"Because I didn't want to hurt you. It felt at the time, and it still feels, like an impossible situation. I thought the truth would only make it worse. I didn't want you to carry the burden of all our secrets."

Ada was silent as she stared into the hot lavender tea her mother made for her.

"Captain Claybourne and Aunt Charmaine know more about my life than I do," she whispered into the steam. Over the course of the night, the raw edges of her anger had worn down with weariness.

"Captain Claybourne knows about me and the fact that you are my daughter. He doesn't know about your father, how you lost your leg, or anything else." Lilavois was glad to see Ada's shoulders release some of its tension.

"Aunt Charmaine is the only one who knows everything," Lilavois continued. "I wouldn't have shared any of it with her, except I needed someone I could trust to keep the truth for you if something happened to me." When Ada did not respond, Lilavois added, "This is only part of your life, Ada. It doesn't have to define you."

"How can you say that?" Ada snapped, pushing her tea away. "I killed someone last night! Someone I wasn't even supposed to be able to kill. Someone who's hated me ever since I was a baby because my father dared to protect me. A father I thought was dead, who you now tell me is alive!" Ada lifted her hands, remembering the glow that lit them from within.

"Part of me is a demon who can kill other demons. I didn't go looking for this, but it found me and almost killed Simon. Not knowing hasn't helped me . . ." Ada looked down at her leg.

"For the longest time, I would have these nightmares of this man screaming, 'Ruined. Everything is ruined.' I was so young when they started, I didn't know what ruined meant. I just knew the voice didn't approve of me. That he thought I was wrong somehow because of my leg. I didn't know whose voice it was. But now, I know it was my father's."

Lilavois felt stricken as she listened to her daughter's words.

"That's not true, Ada! Please, you must believe me! Your father blamed himself for the attack and how it hurt you. It wasn't about you at all. He loves you, Ada, so much."

"Then how come he's avoided me? In all these years, he's never come to see me, not even once."

"He has! He's just kept his distance to keep you safe, but he's been there watching you throughout your life. Your first day of school, when you graduated from primary, every birthday."

Ada's eyes widened with shock. "Where? I've never seen him."

Lilavois looked down fiddling with the lace at her wrists, hiding her tears. "Usually, I don't either," she admitted softly. "Most often I'll know he was here because he'll leave a gift or move something or take something of mine as a memento. He'll leave a bushel of rare herbs at an open window or flowers on your birthday, every year."

Ada gasped. "The moonflowers? I thought you bought me those."

"No. You used to pick them with your father in the garden in the home we shared. They were your favorite."

"They still are," she said absently, reaching for a frayed memory she thought she'd imagined of walking through a garden where everything was fragrant and much taller than herself. Yet she felt safe holding on to a strong hand that was soft and warm.

"Sometimes I think I remember him. All these years, I thought that was impossible."

"You were very young. We didn't think you'd remember. Most humans have no memory of their early years."

"But I'm not just human, am I?"

"No, you're not."

"Did you know I could kill a demon?"

"Of course not! I might not have been so worried about you going on that field trip if I had. Your father and I have done everything possible to try to make sure no demon ever came across your path again. That's why he stays away. They tracked his scent before. That's how they found us. He would never make that mistake again and put you in danger."

"But you had to know I would be different. I mean demon children must have some defining characteristics."

"You are not a demon child! Your father was an Angel of the Ever!" Lilavois said firmly. "And there are no others like you. The Fallen have been trying for millennia to have children, but there has never been a single reported case. We had no idea what your potential might be and we didn't care. You're our miracle. We were just glad to have you."

Ada sat with the weight of that, trying to recall the history she had read while taking a sip of the tea that had now gone cold. "Demons can't have children," she muttered.

"It's never happened, before you," Lilavois whispered. "Even before your father was forced to leave, we kept it a secret. We wanted you to have a life — to choose a life of your own."

When Ada said nothing, Lilavois continued.

"You lost your leg because a demon named Nephycil pierced his talon through your shin. The demon poison should have killed you almost instantly, turned you to stone like the victims in the paper, but you survived. By the time I got home, the poison had spread to your knee which is why I chose to amputate at the thigh. That you survived was surely because of your father's contribution to your make-up, but beyond that, I'd never given any thought to why we were able to create you. I was just glad we did."

"That's why you didn't want me to go on the field trip. You thought the Stone Killer might find me."

Lilavois nodded, grateful for her daughter's calmer demeanor and the soothing properties of lavender. "Your father felt sure they would never stop hunting him. Saisho would not have suspected you were alive, but we didn't want to risk the chance that your paths might cross again."

"So you think he was the Stone Killer?"

"Given the cruel and random nature of the attacks, yes. I believed so."

"Do you think that's the reason I was born? To kill them."

Lilavois reached over and gathered both her daughter's hands in hers. "You were born because I dared to love your father and he dared to love me back. That's the most important reason, but I can't deny something new has happened. You didn't just kill him, Ada. You transformed him — made him human so he could die. Do you know why it's forbidden for one demon to kill another?"

"Aunt Charmaine said because they would cease to exist."

"That's right. They have no souls. That's why they don't die. They were created as infinite beings who were never meant to separate from, much less return to, their Creator. They are stuck here forever. Having realized their mistake with no way to go home, existence is their only connection to God. To take that life, to sever their only tie to God forever, it's an unthinkable crime.

"As humans, we have a soul, a key that allows us to return to our Creator when we die. To begin again in another life or stay in the presence of God. I think when you turned that demon human, you didn't just kill him, you gave him a soul, Ada. You allowed him to do the one thing no member of The Fallen has ever done: return home."

Ada shook her head. "I'm not God! No one can do something like that."

"And yet, you did. Maybe God gave you a different type of magic. One that can restore connection. Claybourne said the light of your magic was different. He said it was as bright as the sun."

Ada sat in silence, feeling the last of her anger leached away by bewilderment and the staggering implications of her mother's words. Feeling the weight of it, she was suddenly grateful for all the time her parents had afforded her to live without any notion of the burden she now carried. But now that she knew, she needed more answers.

"Do you have a way to reach my father?"

"Yes, in case of emergencies."

"I need to speak with him.

"Ada, I . . ."

Sensing her mother's hesitation, Ada pushed forward. "It's my birthday in a few weeks, anyway. He'll bring flowers, won't he?"

Lilavois smiled. "Yes. I'm sure of it."

"Then send him a message. We can meet far away from here to make it safer, if he'd prefer, but I need to meet him."

Lilavois watched her daughter rise from the table and head towards the steps. The clock in the hall chimed softly. It was a quarter past three in the morning.

"Where are you going?" Lilavois asked. "You haven't slept. I wasn't planning for you to go to school today."

Ada paused on the steps.

"I can still catch a few hours, but I need to go to school. I have to tell Simon."

"Ada," Lilavois began, cautiously.

"He would never hurt me. You know that. He was there. He saw the light in me before I even knew what was happening. I need him to know."

chapter eleven

AFTERMATH

DESPITE her lack of sleep, Ada hoped going to school would provide a sense of normalcy after the turmoil of the last two days. But as she walked to Phule Academy, quietly sharing with Simon the revelations she had learned the night before, it became clear that the consequences of what they experienced in Kemet had followed them home. From the morning's newspaper to the chatter that filled every storefront, street corner, and classroom, the people of Liren were obsessed with the mysterious murder that had taken place minutes away from the hotel where so many students had stayed.

Worse, the mystery of the Stone Killer, which Lilavois thought Ada had solved with Saisho's death, proved very much alive. Over the next two weeks, three new Stone Murders were reported.

The first killings happened just three days after returning home. According to the night clerk on duty at the morgue where Saisho was being held, the coroner and a security guard were attacked in the night by two demons, who stole the body of an unidentified man and destroyed the morgue. No other bodies were reported missing.

The biggest mystery on everyone's mind seemed to be where this unidentified victim had come from and why a pair of demons would be so invested in the murder of a human. The theories ran to every corner of speculation. In the paper, the crime editor posited that the missing body belonged to a loyal servant who had been killed by a warring gang of demons.

In school, the prevailing rumor was that the Stone Murders were a sign of a new demon scourge that would wreak havoc on the human world again. The Covenant who fought against the first scourge had not been seen for many years. Perhaps demons thought, in the Covenant's absence, they could now reemerge unchecked. During the lively discussions that continued from class to the lunchroom and back again, Simon and Ada sat quietly, praying no one noticed the strangely guarded looks on their faces.

In the marketplace, the theories were more salacious, casting the human as a demon lover who got caught cheating with another.

The day before Ada's sixteenth birthday, Simon waited until they were outside the gate of her home to show her the latest newspaper headline.

"Stone Killer Murder Found Close to Home!"

The Crimson Herald reported that the latest victim, described only as a "young woman" was found just outside Bonne, twenty miles from Liren.

They took the route to school in silence for several minutes, too frightened to say aloud what they both feared was true. The Stone Killer was getting closer and coming for her.

Simon took her hand and held it tightly. "They won't find us," he whispered. Ada squeezed back, trying to hold on to his assurance, but as she looked at the faces of the pedestrians and storekeepers they passed, she could not help but notice the shift in their gazes. The constant chatter and speculation that had livened every doorway and street corner over the past two weeks was suddenly gone. In its place, an anxious silence descended, telling her that she and Simon were not alone in their fears.

While Ada and Simon were still getting used to carrying the weight of her secret, Lilavois navigated life as she always did, keeping her appointments as a means to both conduct her business and gather the information needed to keep her child and her community safe. It didn't hurt that one of her most regular patients was Lieutenant Rhyss Fenton, the head of Liren's police department who was always more than happy to ply Lilavois with the latest news or her favorite macaroons; anything to prolong her stay during their weekly Tuesday and Thursday appointments to manage the mysterious pain in his elbow.

Though the latest news from Bonne was disturbing, Lilavois tried to remain calm. *RaZiel will be here tomorrow*, she reasoned. *If there is any danger, we will keep her safe.*

Yet the excitement in her heart was wild. It had been thirteen years since last she'd held him, since last they had all shared the same space. She could only imagine the immense joy he must feel at finally being able to speak to their daughter. No amount of danger could dampen the moment.

On the way home from her rounds, Lilavois picked up Ada's birthday cake from the baker, along with the magnifying glass and latest compendium of Madame Curie's *Discoveries* that Ada had been asking for, and rushed home to hide them before she returned from school. During dinner, Lilavois tried to keep the conversation light, despite the worry in her daughter's eyes. She waited until Ada had gone to bed before wrapping her presents, along with a priceless necklace made of gold and Larimar that had belonged to their grandmother. Charmaine insisted it would be the "*perfect little bauble*" for her niece. Quietly, Lilavois crept into her daughter's room and arranged the presents on her dressing table along with an empty vase with water, knowing they would be filled with moonflowers by morning.

chapter twelve

BIRTHDAY

ADA opened her eyes to find her favorite vase was empty. The other presents were lovely, but the flowers, her father's flowers — his presence — were the only thing she truly wanted.

When Ada came downstairs, Lilavois greeted her with birthday wishes and valiant assurances that RaZiel must be planning to deliver them himself later on today when it might be safer for him to appear. Wanting her mother's words to be true, Ada was effusive in her expressions of gratitude for her presents. But behind their smiling eyes, both women looked at each other and knew something was very, very wrong.

Lilavois held back her tears until Ada and Simon were out of the house and well on their way to school.

After making a few sick patients visits that could not be postponed, Lilavois headed for the police station. If there was news of anything amiss, it would be the best place to find out. Lieutenant Fenton always got the updates on the latest news via telegram before it hit the paper, which meant Lilavois did as well. Though she would have found an excuse to come anyway, it helped that her growing terror fit neatly into her Thursday patient schedule so as not to arouse suspicion or curiosity.

Just before noon, Lilavois walked into the station and was greeted with an empty front desk, a rumble of sound coming from the back of the station, and no setting of macaroons and lemon ginger tea. She put down her medicine bag and pulled out the pistol in her skirt pocket.

"Lieutenant Fenton? Are you there?" she called, inching slowly towards the commotion. She had made it halfway before three officers came out. With hasty nods and grave expressions, they rushed past her and out to the horses that were harnessed just outside the police station. Lieutenant Fenton came out last, breathless and flustered.

"I'm so sorry, Ms. St. James," he offered, barely noting Lilavois's gun as she placed it back in her pocket. "I must postpone our appointment today. God help us! There's been a murder here in Liren. Just down the road."

Fear lanced through her. There had never been a murder in Liren. It was one of the reasons she had chosen to raise her child here.

"Who?" she asked.

"The Kipling boy. Only fifteen, poor thing. I understand he was home from school with a cold, watching the print shop while his father made a delivery. He's one of your patients, isn't he?"

For an instant, the shock was so great Lilavois could not speak. "He is," she said finally. "I made him a prosthetic last year after his hiking accident."

"Hmm," Lieutenant Fenton replied, avoiding her gaze in a way that said he knew much more than he was letting on.

"I'll come with you," Lilavois declared, grabbing her medicine bag before easily matching his steps as he walked to the front door.

Lieutenant Fenton turned to block her path. "No! I can't allow you to put yourself in such danger. This … is no ordinary murder. We've sent a message to the Sisters of the Light."

Lilavois shivered at hearing her deepest worries confirmed.

Lieutenant Fenton leaned in and squeezed her hand, mistaking her fear for frailty. "This is a Stone Murder," he whispered. "Evil has passed through our gates, and I cannot in good conscience put you in harm's way."

Recognizing his misguided concern, Lilavois forced her tone to steady. "I appreciate your concern, Rhyss, but you forget that I have been trained by the Sisterhood. My skills as a surgeon and a former member may be needed."

Lieutenant Fenton hesitated. As one of the few in town who knew her association with the Sisterhood, he was unable to deny the soundness of her logic despite the yearning in his heart to keep her safe.

"I, too, am bound to protect the safety of our community. Please," she added. "Let me help you."

With no more time to tarry and even less desire to resist her, Lieutenant Fenton locked the police station and escorted Lilavois to his buggy.

They arrived at the print shop to find half the town was gathered. The crowd pressed in with panicked questions as Liren's entire police force — of three officers — struggled to hold them back and keep the crime scene secure. Lilavois saw some Phule students in the crowd but was relieved that Ada was not among them.

Perhaps, she thought, the news had not made it to school before dismissal.

Once they were spotted, Officer Bashar broke away to lead Lieutenant Fenton and Lilavois to the back door where the intruders had entered.

"Lieutenant, we need more help. We can't hold them all night."

Fenton sighed heavily while patting the young officer on the shoulder. "I know, Abdul. Return to your post. I've sent word to Bonne for reinforcements. They'll be here by nightfall."

"Thank you, Sir," Officer Bashar replied before leaving the Lieutenant and Lilavois to follow the low wail of Harold and Sarai Kipling's grief on their own.

Prostrate over the body of their only child, their cries were the very pitch of agony.

Lilavois's stomach seized with the memory of the anguish required to make such a sound. Though she had been spared the ultimate loss, Lilavois had never fully recovered from the wound. While Lieutenant Fenton tried to reassure and comfort the Kiplings, Lilavois kept her distance, knowing there was nothing she could do and nothing she could offer to ease their pain. Instead, she circled the perimeter of the shop, noting the small puncture wound just above Miles' abdomen. His body was rigid, as if frozen in place with striated black and white lines across his face and hands — all evidence of demon poisoning.

From what Lilavois could see, there was little sign of struggle. The door was broken off its hinges and splintered from the center as if kicked in. It would have caught Miles by surprise, she thought, looking over to where he lay next to a book that had fallen to the floor beside an overturned stool. Lilavois could almost see him sitting with his back to the door. By the time he heard the sound, there would have been no time to run, not that it would have mattered either way. Miles would have had no chance to escape.

Yet despite her heartbreak for Miles and his family, only one thing made her body tremble. In the corner of the small shop, torn in two lay a prosthetic limb, the one Lilavois had custom-made for Miles a year ago.

Lilavois felt sick. Looking at the broken pieces of her creation, she knew that the demons who had slain Miles had come looking for it, tracking the prosthetic and its maker in hopes of finding the one who killed Saisho. Miles had merely been in their way.

They're here, she thought with a violent shudder.

Ada would be out of school any moment. Refusing to succumb to her panic, Lilavois willed herself to move. On her way out, she left a small bottle of laudanum on the counter to help the Kiplings rest when their grief became too much to bear. She was almost through the doorway when she ran into the very people she did not want to see.

"Ada! Simon! You shouldn't be here."

Lilavois tried to block their path, to shield her from the worst of it, but by the horror in her wide-eyed glare, Ada had already seen too much. It took her only a second to scan the room and see Miles' rigid body, to see the puncture in his chest and the broken remnants of his prosthetic leg. Helplessly, Lilavois recognized the exact moment when Ada understood the meaning behind the tragedy before them.

Ada let out a deep sob as her lips began to tremble.

Lilavois grabbed Ada's arm and pushed her outside, grateful that her daughter's momentary shock made her so pliable. "Simon, come on! We need to go. Now."

Desperate to put as much distance as possible between the scene of the crime and her daughter, Lilavois grabbed the first idle carriage she saw, whispered their destination to the driver, then ushered the three of them inside. While holding her shaking daughter in her arms, from the opposite side of the carriage, Simon leaned forward.

"You don't think they were looking for —" he began before Lilavois silenced him with a shake of her head.

"Not here. Wait until we get someplace safe."

Simon did not miss that Lilavois had not said they were going 'home' but did not utter another word until they pulled up to a massive warehouse in the middle of the manufacturing district that he'd never seen before. Simon waited until their carriage had rolled away.

"What is this place?" he muttered more to himself than Lilavois as she unlocked a soot-covered door. With Ada still tucked into her side, she led them through two more doors. The last door she unlocked opened to a narrow flight of stairs that led to the very back of the building. Simon watched as she unlocked another door and turned on the light illuminating a large room and loft that spanned the entire width of the building.

Ada had not said a word since they got in the carriage but went straight to the ice box and poured herself a glass of cold water from a tall copper pitcher. When she was finished, she wiped her tear-stained face with her sleeve and poured two more glasses, while Lilavois opened a large wooden cabinet filled with weapons. Though Simon had no idea where they were, it was clear they both knew this place well.

"Here," Ada said, unable to meet his gaze as she handed him the cool glass. Simon followed her in a daze as she walked to a plush red couch that seemed out of place within their industrial surroundings. Ada slipped off Esha, the copper prosthetic that she'd worn to school that day, then rubbed her thigh with a methodical focus to ease the tension in her muscles and the worry in her mind.

"This is our safe house, Simon," Lilavois replied to his unanswered question while taking out the weapons she had created for a moment just like this, a moment she'd hoped would never come. She inspected them carefully before arranging them on a large table at the center of the room. "I built this place just in case they ever found us."

"She told *me* it was an extra workshop," Ada murmured absently.

Simon looked around. The space was clean and well maintained, opulent even, despite the exposed metal pipes and grime clinging to the outside of the large warehouse windows. He had so many questions. Did Lilavois know the demons searching for Ada? When had the woman who seemed so busy making rounds to her patients, developing medicines, crafting magical prosthetics, and taking care of her daughter have time to create a safe house? How long had Ada known about this place, yet never told him, and where was the washroom?

He decided not to voice any of these, instead saying, "And you believe they found you, that the reason they came here was for Ada, to seek revenge for the demon she killed?"

"The patterns of the recent killings suggest at least that much," Lilavois answered. Walking to the other side of the room, she pulled down a black satin cloth to reveal a detailed map littered with notes pinned to various locations and news clippings, all related to the Stone Murders.

"Before your class trip to Kemet, the Stone Murders were clustered in mostly urban areas. Finne, Abu Gar, Lessto, and Prakesh." Lilavois pointed to the news clippings that accompanied their circled locations. "I'd assumed Saisho was responsible for these. But after the attacks in Kemet." Lilavois paused, shifting her gaze to Ada. Despite her pensive and slightly withdrawn demeanor, she was clearly paying attention. "A new cluster of activity began in Kemet, then Bonne, then here."

"You think someone else has continued his attacks?" Simon asked.

"Or shifted their efforts to find his killer. There was no discernible pattern before Kemet. But, now, with Miles' murder and his leg . . ."

"There was no one on the street when we were attacked," Simon replied. "I don't see how anyone would know who we are."

Lilavois nodded. "I don't think they do. Not exactly. Captain Claybourne shares your perspective, but it's clear someone saw something, specifically

Ada's prosthetic. That person must have mentioned it. Why else would they have tracked down poor Miles, killed him, and dismantled his prosthetic? I think they were looking for its maker in hopes that that person would lead them to Ada.

"I just haven't figured out why the killings began in the first place. Even if Saisho was the Stone Killer, I could never figure out why they started again after so many years. At first, I thought it might have been an attempt to draw RaZiel out by taking his revenge on innocent people."

"How did he recognize her if the last time he saw her was when she was a baby?"

"He said he knew my scent," Ada explained, remembering that Simon was most likely unconscious for that part of their introduction.

"Yes," Lilavois added. "Every human has a distinct scent that all demons can smell. It is present at birth and does not change throughout our lives. Demons are incapable of forgetting, so there would have been no way he wouldn't recognize her. Ada's father, RaZiel, said that Saisho resented that he was willing to kill his own kind to protect us. Assuming Ada was dead, I thought Saisho might have been looking for me as a means to punish RaZiel for killing the others. Ada's father left because he feared we would be held accountable for what he did. His hope was that by separating, we would be safe. Saisho might have eventually found me if he hadn't run into Ada. But with all that's happened, I can't help but ask myself, what if Saisho was never the Stone Killer to begin with?"

Ada shook her head, fresh tears welling in her eyes. "None of this matters! If I had been there, I could have saved Miles. He died because of me."

Lilavois felt a sad relief at hearing her daughter say aloud what she knew Ada had been thinking.

"Miles died because they decided to kill an innocent child. You're powerful, but not powerful enough to control the decisions of an eternal being,"

Lilavois replied.

"But if I had been there, I could have stopped them!"

"Or you could have been killed," Simon said softly, reaching for her hand. "Just because you can kill them doesn't mean they can't kill you."

Ada shook her head, refusing the small reprieve he offered. "I won't sit here and let anyone else die because of me. How many other people are there with prosthetics in this town?"

Of course, Lilavois knew the answer. "Five, but you're the only girl with a leg prosthetic."

"That didn't save Miles," Ada replied. "We have to stop them before they hurt anyone else."

"I know," Lilavois agreed. "Which is why I've bought you here. I'm headed back to the house. If Miles was able to tell them where his prosthetic was made, they might already be there."

Ada pushed up from the couch, balancing on one leg with her hands clenched into fists. "You expect me to stay here? While you walk into a house full of demons by yourself? On my birthday!"

"Ada, it's too dangerous! I've been trained for this. You haven't. I can protect myself. Besides, I don't know what happened this morning with your flowers, but I know your father wouldn't miss your birthday. He's probably waiting for us at home, and if he is there, I have nothing to fear. We'll come back to get you both when it's safe."

"But you don't know that. You have no idea how many there are."

"Ada, even if RaZiel isn't there, I can handle myself. You need to stay here."

At first, Lilavois assumed the brightness glistening in Ada's eyes was anger, until her daughter's lips began to quiver.

"Please, don't go," Ada said, struggling to keep her voice steady. "I can't lose you, too."

Lilavois crossed the room and held her daughter tightly. "I won't let anything take me from you," she whispered fiercely.

"Then don't. We're a family. If we fight, we should fight together."

Everything in Lilavois wanted to keep Ada away. But the truth was she could not guarantee her own safety. Though she had been trained, she had never fought a demon before, much less killed one. Even with all their training, the Sisters of the Light never fought alone. If it came to that, she would need all the help she could get.

"All right," she conceded pulling away to let her daughter see the warning in her eyes. "I'll go in first. You're allowed to come in *only* if there's trouble or I say the coast is clear."

"Okay," Ada agreed as Simon stood up beside her.

Lilavois shook her head. "No, Simon. You should go home. We can't risk anything happening to you."

"There's no one at home to worry about me," he said simply. "Please. Tell me how I can help."

"That may be true, but I know your father well enough to know that if he were here, he would be very worried about you. And he's not alone. Your aunt would be worried. I'm worried. If something happened to you, I would never . . ." Lilavois paused, swallowing the tears and the image of Miles' body cold and stiff on the ground. "I don't want you involved."

Simon stepped forward. "I know you care what happens to me, but I'm already involved. I was there that night in Kemet, too. Whoever saw Ada saw me as well. They could be looking for both of us, and if they are, I'm safer with you, aren't I?"

Lilavois's thoughts settled on a new possibility — one she hadn't considered before. Miles and he were the same general build and height with roughly the same skin tone. Lilavois had assumed that the prosthetic was the only reason they sought him out, but what if they were simply looking for a young man that matched Simon's description? If Simon were alone, like Miles had been, he wouldn't have a fighting chance, and that was a risk she could not take. Like it or not, Simon was right.

Resigned that she would not be going alone, she went to the cabinet and pulled out her lasso of El that she'd imbued with her own mooncraft, secured it to her belt, then turned back to Simon and Ada.

"Since you're both coming, you'll need weapons." Lilavois motioned towards the table. "Each of these is made with demon claw shards to penetrate the skin. Choose whichever one you're most comfortable using."

Both Ada and Simon went for the crossbows.

"I wish I hadn't left my Iron Stocking at home," Ada mumbled, lowering herself back to the couch to reattach Esha.

"No need to wish."

Ada looked up to see her mother holding out a leg that was almost identical to the one she'd worn in Kemet.

"I made a spare."

At ten past nine o'clock in the evening, their entire block was still. With ash trees lining the sidewalks, it looked like almost any street in Liren, softly lit and mostly quiet. Lilavois picked the town because it was small enough to easily detect strangers, yet it was also a well-educated enclave. Whether self-taught or formally educated, the people of Liren valued the nurturing of ideas and critical thinking. Their libraries were well known throughout the region and regularly frequented by locals. Once a month, the library hosted free workshops run by anyone from the town who had a skill they wanted to share. Lilavois had conducted several on the importance of washing your hands before food preparation and meals and how to use different herbs to promote better health.

The storefront and home Lilavois had built blended in well with the other homes on their block, which contained a mix of private homes and small businesses. Their neighbors were always friendly, with a curiosity about them that never crossed the line.

At this hour, every household had doused their lights long ago, with two exceptions. At the corner, Mrs. Emery kept her bedroom light burning as she worked into the wee hours of the morning writing her popular ghost novel series. The other exception was their home, where a decidedly bright lantern light burned at their kitchen window, one she had not left on this morning. Nothing else about the house looked amiss.

From the alley where they hid, Ada and Lilavois turned to each other with the same unguarded hope in their eyes.

RaZiel.

"Please. Stay here. I just need to be sure," Lilavois whispered. She did not wait for a reply before stepping out of the shadows and into the street. It took all her concentration not to run, not to cast down all her defenses and shout RaZiel's name knowing that he would come rushing out the door to greet her.

From an opening in the curtains, she could see a vase at the center of the kitchen table crowded with moonflowers. Tears pricked her eyes. She unlocked the door, forgetting to listen for any sign of commotion inside. Who else could it be?

Lilavois crossed the threshold into the kitchen with only enough of a glance around to note that nothing seemed out of place. Her heart raced as she pushed through the kitchen door — and stopped, frozen by the sight of a tall, angelic woman she'd never seen before standing at the far side of the room. It took only a second for instinct to override her confusion. Lilavois stepped back and conjured her shield.

The woman before her sighed. "Calm yourself. I am SeKet, RaZiel's sister. I have not come to harm you. I have news of my brother and a promise to keep to his child." SeKet nodded towards the flowers.

Though Lilavois did not move, the heartbreak was already welling in her eyes. She had barely begun processing the words before Ada and Simon stepped through the kitchen with their weapons drawn.

"Who are you? Where's my father?" Ada said with fear and disappointment warring in her voice.

SeKet stared at Ada for several moments. The resemblance to RaZiel was undeniable, yet she still found herself struggling to comprehend the existence of a person she had heard so much about but barely believed was real.

"Forgive me," SeKet began, recognizing Ada's obvious discomfort under her gaze. "Your father has told me many things about you, but to see you with my own eyes … I … You are so much like him."

Ada lowered her crossbow. "Then why isn't he here? My mother sent word that I knew the truth and wanted to meet him."

"Yes, the message was sent to me. I went looking for him to deliver it but arrived too late. There were signs of a struggle. I believe he's been captured to be brought before the Council for trial."

"The Council?" Ada asked.
"It's where Obi and those who follow him judge any of The Fallen who

break our rules. Once I realized he was missing, my first thought was to find him. Obi's so-called trials are a farce. Once RaZiel is taken before the Council, he'll barely have a chance to speak for himself, much less have anyone else speak on his behalf. He will either be sentenced to death or confined to prison forever, unable to see the light of day again."

Lilavois retracted her shield and sank into one of the chairs at her kitchen table. She remembered RaZiel warning her of this place, a cave that was like a living hell for angels on earth. A place he had managed to evade until now.

"Why didn't you go after him?" Ada asked, tears of pain and regret shining in her eyes.

"In part because I don't know where they've taken him, and even if I did, I could not rescue RaZiel alone. Wherever he is, I'm certain he's heavily guarded. Fortunately, the Council must send notice before his trial begins. They will wait until all The Fallen, except for Lucifer, are assembled. It will give me the time I need to gather those who are loyal to your father and me."

Ada frowned in confusion. A trial for demons? The process SeKet described was so foreign, she had to ask, "Why not Lucifer?"

SeKet's eyes filled with tears. "Our kin was forbidden from gathering with the other Fallen centuries ago."

Ada nodded, "So if we leave now, before his trial is announced, we'll have more time to find my father, right?"

SeKet smiled at the eagerness in Ada's gaze. "That's true, but then I would have broken my promise." SeKet motioned towards the moonflowers. "Your father made me swear to deliver those to you if he was ever unable to do so. Every birthday for the rest of your life, so that you would know how much he loves you.

"I also knew that, more than his own safety, RaZiel would want me to make sure you were safe. Without his protection, I thought you might be vulnerable."

Lilavois stood abruptly. "When you arrived, did you find any of The Fallen? A boy was killed earlier today. They're looking for Ada."

"There was no one here when I arrived," SeKet replied. "But I don't understand. Why would they be looking for her at all? How could they know she's alive? The only beings who know of Ada besides RaZiel are in this room." She glanced at Simon who did not shrink beneath her gaze before continuing. "And none of us would ever betray her."

Ada looked at Lilavois who nodded for her to answer truthfully.

"I ran into one of them while I was in Kemet a few weeks ago. He said he recognized my scent from when I was a baby."

"Saisho," SeKet spat. "How did you escape him?"

"I didn't. I killed him."

SeKet stared at her in disbelief, but from the steady beat of Ada's heart, she knew the young woman was not lying.

"I stabbed him through the heart with this." Ada reaching down to pull the blade from the hidden compartment in her leg, then handed it to SeKet.

SeKet took it carefully. "This alone would not be enough to kill one of us. We must release the venom in our claws. Perhaps, he was only deeply wounded, and you thought he was dead . . ."

"At first it wasn't," Ada agreed. "But then he changed. He turned human and started bleeding. That's when he died."

"You saw a body?"

"Yes, he died in the middle of the street."

SeKet let out a shuddering breath. "That's not possible. We can be killed, but only by the hands of our kin," she whispered. "We do not die; we disintegrate into nothing."

"I saw him bleeding. He thanked me before he died."

"I saw it, too," Simon added.

"You gave him a soul?" SeKet uttered the words without comprehension. "How? Only Rah has such power."

"When she stabbed him, a light opened up inside her. We think that's what changed him," Lilavois explained.

"Like the magic of the Sisters of the Light?"

"No, it was yellow and bright, like the Sun," Simon replied.

"A portal," SeKet gasped.

"A what?" Ada asked in confusion. "I only saw the light in my hands for a second. I don't know how it came, I haven't seen it since, and I don't know how to conjure it. I've tried."

SeKet smiled, tears of wonder brimming in her eyes.

"You cannot conjure it because you *are* it. In the Ever, Rah created portals to allow us to move across great distances, but never have I seen one embodied in a person."

Ada stepped back. "I'm just a girl."

"No," SeKet smiled. "You are a gift. A miracle! You are a portal able to summon the light of Rah to deliver us from eternal life."
Ada was not sure she wanted to be.

On the other side of the room, Lilavois, who had always considered her daughter a gift, was teasing out another problem.

“SeKet, do you know when RaZiel was captured? It seems too much of a coincidence that he would be caught around the same time that Saisho was killed.”

SeKet nodded. “I agree. Those hunting you follow Obi, and for the death of our own, he would certainly seek revenge. More than that, he would want answers. What happened to Saisho is not only unprecedented — in Obi’s mind, it would be a threat to those like him who believe it is the right of The Fallen to rule this realm. Obi knows that RaZiel and I formed the Covenant to fight against him. If he thought there was even a chance that RaZiel had something to do with Saisho’s death, Obi would stop at nothing to find him. RaZiel was always very careful. Only a few of us knew where he was, but it’s possible he was betrayed. Obi’s followers might have threatened death, which most of us would do anything to avoid.”

“I thought The Fallen hated being here. Wouldn’t death be a welcome escape?” Ada asked.

SeKet smiled sadly. “Only your father felt so. Most of us view our existence as a chance to be redeemed in some way. Despite the fear of death humans often harbor, death brings renewal for your kind. For us, it is final. This life is the only connection we have left to the Ever.”

“So then it’s likely that the demons hunting us would know where RaZiel is?” Lilavois said.

“Yes,” SeKet agreed, eyes sharpening as she followed Lilavois train of thought. “You mean to lay a trap for them to find RaZiel.”

Lilavois nodded. “If their plan is to track the maker of the prosthetic to lead them to Saisho’s killer, then we can use that to our advantage. The fact that they didn’t come here after killing Miles must mean they still don’t know who made the prosthetic. If they come looking again tomorrow, we can make sure we lead them here. They've never seen me before. For all they know, I could be his killer. We could capture them and find out where they're keeping RaZiel."

"Capturing them doesn't mean they'll tell us anything?" SeKet countered.

Ada picked up her blade from the counter where SeKet had laid it down.

"They will because we have something they fear."

chapter thirteen

THE PLAN

ADA'S birthday cake sat uneaten. Ada didn't want it, and Lilavois couldn't blame her. It was the worst birthday Ada could remember besides the day she thought her father died which made her all the more anxious to have some part in bringing him back.

At first, Ada thought she was actually going to be a part of the plan to rescue RaZiel, to use her skills to reconnect with the parent she now knew was still alive and loved her. But it did not take long for her to understand that Lilavois had no intention of including her.

Once the cake was stored away, SeKet and Lilavois sat together at the kitchen table for twenty minutes plotting as if she were not even there, without any mention of her involvement.

"Excuse me!" Ada interrupted. "I'm the one who's actually killed a demon. Shouldn't I be included here?"

"Absolutely not!" Lilavois replied. "You can't imagine I would use my own child as bait. You know me better than that! As soon as SeKet says it's safe, we'll drop Simon to his aunt's, then you will be going back to the safe house."

"But I can help," Ada pleaded.

"Yes, you can, by going to school and keeping yourself as inconspicuous as possible."

Ada sank back in her chair and sulked. Every fiber in her wanted to protest, but in the end, she knew her mother better than to think she could convince her otherwise.

"Do not fret, Ada. I will watch over your mother."

"But what if there are a lot of them?"

SeKet smiled shrewdly, "Then they would be wise to stay out of my way."

Even in her sour mood, Ada took in the confident stillness in SeKet's amber eyes along with her seven-foot five-inch frame and had to agree.

"I'd like to stay with you all, if that's all right," Simon chimed in beside her. "I can send word to my aunt. I'm sure she wouldn't mind."

Lilavois smiled, noting his proximity to her daughter.

"Thank you, Simon. But I'm fairly certain your aunt would mind. With Miles' death, everyone is on edge. SeKet and I will take you to her soon. We need you to stay there tonight. You can meet Ada at school in the morning." Disappointed but resigned to his fate, Simon took comfort in the fact that they wouldn't be apart for long.

"It would be good for you both to keep things as normal as possible even though I suspect they will be watching the school."

Lilavois turned to Ada. "Make sure you pack your black skirts for tomorrow." Lilavois paused at the unspoken question on Ada's face. "As a show of respect for Miles."

"Okay," Ada sighed, saddened by the memory of her classmate lying frozen on the ground and frustrated that she was unable to do anything about it.

"We must assume they're nearby," SeKet added. "I'll patrol between your houses tonight. In the morning, we'll put our plan in motion."

Lilavois used her own carriage to drop Simon off first before heading to the safe house to rest. When they arrived, Lilavois and SeKet pored over the maps she had been using to track the Stone Killer and finalized their plans for tomorrow while Ada was sent to the sleeping loft to get ready for bed.

Despite her desire to be included in their plans, Ada was exhausted. By the time she bathed and changed her clothes for bed, she heard enough to know that their plans involved Lilavois dropping her off to school, then posing as Ada to lure the demons to her shop. Once the demons arrived, Lilavois and SeKet would subdue them and learn RaZiel's location. As Ada fell asleep, she noted that they both seemed confident enough that the whole matter would be over by the time her mother picked her up from school.

chapter fourteen

STAY CLOSE

THE sky was grey, and the air was still with quiet mourning. On the streets, every lamp post and corner of Liren was hung with black ribbon in honor of Miles Kipling's death.

To see her own grief so publicly displayed shook Ada to her core. She reached out for her mother's hand and held it tightly as they made their way by carriage to the Academy.

"This is all my fault," Ada murmured with tears in her eyes as Lilavois eased the carriage into a space just left of the school entrance.

Her mother turned to her and took both of Ada's trembling hands in her own with a tight grip.

"Listen to me," Lilavois began, determined to extract the doubt from her daughter like the poison it was. "You did not kill Miles. You did not bring whatever killed him here. You did not attack yourself in Kemet. You did not choose to have the gift you do, but if you didn't use it, both you and Simon would be dead.

"What's happened is horrible, but you did not *cause* this. The cruelty that earned the demons their name began thousands of years ago. You lost your leg because of that cruelty. They tore our family apart because of that cruelty. But *you* aren't responsible for any of that. Do you hear me?"

There was something hard and unyielding in Lilavois's voice that forced Ada to listen and compelled her to understand. The tears receded.

"What we get to do now is choose how we respond. We will not let Miles' death be in vain. We will find those who did this, and we will hold them accountable. We will find your father and bring him back to you. We will defend ourselves and our community because that is our right, and no one can take it from us. That's what we're going to do now. What we do next is ours to own, and guilt has no place in it. It will not bring Miles back. It will not help us face what lies ahead and it cannot help us prevail. I want you to leave it behind — right now. You will leave this carriage with your head held high."

Only when her daughter collapsed into her arms and hugged her fiercely did Lilavois allow her own tears to fall.

"Thank you, Mama," Ada whispered before pulling back. "Why are you crying?" she asked, with a watery laugh.

"Because I'm proud of you," Lilavois whispered while brushing her tears away. "Come on. We got here early. Now we're almost late. I'll walk you in."

They didn't see the small crowd that had begun to form outside at the school entrance until they stepped outside the carriage. To the right, Headmistress Mwaso stood just inside the doorway, across from someone Lilavois had not seen in over sixteen years. Her footsteps halted as Ada moved forward into the crowd of students.

"Who's that lady standing next to the Headmistress?" Ada wondered to Leisel who, at only four-foot-nine, was jostling about for a better look.

"Maybe it's a new teacher, but I don't know why she would be wearing a length of rope on her belt."

Ada recognized the lasso of El immediately then turned to her mother, only to find Lilavois frozen in place several steps behind. She didn't need any confirmation beyond Lilavois's tense expression to know the woman standing at the door was from the Sisterhood.

Ada came closer and kept her voice low. "Mama, do you know her?"

"Stay close," was Lilavois's only reply as they neared the entrance.

"Single file, please. Lieutenant Fenton has a few questions for our third-year students. Those who attended the Kemet trip can move to the left of the hall. All other students, please proceed to your classes as quickly as possible."

Ada noticed that her mother purposely averted her gaze until they were close to the door then met the strange woman's eyes squarely as they passed through the doorway. Lilavois used her hand to usher Ada ahead of her then turned to the woman. At several inches taller, Ada noticed that her mother's chosen position just inside the doorway was an attempt to block the woman's view of her.

"Jhonna. Though the circumstances of our meeting are tragic, it's good to see you again," Lilavois began in a voice that was sincere though something slightly less than warm.

"Lilavois," Jhonna replied coolly. "I would say the same. Sabine and I had hoped you'd keep in better touch all those years ago." Ada watched as Jhonna's eyes roamed over her mother with a calculating indifference as if Lilavois was something she might dissect. While the scrutiny made her mother stand a little taller, Ada knew right then and there she did not like her.

"But I see you've had your hands full. Is that your child?" Jhonna angled her head towards Ada who stared back at her indignantly before walking away to take a seat on the bench across from the Headmistress' office.

"Yes."

"I didn't see the father in line with you. Nor do I see a marriage band on your hand. I take it things did not work out as you'd hoped."

Lilavois's smile was keen and firmly set. "They did not."

"I'm sorry to hear it. You gave up so much."

"And gained more."

"Of course," Jhonna replied. "I'm sure your daughter has inherited many of your talents. Perhaps you'll encourage her to join us. With the Stone Killer running rampant, the relevance of the Sisterhood is no longer in question. In fact, very soon, our ranks may need replenishing."

Lilavois ignored the invitation. "How is Sabine?"

Jhonna's smug expression slipped. "She's been on special assignment with Reverend Sister Imoleina Kai for over a year now. I haven't heard from her for a while, but I believe she is well."

Despite Jhonna's coldness, Lilavois felt a sting of regret at having broached a topic that brought her former friend such sadness. "I see. And you're here with Lieutenant Fenton to help with Miles Kipling's murder?"

"Yes, we were called in yesterday from Bonne. There may be a pattern emerging in the most recent killings that we wanted to investigate."

A prickle of fear shot through Lilavois's body. "What pattern? "

"Ah, Ms. St. James! How fortuitous! I see you've found your old colleague," Lieutenant Fenton interrupted as he walked over to them from the Headmistress' office. "Did you two attend convent together?"

"Briefly," Jhonna replied. "Did you learn anything new, Lieutenant?"

Lilavois looked over to where Simon was exiting the Headmistress' office. He gave a quick glance around the hall before giving Ada a cautious nod then heading off to class.

"Not really. We only have a few students left," Lieutenant Fenton began before turning to Lilavois. "Since you're here, perhaps we'll question Ada next."

"What exactly are you trying to determine by questioning the students from the field trip? Is there something new that links them specifically to the murders?" Lilavois asked in a voice she hoped was more curious than pressing.

Lieutenant Fenton moved in closer. "The last two victims have been amputees," he whispered.

Lilavois felt faint. "The victim in Bonne as well? The papers didn't mention it."

"Yes. We asked to keep that detail close because we weren't sure what to make of it, but if there is a connection — Ada may be in danger."

Jhonna's eyes snapped to Ada, inspecting her carefully. The long skirt that Lilavois had insisted Ada wear had no split down the left side, making it impossible to see her prosthetic. "Your daughter's a cripple?"

Before Lilavois could say anything, Ada was already striding over with a vengeance. "Don't call me that! I'm not crippled. I lost my leg in an accident, but it doesn't stop me from doing anything and it didn't stop Miles either."

"Of course not, dear. I meant no offense," Jhonna smiled condescendingly before turning to Lilavois. "Her gait is flawless. Who made her prosthetic? Is it the same maker as the Kipling boy's?"

"I did," Lilavois said, placing an arm around Ada's shoulder to ease her rage.

Jhonna's eyes narrowed on Lilavois. "I see your attraction to trouble has not waned. Curious that the demons who killed him were so fixated on his prosthetic and you should be at the center of all these clues."

Lieutenant Fenton let out an indignant huff. "I'm not sure what you're implying, Sister, but Ms. St. James is the best surgeon in these parts and an upstanding member of our community. She wasn't even in Kemet at the time of the murders. And the victim in Bonne had no association with Ms. St. James. It would be best to stick to the evidence at hand."

"I have no other intent, Lieutenant Fenton. I merely want to protect a dear old friend and her daughter. It's unlikely that the prosthetic connection is simply a coincidence. It would behoove us to take extra precautions to keep Lilavois and her daughter safe as we discern what the killer's motives might be."

Smoothly and connivingly put, Lilavois noted. Jhonna had changed much since their school days.

"While Ada and I appreciate your concern, Jhonna, Lieutenant Fenton is correct. While I did fashion the prosthetics for Ada and Miles, that is hardly a coincidence. I'm the only surgeon in the area with the skill to do such work. As you can imagine, the pool of qualified prosthetic makers is small. Nonetheless, the latest victim in Bonne, Ms. Abbe, if I recall the news correctly, was not a patient of mine. In your zeal to solve these murders, I believe you're conflating correlation with causation on this point."

Though Jhonna's face remained calm, Lilavois did not miss the telltale reddening around her neck and ears.

"You may be right, Lilavois. But the E'gida will be diligent in examining every facet of these murders so that we may find the culprit before they strike again. We wouldn't want you or anyone else to fall into danger."

Lilavois turned from Jhonna. "Lieutenant Fenton, is there anything you wanted to ask Ada? Her classes have surely begun, and I wouldn't want her to miss instruction unnecessarily."

"Of course not," he replied. "Forgive me. Ada, do you recall any unusual incidents happening during your stay, strange people following you or watching you closely?"

Ada tried her best to suppress a shudder at the memory of Saisho jumping down from the rooftop.

"No, sir," she replied simply. Being the terrible liar she always was, Ada could see that between Jhonna's narrowed gaze and Lieutenant Fenton's kind smile, no one believed her.

"Are you sure, Ada?" he asked gently. "You seem a bit upset."

Ada's eyes shifted to her mother's, who squeezed her shoulders gently and kissed her on her forehead.

"You are correct, Lieutenant Fenton," Lilavois began. "It was a difficult night. Ada was at the Kiplings' shop yesterday, shortly after you and I arrived. She saw Miles' body and has been crying all night. I saw her to school this morning because I knew how difficult it would be walking into school with the memories so fresh in her mind."

Lieutenant Fenton frowned. "Of course, dear. I'm so sorry you had to see that. Go on to class and try your best not to worry. We'll keep you safe."

"Everything will be fine," Lilavois added. "I'll see you later today." After a brief hug, Lilavois released her daughter and watched her walk away.

Keeping her daughter safe was exactly what she planned to do, and she was already behind schedule.

"Thank you for your understanding, Lieutenant Fenton," she began once

Ada was out of sight. "Jhonna. I wish you and the Sisterhood much success in finding the culprits of these heinous crimes. If you'll both excuse me, I must begin my rounds."

chapter fifteen

BAIT

IT went against Lilavois's instincts to walk away from her child, but today of all days, she needed Ada as far away from her as possible. While Phule was not the most secure place, they did keep a close watch on their students, which suited her purposes.

Recent murders aside, since the Scourge, demon attacks were rare and almost never in broad daylight or in crowded places. But demons were not her only concern. If left at the safe house or their home, there was no doubt in Lilavois's mind that Ada, and most likely Simon, would find a way to stay decidedly out of hiding and interfere with their plans. Lilavois could not take the risk, making school the best option.

Their plan was a simple one. After dropping Ada off to school, Lilavois would lure them in while SeKet watched from an undetectable distance. After leaving Phule Academy, Lilavois parked her carriage at the town stall then began her rounds on foot, parting the split in her own skirt to reveal a painted mold of the prosthetic design she crafted for Ada strapped to her leg. She created molds with every leg she designed to test for basic comfort, weight, and mobility. This, however, was the first time she had ever worn one outside. It would be easy to detect as a fake if someone came close, but to a demon observing her from the shadows, they would think exactly what she wanted them to think: that she was the person with the prosthetic who managed to kill one of their own. It would be enough to catch their attention and hold it.

Lilavois made her rounds to every patient, ensuring that whoever might be following her would know that *she* rather than *they* was the target. When she told her patients she was testing out a new design they thought nothing of it. It had taken her less than two hours, but by the time she was through, Lilavois felt certain she was being followed. Holding the uneasy feeling in her chest, Lilavois weaved through the main streets of the town and back to her storefront where SeKet would wait with her until the demons arrived.

She hummed to calm her nerves as she turned the key to her shop and closed the door behind her while leaving the closed sign in place. She did not want one of her customers to happen upon whatever battle was about to ensue. But as she stepped into the store fully, she felt a stillness that should not have been. Lilavois tried to steady the jolt in her heart as she made her way to the long mahogany counter that separated the usual customers from her floor-to-ceiling cabinets of herbs, potions, and salves, toward the private door that led into her home.

"SeKet," she whispered before flipping the counter open, but no one answered. Lilavois pulled a dagger identical to her daughter's from a hidden compartment in her jacket and opened the door that led to her kitchen. She was met with silence. Dread crept in as she called SeKet's name over and over with only the faint echo of her own voice in response. Unable to stop herself, she raced through her house and the back porch to her workshop only to find the weapons carefully placed where they had planned with no SeKet to wield them. There was no sign of struggle.

"Why would she leave?" Lilavois wondered aloud, recounting the plan in her mind. She knew Jhonna's presence at the school held her up a bit, but not enough to derail their plans. Ada would not be out of school for hours — plenty of time to execute their plan without risk of her involvement.

Lilavois shook her head. Instinctively, she knew as she crossed through the kitchen door back to the storefront that SeKet would not have left unless something was terribly wrong.

Ada.

She was on her way back out when Lilavois saw it — a piece of white paper on the floor that she had not noticed on her way in. Curiosity turned to full blown panic as she stepped closer and saw the handwriting in black ink.

They've discovered our plan. I've gone to get Ada. Meet me at the safe house!

A second later, Lilavois was running down the street without the slightest thought of locking the storefront door behind her.

The low drone of Professor Castille's trigonometry lecture combined with the unrelenting anxious tap of Ada's foot against the leg of his desk was driving Simon mad. Yet he said nothing, choosing instead to watch the clock like she was, counting down the hours until they would be allowed to find out if her mother's plan had worked. When Professor Castille told Ada that her presence was requested in the Principal's office, she practically bolted out of her seat. Before crossing the doorway, she glanced back at Simon with fire in her eyes. He barely suppressed his instinct to follow.

Ada ran down the main staircase with a cautious excitement, trying to resist all the visions in her mind of what might have happened, but the sight of SeKet standing in the Headmistess's office stunned her. In fact, they both looked at each other in shock with Headmistress Mwaso sitting very uncomfortably between them.

"Where's my mother?" Ada blurted out. "I thought you were together."

"I received this note from her. I thought she was here with you."

SeKet handed Ada a piece of stationery from her mother's store. Everything looked right, except the handwriting on the page was not Lilavois's.

chapter sixteen

SILENCE

LILAVOIS flew up the steps, tearing the scarf from her neck as she ran. Her gold locket beat against her chest like a reminder of everything that was at stake if SeKet had not reached Ada in time — if her daughter was not upstairs, safe and sound.

Relief swelled in her heart as she saw the door to her flat ajar. If she had not been in such a rush, if her heart had raced a little less, she might have noticed the silence.

But she did not and so the door closed behind her just as she called her daughter's name and then sensed, a moment too late, that something stood behind her. Despite the sudden pounding in her ears, her sense of smell did not fail her. With the door closed, the fragrance of wisteria and lilacs coiled around her nostrils like a clinging vine. Lilavois turned around to find a demon with dark skin, sharp features, and eyes the color of milk smiling at her.

"That was easy." Her voice was heavenly like the tinkling of wind chimes … echoing within a mouth full of short, pointed teeth.

"I was expecting more of a fight from the person who killed my brother."

Lilavois's gaze swept the room looking for signs that Ada or SeKet had been there, but everything looked the way they had left it this morning. Satisfied that it did not appear Ada was there, Lilavois stepped back, creating what she hoped would be enough distance between them to mount a defense.

"Who are you?"

"I am called Al-Yah."

Remembering how fast RaZiel was and assuming the lithe creature before her was at least as quick, Lilavois decided to stall in hopes of creating more distance between them.

"You wrote the note? You were there at my shop."

Al-Yah shrugged. "Penmanship is a hobby of mine. Something I've picked up here, since writing is not necessary in the Ever. I grew tired of watching you prance around with SeKet hovering over your every move like a loyal dog. I needed to get her away from you. The child proved a helpful distraction. It is only you I mean to kill."

Ignoring the slight that told her that at least part of her plan had worked, Lilavois kept up the charade, taking another step back.

"Your brother attacked me first. I had no choice."

Al-Yah took two sniffs and shook her head.

"I can smell the lies on you. I've seen your weapons. All of them." She motioned towards the cabinet that was merely half full. "You are one of the Sisters of the Light, are you not? You've been hunting us for years, and now your magic has taught you to kill us, but we will not be condemned to death by your kind. We are supreme here! You have no rights over us."

"I have every right!" Lilavois replied, unable to resist the risk. "Your brother killed my child, then drove RaZiel away!"

"Do not speak that name! He betrayed us to protect what? A human child and —" Al-Yah looked her over in disgust. "And its mother. He will meet his fate soon enough."

The confirmation that RaZiel was still alive took her breath away.

"Please, don't hurt him," Lilavois begged, with true tears in her eyes. "He did what he did to protect us. I will pay for his crimes. Just release him."

"You and all the others you've taught to use your foul magic to undo us."

"I've taught no one else," she answered truthfully. "Who else would I teach? I left the Sisterhood years ago to be with RaZiel."

Sensing truth, Al-Yah pondered a moment before shaking her head slowly.

"No," she replied. "I think, for the death of my kin, you both will pay. I will take you to RaHabel where you both will answer for your crimes, and he will watch you die before he meets his own fate. Now unsheathe your weapons and understand it will not pain me to kill you here and leave your remains for your child to find."

"I understand," Lilavois replied. She removed her weapons with careful purpose, disguising her relief that the ruin of their plans had still worked out so well. Her only task now was to leave some clue that would help SeKet find her and RaZiel and rescue them if she was able.

SeKet knew they were too late the moment she reached the back alley of the safe house. They had gone to the house first, which meant she and Ada had lost precious time. SeKet glanced over to Ada. To her credit, the young girl beside her, the one now facing the possibility of having lost both her parents, was stoic. The blade in her hand trembled, but only a little.

The door to the safe house was wide open, but at least there was no body.

Ada let out a short trembling breath as she lowered her blade. "They've taken her, haven't they."

"I believe so," SeKet answered quietly.

Ada could not hold back her sob. "How . . . How will we find her?"

SeKet walked towards her and wrapped her long arms around the strong girl who felt so frail in that moment. To SeKet's surprise, Ada clung to her, digging her fingers into the soft cotton of SeKet's blouse.

"I don't know, but I will do everything in my power to bring her back."

They stood there for a moment, sharing their grief until Ada pulled away. She looked around the room finding little sign of struggle until her eyes landed on the large table at the center of the room.

"She didn't even get to take a weapon to defend herself." Ada's voice was wobbly as she walked over and looked at her mother's weapons and medical supplies laid out on the table. Her mother's style of dress was always so streamlined and elegant that it was easy to forget all the things she carried with her. All tools, the potions and medicines, and the magical defenses that made up the life of a complex woman, one who had carried her secrets alone for so many years. Ada took a moment to marvel at how neatly everything was arranged on the table as if even in capture she could not resist organizing her possessions. With a gasp, Ada stepped back taking in the placement of the turquoise vials and scalpels, the blades and the rolls of bandages until she recognized the pattern before her was not a design but a word. A location.

"I know where she is! She spelled it out for us right here!"

SeKet moved to stand beside Ada. "RaHabel," she gasped. "This is the place where RaZiel will face the Council."

"My father's there?"

"Yes."

"How do we get there?"

"We'll have to take a train," Simon said breathlessly as he stood in the doorway, grateful his sprinting had paid off as he crossed the doorway. "Then hike a bit. RaHabel is its old name meaning Mount of the Gods. People used to bring offerings to The Fallen there in ancient times. Now it's called the Devil's Pit."

SeKet looked at him incredulously. "How would you know this?"

Simon opened his satchel and pulled out his travel journal. "It was featured in a travel guide a few years ago. Here," he said handing her his notebook which held a clipping titled, *Five Sites of Antiquity*.

SeKet glanced over the article remembering a time when The Fallen had no secrets to hide.

"We?" SeKet asked.

"I ran from school to your house, all the way here for one reason, so that you wouldn't leave without me."

chapter seventeen

RAHABEL

RAZIEL sat with his back against a jagged stone wall. Outside his cell where the Court of The Fallen kept him, the sounds of arguing, cruelty, and debauchery were everywhere.

His kin had created a place for themselves to bask in their bitterness while still imagining their own dominion. Human servants scurried about the massive underground caves, eager to please in any way The Fallen deemed necessary in the hope that they would be elevated to higher and higher ranks of servitude. And in between the sloth and the waste of this kin, they fought about everything. Who was best at what, who was most beloved by the people, and even, most absurdly, who God had loved best.

RaZiel had been a prisoner for six days.

For many years after he left Lilavois and Ada, he'd resisted making a home for himself. Without his family, he could not imagine how to fill a space, but when it became harder to find the moonflowers he needed to deliver on Ada's birthday, RaZiel decided to grow them himself. He settled inside an abandoned shack on a small plot of land. What began as a simple goal grew into a thriving garden, a replica in many ways of the garden he, Lilavois, and Ada had built together. In it, he kept the scent of his memories. Lilies for her name. Roses that smelled of Lilavois's hair. Lavender, which reminded him of the oils she used in her nightly baths and that first night when they had made love. Chamomile and mint for the teas Ada liked to sip with her morning biscuits. And moonflowers, delicate and rare, like his daughter.

The townsfolk were welcome to pick anything from the garden to use or sell in exchange for a loaf of bread, a cut of meat, or a pair of used pants in his size. Every morning, they came before the market opened and their day began. The only thing they were not allowed to take was the moonflowers; those he kept for himself. Most days, he smiled in greeting, but rarely spoke, leaving his visitors to take what they needed and be on their way. Yet word of him and the abundance of his garden had begun to spread in ways his heart was too broken to recognize. He could have left sooner. He should have, but he could not leave Ada's garden again.

The morning before her birthday, the day he was captured, RaZiel opened his eyes and greeted the gift of the new day with a song of praise. He laid on his pallet longer than usual, replaying memories of how happy his family had been. It was a rare indulgence reserved for when the longing for them became too heavy to bear. If he allowed himself to think of them daily, he would not have been able to resist racing back to where he knew they were. He had given in more times than they knew just to watch Ada walk to school or marvel at Lilavois picking herbs in her garden. But he made no excuses for Ada's birthday. A father had a right to celebrate the miracle of his child. And so, the tradition of the moonflowers began.

By the time he got up to gather water from the nearby river, the garden was already bustling with its first visitors. He returned a while later to find the garden silent with baskets of flowers and herbs scattered on the road. When he caught his kin's scent, he barely had the fight within him to resist.

RaZiel had wept his first night at RaHabel. His heart broken by how low his kin had sunk — from divine beings of infinite light, harmony, and wisdom to creatures who hid from the sun in dark caves to fight amongst themselves.

Before Lilavois and Ada, RaZiel had spent the last four thousand years begging for death. Yet, until he came to RaHabel, he had never understood what death was, or rather how many kinds of death there could be. In the last six days, he had witnessed the meaning of true death, to exist as only a twisted shell of oneself, forsaking every good thing you ever knew — and he wanted no part of it.

If these were truly the last moments of his existence, with no hope of ever seeing his family again, he took comfort in knowing that his end would secure their safety. He had never missed a birthday, not a single one until five days ago. He hoped SeKet had delivered the flowers and apologized for her father's absence. He knew she would watch over them both, keeping them safe as long as they lived, the way he would no longer be able to do.

Closing his eyes against the chaos outside the rough blue jade bars of his cell, he thought of the bliss he had once known. The smell of Lilavois's hair as she curled up next to him in the morning. The sound of her laugh as she teased his poor sense of fashion, the taste of her mouth when he kissed her. And finally, the feel of his daughter's tiny palm on his cheek and the way her sweet voice quivered around the sacred sounds they sang together each morning. The images were so clear in his mind he could smell traces of Lilavois's perfume. At first, he smiled, inhaling the illusion deeply until he caught the fear mingled in her scent.

His eyes flashed open, every sense heightened at the familiar cadence of two feet making their way to him. He sprang up wishing, dreading, and hoping as the sound grew nearer. Obscured behind the hulking mass of Judah, who insisted on maintaining his half-lion half-bear form wherever he went, RaZiel could not see her clearly. But he could read the story of how Lilavois had come to RaHabel from the presence of Al-Yah behind her and the pine smoke and feathers that clung to the flashes of her garment that he could see. As they rounded the corner, Judah picked up his pace, allowing Lilavois to finally come into view. Though her face was drawn with exhaustion, Lilavois's eyes were sharp, scanning each cell and corner they passed.

She's looking for me.

His chest constricted with the understanding that he still meant so much to her, and the utter conviction that she *should not* be here. Though he sensed no injury in her movements, RaZiel had already decided he would kill at least one more of his kin before they took his life.

Aside from his rage, RaZiel could also admit that he was selfishly, nonsensically grateful for the sight of her.

"I brought you some company, brother," Al-Yah smiled from behind Lilavois. "I believe you know each other."

Ignoring the biting edge of blue jade against his skin, RaZiel reached for her.

"Lilavois!"

"RaZiel!" Lilavois rushed forward, hands grasping for him, but she was not quick enough. Before their fingertips could touch, Al-Yah grabbed the collar of Lilavois's coat and yanked back.

"Spare me!" Al-Yah snapped as she pushed Lilavois into the open cell beside him with such force, she lost her balance and fell to the ground. "Keep your pining out of my sight. I brought her to you so you can watch her die. Her trial begins tomorrow."

RaZiel looked between Al-Yah and Lilavois, frantic and confused. "She has committed no crime!" he bellowed.

"She killed Saisho!" Al-Yah hissed. "She is a murderer like you, and tomorrow you both will pay for it with your lives."

Seeing the devastation on RaZiel's face, Al-Yah shook her head in disgust then turned to Judah. "Leave them here. Obi will put an end to this soon enough."

The moment they left, before any answers, before even understanding, they reached for each other, kissing, touching, and holding whatever they could reach. To think there could be joy in such a hopeless moment, in such a soulless place, would have seemed ludicrous and yet suddenly there was. The touch of his lips to hers felt more magical than any power she had ever conjured and the smile on her face when RaZiel stepped back to look at her warmed him more than any light the sun could shine.

"How? How have you come here?" Anguish burned the edges of his happiness to see her in this horrid place.

"I came for you."

"But how? What did Al-Yah mean by you killed Saisho? She knows that's impossible."

Lilavois drew him close and whispered directly in his ear. "It is for me, but not for Ada."

RaZiel shook his head. Words failed him.

"Saisho found her in Kemet a few weeks ago. He attacked Ada and Simon on the street. Simon is her . . ."

"I know who Simon is," RaZiel interrupted. "Please, go on."

Lilavois looked at him quizzically, before continuing. "Ada stabbed Saisho with a dagger I made from the talons you left me. He was wounded at first, but then he changed, RaZiel. Somehow, Ada made him mortal."

"Mortal?"

"Ada, Simon, and Captain Claybourne saw Saisho turn then bleed to death."

RaZiel held on to Lilavois's hand as he sank to his knees, eyes ablaze in amazement and wonder.

"Bleed. Our daughter did this?"

Lilavois settled down in front of him as best she could through the bars. "Yes. SeKet thinks Ada is a soul portal. Through her magic, she's able to give demons a soul so that they can return."

"What kind of mooncraft can do this?"

"This isn't mooncraft. This magic is Ada's alone."

Understanding came slowly. "She is a gift," he said finally. "Not only to us, but to all my kind."

"I think so," Lilavois agreed. "Maybe this is why God gave her to us."

"But if Ada is the one who destroyed Saisho, how are you here?"

Lilavois shifted her skirt to reveal the mold still strapped to her leg.

"They think you're Ada."

RaZiel kissed her then out of love and deep understanding for the bargain she made.

"We will find a way to get you out of here."

"We are her parents," Lilavois countered. "If we die here, the search will be over. She'll be free."

"They've already taken me from her. I won't let them take you from her, as well. I will not watch you die."

"I left a clue for SeKet to follow. She may find us."

"It will take more than SeKet to save us. No one knows that better than her. If she is able, I know she will, but I will not leave your survival to chance. We must find another way. Do you have a weapon?"

Lilavois smiled, pulling back her skirt and whispering the spell that revealed a small dagger at her thigh, the prototype of the one she had given Ada.

"Good," he said, determination shining in his eyes. "Keep it close."

chapter eighteen

THE TRIAL

LILAVOIS and RaZiel woke to the sensation of being torn apart. In the dim confines of their cells, it was impossible to tell the time. After hours of talking, they had fallen asleep side by side, hands intertwined between the bars of their cells.

"Judah! Alekwu! Get them up! Obi wants them now. Our kin have arrived."

Lilavois stumbled to her feet, struggling to recover from being jolted awake. When she looked up, she found RaZiel strangely calm and steady. He stared at her with singular purpose, holding her attention before giving her a slight nod. Instantly she was alert, realizing that now was their chance. To her left, Al-Yah stood over her, sneering as she pushed Lilavois towards the open cell door.

Lilavois noted that RaZiel had two guards to her one. His hands were bound. Hers were not. She was apparently considered the lesser threat. Realizing it would be easier for her to start a distraction, she pretended to stumble, moaning loudly as she stepped over the threshold of her cell.

"What's wrong with you," Al-Yah snapped.

"My leg. It's stiff from sleeping on the ground. Please, I just need a moment." Even though Lilavois had slipped off the prosthetic mold during the night, it was still true. She had meant to put it back on before they arrived, but there was no time. Thankfully, they had not noticed it laying in a dark corner of her cell.

And if I keep Al-Yah's attention on me, they won't.

Lilavois took her time. She bent over, pretending to massage her leg while waiting for Al-Yah to step closer.

"We don't wait for murderers!" Al-Yah seethed, yanking her up by her arm. But Lilavois was prepared for Al-Yah's roughness. Using the demon's momentum, she swung her free hand around and stabbed Al-Yah underneath her ribs in an upward movement. If Al-Yah were human, the blade would have penetrated her heart and killed her. Instead, Al-Yah staggered back as Lilavois withdrew her blade then fell onto the cell floor.

Beside her, RaZiel was also in motion, using his shoulder to shove Judah to the ground. He fell back while RaZiel hurled into Alekwu, the demon on his right, pushing him back into the cell and closing the door behind him.

"Run, Lilavois!" RaZiel roared, but she had no intention of leaving him. Lilavois locked her own cell door just before Al-Yah got back on her feet, then readied herself to help RaZiel in any way she could. But it was hard to find a good angle to strike. RaZiel wrestled with his kin, crashing into the walls around them while Al-Yah and Alekwu shouted curses and thrashed against their cell bars.

They are making too much noise, Lilavois thought. *If we don't get out soon, others will come, and we'll miss our chance to escape.*

"RaZiel, step back!" Lilavois yelled, determined to get a clear angle to strike. Understanding her intent, RaZiel released his hold, flinging his kin away from his body. She aimed for his chest but got the side of his neck. They did not wait for his body to fall. RaZiel grabbed Lilavois's hand and a torch light then ran. The caves surrounding their cells were poorly lit and almost completely indistinguishable from one another, with no sign or clear direction on where any path lead.

"Al-Yah blindfolded me for most of the way here. I don't know the way," Lilavois admitted.

"They did the same to me," RaZiel confided, his hand gripping hers tightly.

"Then how will we know where to go?"

"Smell. There's fresh air this way."

It was a struggle to keep his pace, but she refused to slow down. All around them the shrieks of disarray were growing louder, and the ground trembled with frenzied demons giving chase. They did not stop until the footsteps faded and they could feel the current of fresh air rushing towards them from some open space ahead. As they moved down a narrow tunnel, the way ahead became clearer with light reflecting off the walls from a nearby source. Lilavois could feel the full force of the wind whipping the edges of her skirt when RaZiel's body went rigid. He held her behind him, blocking her from view.

"Hello brother," Obi said, his voice light and melodic. "It has been too long."

And then the tunnel went pitch black as RaZiel collapsed over her body creating a cocoon of protection where only his screams of pain could break through.

chapter nineteen

BELOVED

LILAVOIS did not see light again until her knees hit a smooth dirt floor and Al-Yah pulled a hood off her head. She opened her eyes to find herself in the middle of a circular stone amphitheater lit with dozens of torches. Demons in various forms filled the room on all sides. To her left, RaZiel knelt, bound by a shackle that was bolted to the floor. His head was low to the ground with his arms outstretched. His shirt had been stripped away, revealing a tapestry of bruises and torn flesh.

"RaZiel!" Lilavois scrambled to her feet only to realize she was similarly tethered by her ankle. Still, the chains did not stop her from reaching out to touch his shoulder.

"My love," she whispered, ignoring the gasps around the room. "Are you all right?" It was only as she inched forward that she realized he was praying. Resting her head on his shoulder as much as she could, Lilavois strained to listen to the familiar words she had not heard in so long.

"Thank you for my wife, my heart, my purpose. Thank you for the miracle that you saw fit to grant us, though I am unworthy. I ask that you watch over them, protect them, and keep them safe, Abba, even as I fail, now and forever. Ashe."

RaZiel sat up and took her face in his shackled hands. His eyes were ravaged by anguish.

"Are you hurt?" A tear rushed down his cheek at the mere thought.

"No," she answered honestly. "You protected me well."

"Not well enough," he said sadly.

"Silence!" Obi roared as he entered the amphitheater and shattered their peace. "Get this witch away from him."

Two demons rushed in to pull her out of RaZiel's grasp.

"Obi!" RaZiel bellowed, fighting against his chains. "Let her go. She has nothing to do with this!"

"She has everything to do with this, traitor! She is the reason you killed three of our kin. Your actions emboldened her to do the same. Because of you, Saisho has been lost. Today, you both will face the consequences of your actions."

Obi's declaration set off a flurry of whispers throughout the gathering of The Fallen and the members of the Demon Council. The trial was supposed to be an objective review of facts, yet Obi was already declaring the outcome.

Standing by the dais, a tall demon with dark skin and sable hair that flowed to her thighs shook her head in reproach. "Obi!" Giada, the archivist and a member of the Council called with a cautioning glare. "Restore yourself!"

Obi's outburst threatened to betray his plans before the trial had even begun. If he wanted to maintain control over the proceedings, he needed to do a better job of masking his true intentions.

"Forgive me, Beloveds. My grief is too near," he demurred. "Rest assured, I will not forsake the sanctity of this gathering."

He walked to the center of the dais where the Council presided. Lucifer established the Council shortly after their time on Earth began as a means of managing conflict between the members of The Fallen. After Lucifer was exiled, those who remained kept the tradition. Seven councilors were elected to serve every millennium. With his panache for politics and power, Obi was the Council's longest standing member. Though the majesty of the Council had waned over the millennia, it was still considered one of their most sacred traditions. When a gathering of the Council was called, every demon from every corner of the earth came to RaHabel. No human had ever entered this space before. Not even the servants were allowed. As Obi and the Council counted those in attendance, they were pleased to see that most but not all were in attendance.

"Where are SeKet, Heka, Lono, and Tlaloc?" Vishin, the newly elected member of the Council, asked.

"Maybe they took up with Lucifer," Ahmed, another member of the Council quipped. The Council members shook their heads in quiet amusement. Obi was careful to look impartial, scanning the room as if surprised by Vishin's observation.

"Has anyone seen them?" Ahmed called before turning to the Council archivist whose task it was to preside over the proceedings.

"Giada, are you sure the messages were sent?"

"All were sent," she replied.

Obi frowned. "This is deeply disturbing. With the recent attacks on our kin, we should dedicate a contingent of the Beloved to find them and ensure their safety. SeKet has always trusted the humans. I pray they have not turned against her."

A murmur of concern rippled through the amphitheater as others agreed.

"But, for now," Obi continued, "I move that we proceed with the gathering."

"Agreed," the councilors murmured.

From the crowd, Persephone stood up. "Should we not wait? We have always done so before. Perhaps SeKet and the others can't move freely. There is no hurry."

"Yes," another demon agreed from the crowd. "We must respect our traditions."

"Tlaloc is probably off in some poor village taking credit for the rain again," another joked. To Obi's dismay, others chimed in, calling for a delay.

Obi smiled through the disdain he had always felt for Persephone and her contrary nature.

"Under normal circumstances, I would wholeheartedly agree with you," he began, keeping his voice tranquil. "But I believe the matter is too urgent. It has taken us years to find RaZiel to answer for the deaths of Nephycil, Vitas, and Ilhan. Yet if that was the only matter before us, I would surely wait. But there is a far more pressing threat we must address; more disturbing still is the reason why we have brought a human into our sanctuary."

"Four weeks ago, Saisho was slain. All evidence points to a human, this human, who used her mooncraft as a member of the Sisters of the Light to not only maim Saisho, but render him mortal."

The gathering erupted in disbelief.

"That's impossible!"

"There is no magic that can do this."

"Blasphemy!"

Obi raised his hand to calm the crowd. "As incredible as it sounds, I assure you we have evidence that this is true. Which means every member of our kin is in danger until we discern the truth. For our safety and survival, I fear we must proceed."

Obi looked over the gathering of his kin, cataloguing the fear and confusion on their faces, and knew he had them exactly where he wanted them. He looked over to RaZiel who had been watching Obi carefully and gave him a sly smirk.

"Archivist, please call the gathering to order," he announced.

"Beloveds, today we come together to hear charges of murder against our kin, RaZiel, who is accused of the murder of Nephycil, Vitus, and Ilhan." Giada turned to RaZiel. "Do you deny these accusations, brother?"

RaZiel stood tall against the length of chains that held him. "I do not," he said plainly. "I am guilty." A low murmur of surprise rippled across the gathering.

"The consequences of such an act against your kin is death," Giada continued. "Do you accept this judgment against you?"

"I do not," RaZiel replied. His gaze traveled the amphitheater before settling on Obi. "They attacked me and threatened my family. I begged them to leave, but they refused. To protect those I love, I had no choice but to challenge them."

"What evidence do you have of this?" Vishin asked from the dais.

"None, but I swear it to be true. Saisho escaped. He saw."

"But Saisho is dead now," Obi interjected. "Killed by the woman you chose

as your mate."
RaZiel turned to Lilavois. Although she was too far to touch, her gaze held him firm. He could feel her strength, her resolve, and her fear. The choice they made to save Ada bound them together, but he could not bring himself to say the words.

"I do not deny it," she said turning from RaZiel to face Obi. "He attacked. I have a right to defend myself."

"Perhaps," Giada replied. "But you are a member of the Sisters of the Light? Your stance against us is well known. Even within your own human customs, which condone so many ills, to take a life is still a crime — is it not?"

"It was not my intention to take his life," she answered carefully, knowing any lie she uttered would be sensed immediately.

Obi shook his head in frustration. "Whether you meant to or not is irrelevant! The fact remains he is dead by your hand. Bring in the body!"

At the opposite side of the dais, two large doors opened. On a portable stretcher made of raw silk, two demons carried Saisho's body to the center of the amphitheater, stopping between RaZiel and Lilavois.

"Observe for yourself, the remains of our kin!" Obi bellowed, stepping down from the dais. "His immortality stolen from him by some foul craft!"

Lilavois tried not to look like she was seeing Saisho for the very first time. Even though he had been dead for weeks, he still smelled faintly of lilacs. Death had not diminished the angelic beauty of his features, or the peaceful smile Ada and Simon had described, still frozen on his face.

"Is that . . . blood?" a demon gasped before leaving their seat for a closer look. Others followed, until there was a crush of bodies, all staring in amazement. Amidst the shock of their kin's death, they looked at Saisho and saw not only tragedy, but the advent of something truly new dawning.

Lilavois was so distracted watching the demons' expressions as realization took hold of them that she did not notice Obi move from the dais to stand beside her.

"Tell us how you defiled our brethren!"

"I don't know," she answered honestly.

Unable to detect her lie, Obi drew out his claws and tracked them gently down her face. "You will tell us," he sneered.

"Stop, Obi!" Persephone ordered. "If she made him human, he must have a soul. Maybe this is a sign, a sign from Yahweh! A way home!"

The expressions of confusion, anguish, and frail hope on the faces of The Fallen brought tears to Lilavois's eyes. She knew that look. RaZiel had carried it when they first met all those years ago, when she had been foolish enough to try to kill him. As if hope was so foreign to them the thought alone was too much to bear. Some dropped to their knees, others wept, and others still recoiled in disgust.

Beside her, RaZiel shined with a deep pride no one but Lilavois could understand.

Between them, Obi trembled with rage. "This is no sign! This is a curse! This woman, this human, means to humble us! The Sisters of the Light mean to conquer us. We cannot let this witchcraft spread. We must cut it off at the root," Obi spat, pointing to Lilavois. "We will destroy her and this foul magic with her!"

RaZiel lunged, but the chains prevented him from closing the distance. "Don't touch her!"

Ignoring his brother's protests, Obi grabbed Lilavois by the neck.

"This is highly improper!" Giada yelled, reaching between them. "The

Council has not issued a judgment!"

I am the Council, Obi wanted to yell, but had sense enough not to give his conviction voice. It was true. He made it true, though he dared not say the words out loud. He loosened his grip on her neck, but only a little.

"Then let the Council do it now so I may deliver the sentence."

"Stop! All of you!" Al-Yah said, bursting through the amphitheater doors behind them. "She is an imposter! She is not the one we seek." In her hands, she held up the mold of Ada's prosthetic before throwing it across the room until it landed at Lilavois's feet.

"When Judah and I went to Kemet to investigate Saisho's murder, the doorman at the hotel said that a girl with a prosthetic leg and a young man snuck out of the hotel and came back injured the night Saisho was killed. This is not her!"

Obi looked between Al-Yah, the prosthetic mold on the floor, and Lilavois. Glaring at Al-Yah in disgust, he threw Lilavois to the ground. "Then why did you bring her here?"

Al-Yah stepped forward, refusing to be cowed by Obi's anger. "At first, we … thought we found the boy who accompanied her, but he just turned out to be another student. When I saw her walking with the prosthetic, I assumed it was her. I checked the other amputees in the area and no one else matched the description the doorman gave. He was very specific. But if she went through such lengths to deceive us, she must know who the real killer is."

Obi grabbed Lilavois off the floor and shook her violently. "Tell us where she is!" Obi shrieked. His voice was loud enough to crack the stone surrounding them. Lilavois's ears rang and her head hurt with the intensity of the sound, but she still managed to look back at him with clear eyes.

"Never," she said simply.

The certainty in her defiance took him by surprise, allowing his rage to boil down from a blunt fury to a fine sharp edge.

Obi smiled. "You don't know the meaning of the word." He set Lilavois on the ground. The nails of his right hand grew long and dark once more before Obi turned toward RaZiel and plunged all five talons into his chest.

chapter twenty

THE GIFT

THE pain was blinding. RaZiel could not make a sound, could not form a thought. His body would not move. All RaZiel could do was feel the sensation of five hot brands igniting at the core of his chest and burning through whatever was left of his insides. RaZiel's knees buckled but Obi held him upright and close enough so that his claws stayed firmly buried inside, preventing his body from knitting itself back together and keeping him in perpetual pain — just as Obi intended. In front of him, Lilavois screamed, pleaded, and cried. The pain had numbed RaZiel's sense of sound, but he did not need to hear her. The terror and anguish she saw on her face told him that she finally understood the reason he had stayed away all these years. What his absence had shielded her from and why, no matter what, she must keep their secret and never hand their daughter over to them.

Watching RaZiel, Lilavois did understand, more than she ever had, RaZiel's insistence on keeping them apart, why he had feared for their daughter enough to break his own heart. In the horror of the moment, she found herself grateful that she had followed him here so he would not die alone, because two things were true. Neither of them would ever give their daughter up and they would never make it out of RaHabel alive.

All she could do now was hasten his relief.

"RaZiel! Can you hear me? It's okay to let go. I love you."

Obi shrugged staring into RaZiel's unfocused eyes. "I think she'd rather see you dead. That's not a good sign. Even your pain will not persuade her. I think your mate doesn't love you as much as you love her," he taunted.

"She loves me enough to love what I love," RaZiel rasped. His eyes fell closed against the pain. "As much as I do."

"And what is it you love so much you would betray your own kin?"

RaZiel opened his eyes and smiled, thinking of the day he brought his daughter from her mother's womb into the world. "Do you not remember love, Obi, or has your hatred burned the memory away completely?" Feeling himself slipping slowly from consciousness, RaZiel closed his eyes just before Obi retracted his claws. With no energy to hold himself up or even scream out in pain, he crashed to the ground in silence.

Obi turned to Lilavois. She was silent too, struggling against the need to help the only man she ever loved and the knowledge that, in this place, she could do nothing.

"Let go?" Obi cooed. His voice echoed across the room with a cold malice. "No, my dear, RaZiel will not be dying anytime soon. If I release my demon poison now, he'd die too quickly. You cannot comprehend the meaning of forever. Your days will be spent long before we're done with him."

She stared back at Obi with tear-glazed eyes, trying to mask her despair at how casually he unfolded all her worst fears, and her deep, mind-splitting need for a blade, her crossbow — anything to challenge him.

Seeing the fine sheen of hatred in her eyes, Obi smiled. "At last, I believe you understand me. I'll ask you one last time. Where is the girl?"

Lilavois tried not to look at RaZiel, but her heart could not ignore his pain and all the terror he would suffer for loving her.

"Please," she said. "You were brothers once."

Obi used his left hand to grab RaZiel by the neck and bring him to his feet once more, then lifted his right hand. RaZiel's wounds were almost healed, but not quite.

"That was before we came here." Obi drew back his arm to strike when the sharp sound of stone cracking above them stayed his hand.

The ground, the walls, everything around them began to shake. Screams erupted throughout the amphitheater as large sections of the amphitheater fell around them until a large piece at the center of the ceiling collapsed. Above them SeKet rode into the amphitheater on a shaft of light, crouched atop the boulder she had used to punch through the mountain top. Heka, Lono, and Tlaloc followed, landing beside her to form a tight circle with a small impenetrable core. At first, the Council and all the Beloved stared at them in shock, until SeKet let out a piercing whistle. A moment later, Ada and Simon rappelled to the center of the circle from a rope they had anchored at the mouth of the opening.

Pristine in armor made with the same blue jade stone as the cells of RaHabel, to Lilavois, SeKet was the picture of an angel who had once guarded the very gates of the Ever. And though she would have wished her to be anywhere else, Lilavois could not deny the joy in her heart at seeing Ada alive and unharmed under SeKet's protection. She was also pleased to see that the other three demons and Simon each bore one of her weapons.

Obi stumbled back as RaZiel stepped forward, pain forgotten as the little girl who knew him once stared back at him cautiously. He returned her gaze with open adoration. SeKet looked between them and pursed her lips. "There will be time for this later," she sighed.

Throwing off her helmet, SeKet paused to survey the gathering.

"You dare begin the Council trial without me?" she began, looking squarely at Obi. "Have all our traditions been broken, or are we casting out punishment before judgment has been made? It is only moments before sundown. We cannot be that late. Is this some new rule of the Council?"

Vishin rose. "The accused has admitted his crimes. We have only discovered that the woman is not the true cause of Saisho's death."

"I killed him," Ada said, stepping forward. In a flash of light, SeKet stood before her, shielding her from attack.

The gathering of demons began inching closer, jostling to get a better look at her leg, shimmering with the blue light of Lilavois's magic, and the demon blade in hand.

"How?" Vishin asked.

Ada looked to her mother who was shaking her head, begging her to be silent. *She wants me to hide*, she thought sadly, *but I can't. Not anymore.*

"With this blade my mother made for me and …" Ada hesitated, struggling for the words to describe something she was just beginning to understand.

Beside her, Simon took her hand and stepped forward. "And magic," he said. "When she stabbed him, a light inside her emerged. It turned him human."

"You are a Sister of the Light?" Giada asked.

"No," Ada answered. "I've never been able to conjure mooncraft that way."

"Then how else could you do this?" Obi sneered. "What you speak of is impossible."

SeKet shook her head and pointed to Al-Yah who had stood by Saisho's corpse, having protected it from falling debris. "You have the evidence right there! Saisho was immortal, and now he is dead in a *human body*. He has a soul and has passed through! He has returned! You know what this means. This child is a gift from Allah. A sign of God's forgiveness that in death, we shall finally be reunited."

"No human has ever been given such power," Giada said. "Have you witnessed this power yourself, SeKet?"

"No," SeKet admitted. "But I believe it because this is no ordinary child." SeKet turned to Ada. It was not her story to tell. Only Ada had that right.

Ada could feel her throat closing around every half-truth she had ever been told, every question she had ever seen her mother evade about their life before Liren. The instinct to shrink back into who she once believed herself to be was powerful, but that door was already closed. She had come here to do whatever was necessary to save her parents, just as they had done what was necessary to save her. Ada forced herself to take a deep breath and exhale.

"I am the daughter of Lilavois St. James and RaZiel of The Fallen. Four of your kin attacked us in our home. There was no cause. We were unarmed. My father, my mother, and I had never hurt anyone. When they came, my father tried to save me from them. That's why he killed them. But one pierced my leg. I survived the attack, but by then, the demon poison had spread."

Despite the cries of disbelief and menacing stares, Ada continued. "Though I was strong enough to survive, my parents had to amputate my leg to stop the poison. At dawn, my father left so that none of you would track him to us and risk my life again."

"This child is a liar, just like all the others," Obi began, stepping forward, but he forgot how close he had been to RaZiel. Too close. RaZiel wrapped his arm around Obi's neck and extended his claws.

"I have killed before, brother. Do not make me kill you too. My daughter tells the truth."

"RaZiel! Release him!" Vishin shouted.

"Not while I breathe," RaZiel answered calmly. "As long as he threatens my child, I will be a threat to him or anyone here. I do not wish it, but I will see it done if I must."

In an instant, the quiet murmurs in the room turned to shouts as those loyal to Obi readied themselves to attack.

From across the room, Lilavois and SeKet looked at each other, feeling, knowing what would come next. Those who might have been drawn to their cause needed more time to be convinced; time they no longer had.

"Kill them!" Obi roared.

"Hold them back!" SeKet bellowed.

The room erupted in chaos, with SeKet and those demons who favored order fighting to hold back those most loyal to Obi — those most willing to kill at a word. SeKet showed why she was once called the Daughter of Lightning, flashing from place to place in bursts of light to keep those who threatened them at bay. To Lilavois's surprise, Al-Yah defended her when a demon loyal to Obi lunged at her.

"Is it true? Is the child truly RaZiel's?" Al-Yah whispered as she shielded Lilavois from the chaos around them with her own body.

"Look at her," Lilavois answered. "How could she be anyone else's?"

Al-Yah watched the girl who looked like a tiny cherub, full of inner light, the same light RaZiel carried, and frowned. "It has never happened in all our years. God has never blessed any of our kind this way. If it is as you say, it must be a sign. Abba does not create life blindly."

Persephone fought her way through the chaos, clearing a path to Ada. When she reached SeKet, she dropped her weapon. "Please," she asked with tears welling in her eyes. "I must know."

SeKet watched her for as long as she could spare before darting to the inner circle to stand beside Ada as Persephone followed.

"Prove it," Persephone said quietly. Slowly, she reached for Ada's hand and raised the blade to her chest. "If you truly have this power, help me."

Ada's hand shook. "Are you sure? It might hurt a lot. I don't know."

Persephone's smile was sad. "I am one who knew God's face and turned away. There is no pain greater than that."

The certainty in Persephone's eyes stilled the trembling of Ada's hand.

"Then I wish you peace," Ada whispered as she pressed her blade into Persephone's chest. The moment the blade cut through her skin, Ada saw the light bursting from her hand, felt power from somewhere deep inside her swell until it lit up the room. It was a swirling light that pulsed and held with Ada's new awareness and acceptance of it.

Tears of joy sprang from Persephone's eyes as she looked down and saw the blood, her blood, slowly seeping from the wound. Ada stepped back, shaken by what she had done and how little it took her to do it. Persephone fell to the ground just as Saisho had, then morphed into shadows of the many forms she had taken until her body settled into its final form — a small woman not much larger than Ada herself.

"I am home," she gasped before blood began to trickle from the corner of her mouth. "I see you," she whispered. "Finally, Abba, I see you."

As Persephone took her last breath, Ada drew the light she now understood as her own inward then flexed it out, testing her control, but now she knew it was hers. She did not know she was in danger until she looked up and saw her mother and father standing beside her along with two dozen other angels. They closed around her like a cocoon of protection. Outside their circle, the rest stood back, in fear, confusion, or rage.

"Murderer!"

"Witch!"

"Liar!"

From just behind her, Simon whispered, "I think it's time to go."

"Though the Council has witnessed this new power, it does not accept your authority," Obi bellowed. "No man will have dominion over us."

"This is not dominion," SeKet answered back. "This is a miracle! A chance to return, Obi. Even you must see that."

"By becoming human?" another demon called out. "Why should we lower ourselves? We are of the Ever."

Obi nodded his head in agreement and sneered. "There is no return. We are forsaken, SeKet. No matter how hard you try to be good, God has turned Their back on us. You will never be forgiven."

A rumble of agreement echoed through the chamber.

"Then you are fools," Al-Yah said, throwing back the key she had used to release Lilavois and RaZiel from their bonds. "I will stand with you no longer."

As Ada looked around, she realized a choice was being made and she was the line dividing those demons that accepted who and what she was from those who would fight against it.

I've started a war, she realized.

The thought made her sick to her stomach. Instinctively she reached for her parents and found them ready. Clasping his strangely familiar hand, she looked up to find RaZiel looking down at her with only love, only joy. If he had known this moment of strife would come, there was no regret in his face to show it.

“This is not the end, Brother,” Obi declared, stepping back with those who followed him.

“No,” RaZiel called back. “It is a new beginning for all of us.”

They left through the opening SeKet had made through the chamber ceiling, each demon transforming into a creature able to carry their charge and still fly towards the sun.

The End….

other books by

CERECE RENNIE MURPHY

SCIENCE FICTION

Order of the Seers

Order of the Seers: The Red Order

Order of the Seers: The Last Seer

FANTASY

The Wolf Queen: The Hope of Aferi

The Wolf Queen: The Promise of Aferi

STEAMPUNK

In The Garden of Light & Shadow: The Chronicles of Ada St. James

SHORT STORIES

Between Two Seas

HISTORICAL ROMANCE

To Find You

CHILDREN'S BOOKS

Ellis & The Magic Mirror

Ellis & The Hidden Cave

Ellis & The Cloud Kingdom

Enchanted: 5 Tales of Magic In the Everyday

ABOUT THE AUTHOR

National bestselling and award-winning author Cerece Rennie Murphy fell in love with science fiction at the age of seven while watching "Star Wars: The Empire Strikes Back".

Since debuting her first novel, *Order of the Seers (Book 1)* in 2012, Ms. Murphy has published twelve speculative fiction novels, short stories, and children's books, including, *In The Garden of Light and Shadow: The Chronicles of Ada St. James*. Ms. Murphy is also the founder of Virtuous Con, an online sci-fi and comic culture convention that celebrates the excellence of BIPOC creators in speculative fiction. She is the recipient of Black Pearl Magazine's Author of the Year Award for Children's Literature, the National Best Sellers designation from the African American Literature Book Club (AALBC), and the Science Fiction Writers of America (SFWA)'s Kate Wilhelm Solstice Award for significant contributions to the science fiction, fantasy, and related genres community. Created in 2008, Ms. Murphy joined the ranks of distinguished previous Solstice Award winners, including Petra Mayer, Carl Sagan, Octavia Butler, and Gardner Dozois.

To learn more about the author and her upcoming projects, please visit her website at cerecerenniemurphy.com

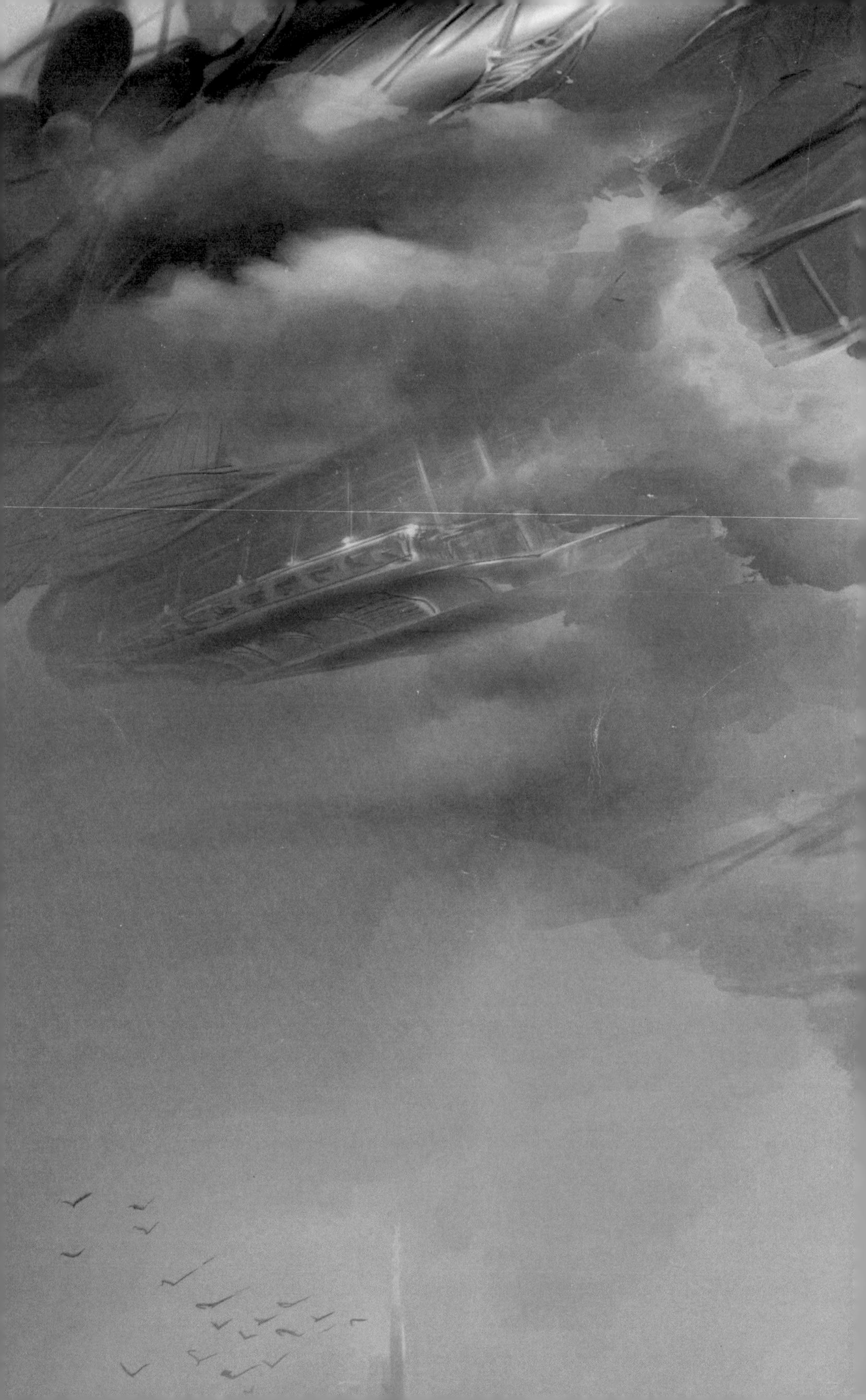